A HUNDRED BILLION GHOSTS

by DM Sinclair

Book 1 of 100,000,000,000.

"In my mind, if there was life after death and there were spirits who survived and could, in any way, communicate with us back here on Earth, it would be incredibly obvious. The afterlife would be as obvious as the existence of Canada. It wouldn't be just some stories that are told between this person and that person. Everybody would see it all the time."

- Sean Carroll, theoretical physicist

ONE

The room held its breath, and so did everyone in it.

A hush spread through the party guests clustered in a horseshoe around the end of the kitchen counter.

The host of the party held up a hand to keep them silent. They listened.

There was a long moment of nothing. Silence and stillness.

And then, faintly, a knock. It came from nowhere specific, had no visible cause. But it did not feel random. It was not a noise of the house.

It felt intentional. *Something* had knocked.

A woman shrieked, and it seemed to give others permission to laugh in disbelief, to whisper in awed tones to each other, to demand that the party host reveal how he was doing this, to insist that it was a trick. But the host shushed them all and denied in a whisper that it was him. Listen now. Listen.

He asked another question into the air. "Are you standing next to me right now? One for yes and two for no."

The guests stood tense as another moment drew out long.

Silence but for the soft white noise of the air conditioning. Nobody breathed.

Knock.

The room jumped, startled. More gasps and laughter.

The host held up a hand again. Silence flooded the room.

He closed his fists, and his eyes. This would be the big one. They could tell.

"Did you die in this house?"

They listened.

The woman who had shrieked before bit her fist to keep

from doing it again.

Some scanned for any hint of movement, for any obvious source of the sound. Maybe to glimpse... something. What, they didn't know.

Listen.

They listened.

The silence pressed in, enveloping them.

At this point, Ryan Matney stepped in from the other room and announced how much he had enjoyed the nachos, but he would have to leave early, and whoever was parked behind him could they come out and move their car?

He wasn't leaving early because of the disembodied knocks. He wasn't leaving because the party wasn't fun. And he wasn't leaving because he didn't like the people at it, most of whom were vague work acquaintances from the call center and the customer service department that he had no particular feelings about.

He was leaving early because it was a work night. And was a couple more hours of party today worth a day spent slightly tired at work tomorrow? Of course it wasn't. He had been slightly tired today, for example, and it had made the day very difficult. Or rather, he suspected it had. He didn't remember much of how his day at work had gone, given how he had spent most of it thinking about coming to this party.

About a half hour after the party started, he began watching for that golden opportunity to leave. There would surely be a lull where he could nab the host, his supervisor Dave, and say it had been great but unfortunately he had a thing and thank you and goodbye.

When a woman that he recognized from order processing whose name he couldn't remember admitted that she recognized him from the call center but didn't know his name, he answered: "Ryan Matney. I will be leaving early." He just thought it prudent to warn her in advance, in case they wound up talking for a long time.

They didn't.

After that, Ryan was mostly thinking about what route he would take to get home. He just needed the perfect opening to say his thank-you's and goodbyes without making a spectacle of his exit.

It came just before ten o'clock.

Dave, whose house this was, had just finished a conversation with a small cluster of people and was moving alone towards the kitchen.

Now. Make your move.

That's when Dave stood up on a chair and announced to the room that this house was haunted, and he could prove it.

Every part of Ryan that could clench, clenched. Now what was he supposed to do?

Dave shut the music off and Ryan realized that he hadn't noticed it was on. He couldn't remember a single song that had played during the entire time he had been there.

As the party flocked to the kitchen area, Ryan attempted to catch Dave's eye with head movements and strong glances and throat clearing, which he regarded as the universal language of "I gotta go". But Dave was busy nodding and assuring everyone he was serious about the haunting, slapping their backs and herding them into the kitchen. Ryan missed his chance.

He hung back in the living room, thinking about how he would definitely be hitting the snooze button tomorrow from staying out too long, and how that had the potential to wreck the whole day.

Things went dead silent in the kitchen for several minutes. Ryan could see people's backs through the doorway, but he couldn't see Dave in the crowd. There were occasional vague remarks and titters, and he thought he heard Dave's voice but he couldn't be sure.

After several minutes of pretending to be checking his

phone, he decided to just go. He got his coat from the bedroom and made one more attempt to see if Dave was reachable through the kitchen door. But he wasn't. So Ryan smiled apologetically in case anyone was glancing his way and slipped out.

A few minutes later he slipped back in because someone was parked behind his car in the driveway.

Everyone was still in the kitchen. People laughed and gasped, and he thought he heard somebody shriek. Everyone's attention was elsewhere, and their backs formed an impenetrable wall across the doorway. This would be tricky. Possibly even impossible. Ryan had never been someone who could stride into the middle of a party, demand everyone's attention, and make an announcement. Nor did he wish to be.

But something had to be done. An entire day of not-being-slightly-tired depended on it.

So he strode into the middle of the party, demanded everyone's attention, and made an announcement.

"I gotta take off! Dave, sorry, I really gotta go. Thanks for everything, it was great. And great to see all of you again! Whoever brought those nachos, wow, those were great! I think I ate, like, half of them. Anyway... oh, who's got the beige Prius? Do you think you could back out for a second so I can get out? Anyone? Beige Prius?"

As soon as he had finished talking, the lights went out.

It was immediately clear that this was not a light bulb popping. Nor was it all the house lights being switched off, or a fuse blowing. Even stray light from the city outside vanished. The house slipped into darkness like a dying ship sinking into an abyss, cold black pressing in on the windows hard enough that they seemed about to crack.

Ryan couldn't help but feel upstaged.

Gasps rippled through the guests and everyone jostled.

Ryan backed off but couldn't escape the press of unseen people in the dark.

Dave was saying something like "It's okay, everyone, just give it a minute." His voice drowned in the murmur of other people voicing theories, reassurances, and fears. Some cracked jokes. "Great party, Dave!", and "Are you trying to get rid of us?"

A few people turned on their cellphone displays and swung them around like hazy floodlights, giving Ryan a vague sense of where everyone was. He navigated through the flickering crowd to a space in the dining area attached to the kitchen. Pushing past a table, he squeezed himself into a corner where there was a patio door looking out over the backyard into the street.

He pulled out his own cellphone to check the time and try to predict what impact this would have on tomorrow. But when the display lit up, it wasn't the time he fixated on.

It was the "No Service" warning in the corner.

He reset the phone, but the warning stayed lit. He had not seen that warning since he bought the phone, and it alarmed him. He looked out the window at the black city.

"Hey," he asked whoever was closest to him, trying to be heard above the general hubbub. "Do you have service?" He waggled his phone.

"Does anybody have service?" whoever was next to him asked the whole party a moment later.

He saw faces light up as cellphone displays were checked. The responses came back.

"No."

"No service."

"Nothing."

Brisk footsteps crossed the kitchen, and somebody fumbled with something plastic. Dave's voice: "Landline is dead too."

The joking stopped. The realization permeated the crowd

that this was serious.

Ryan wanted to get home. Doubly now, because not only was some global disaster apparently happening, but he was also now sure that tomorrow morning at work would be a total wash.

He looked out into the street again, hoping to see street lamps coming on. *There must be emergency generators or something,* he told himself. *They have ways of dealing with stuff like this.*

He was surprised to find that the street was not dark anymore. But the light was not street lamps.

It was people.

Human forms bathed in soft white light, moving. At first he thought it was people out using their cellphones as flashlights to find their way home. But there were too many of them. They were filling the street, and meandering. Not headed anywhere. And he couldn't see them holding any phones or lights at all. Yet their shapes were getting brighter, more distinct by the second, like fluorescent bulbs just switched on and warming up.

In the faint, diffuse light, the people looked almost translucent.

No. They *were* translucent.

Ryan pressed his hands to the glass, trying to make sense of what he was seeing. Some other party people noticed and squeezed in around him. Fresh mutterings of "what is that?" and "do you see that?" circled the kitchen.

Whoever had shrieked before shrieked again from somewhere in the kitchen. And so did somebody else.

Ryan spun around and his breath caught in his throat as he saw what the others had already seen.

There was a semi-transparent, shimmering form of a man standing next to Dave in the kitchen. He was slight, almost skeletal, and a little hunched. And he was dressed in flannel pajamas, what color Ryan couldn't tell because of his transparency.

The man—no, the ghost—appeared surprised, even fearful, to be seen. He let his eyes wander across all the faces. Nobody moved. He looked like a stage actor who had just forgotten his lines.

As they watched, he stretched out a bony arm with trembling trepidation, closed his fist, and knocked on the counter. It took three tries, his fist disappearing into the substance of the counter on each try. But on the third, he made a faint, soft tap.

Everyone screamed again. Including the ghost himself, although he appeared to do so just because he wanted to fit in.

The lights blinked startlingly alive, illuminating the screaming faces. And while the light greatly reduced the generally scary atmosphere of the moment, the ghost was still there. So nobody stopped screaming.

In the midst of all this, Ryan thought if he could find the owner of the Prius, he might still leave early and save tomorrow. The ghosts would probably be gone by then, so he'd have to be ready for a normal day.

He was wrong, though. They weren't gone. By that standard of "normal", the world's normal days were pretty much over.

TWO

Four years later.

When Ryan first moved into his apartment in Cambridge near Harvard Square, there were three ghosts haunting it.

Which was, obviously, far fewer than he expected. Normally for the kind of rent this place was asking, he would have expected to be stuck with a dozen at least.

So he signed a two-year lease even though, aside from the ghosts, the place was a horror show.

It was the third floor of a century-old three-story house. It had creaky floors and low ceilings and walls that slanted and bent alarmingly. The windows were small and narrow, and seemed to allow in only what scant light passed a pat-down and rigorous background check. Its location seemed precisely calculated for maximum inconvenience in commuting anywhere on the T. Everything in it rattled, or creaked, or dripped. The radiator did all three, and yet the heat from it never permeated beyond the three-foot bubble immediately surrounding it. There were frequent other noises from above, below, and all other sides that he variously wrote off as squirrels, water heaters, or "settling". On one occasion he went down to the basement to see if he could make one of the noises stop, and had gotten trapped down there by a sticky door for an entire night. Which was fine, because the rank basement was actually far more comfortable and quiet than his apartment. That had been his best night's sleep in the house so far.

Ryan didn't plan to be there forever. He saw it as a temporary stepping stone on his way to buying a property, perhaps even in two years when his lease was up. Three at most. Then he'd forget that these few years of cold, creaking, and commuting had ever happened. That he was presently forced to live through them was something he put out of his mind.

But only three ghosts was nice. Practically solitude. And solitude was in short supply since the Blackout. In the weeks following that event, most people thought that the solar flare —or whatever it was—had brought all the ghosts back from some other place. But the truth was that they had never actually left. Whatever freakish charge the flare blasted into the Earth's atmosphere, it just made the ghosts of everyone who had ever died much more apparent. And there were, by conservative estimates, about a hundred billion of them. So it was tough afterwards to find a solitary place anywhere in the world, given that ghosts tended to occupy all the spaces people used to have solitude in. And all the other spaces too.

Ghost number one in Ryan's apartment was Benny, killed by heart attack in 1983 at the physical age of thirty-eight and the mental age of about twelve. He had busied himself since his death by scaring people: making things move on shelves, writing threatening messages in dust, and so forth. Before the Blackout, when ghosts were still invisible, he would have been called a "poltergeist". And indeed the movie of that name had come out shortly before his death, and he cited it as inspiration for his post-death hobby. Benny still kept up his old habits even after the Blackout, not bothered by the fact that he could now be seen doing them. What might once have seemed like the machinations of a terrifying trickster spirit, now seemed like a fat guy in a tracksuit being a bit of a jerk. Ryan had one morning caught him on the kitchen counter, trying and failing to open all the cupboard doors. And every time someone knocked at the front door, Benny would bolt for it first with a cry of "I'll get it!". Yet in the years Ryan had been there Benny had never once managed to get it open. These tricks were an annoyance, but Benny was otherwise friendly enough. And he spent a lot of his time out of the apartment, "scaring" people elsewhere. So Ryan didn't mind him.

The second ghost was a man whom Ryan took to be an Algonquian tribesman, likely dead since long before the Europeans had even arrived. He wasn't inclined towards communication, so Ryan didn't know his name or anything about him. He spent nearly all of his time fairly unobtrusively in the fridge. If you opened the fridge door you could see his body up to the neck, and if you opened the freezer door above it you could see his face staring at you in astonishment over a bag of frozen Lima beans. Ryan so rarely saw him that he didn't mind him at all. Ryan would say the occasional hello when he needed to get ice cubes, and the ghost might, on a good day, grunt in reply. But that was about the extent of their interaction.

The third, of course, was Sye. Sye was the problem.

Sye looked to be in his 80's, and although he never spoke, Ryan guessed from his clothes that he had died sometime in the 1940's or perhaps 50's. He never moved from the kitchen chair that had been in the apartment already when Ryan moved in. It was an objectively hideous chair made of some unidentifiable yellowish wood that was somehow developing fresh new knots on top of its old knots as it aged, and it appeared to be lashed together with strips of varnished bark. Ryan kept it when he moved in, partly because he needed another chair, but mostly because he was waiting for Sye to vacate it so that he could remove it discreetly. But Sye never, ever left it. Ryan had to guess that the chair had special meaning for Sye. Maybe he had built it himself. It was old enough. But it didn't seem like an achievement to be proud of, or attached to.

Sye was really only a problem at breakfast.

While it has been asserted that breakfast is the most important meal of the day, Ryan took the concept and ran with it in entirely new directions. It had nothing to do with nutrition. In fact, he specifically avoided nutrition as a factor by selecting only the most honey-coated, multi-colored, vitamin-and-mineral-devoid brands of puffed chemical nonsense on the market. Some had special meaning from his childhood. But he had never stopped discovering new ones, even as he crossed into his 30's. He had become a connoisseur of them, a sommelier of cereals. He was able to assign exactly the right sugar-frosted puffed-corn-and-marshmallow delicacy to each day based on the time of year, the weather, what he had on his agenda, and how long his present supply of milk had been in the fridge. When he got it exactly right, it could set him up for a day of productivity and success. But when he got it wrong or, worse, when he ran out of milk and had to eat his cereal dry, it could put him in a dark frame of mind that made normal functioning nearly impossible.

Ryan rarely ate dinner at the table. He liked to watch TV at dinner time and it was hard to see the TV from the kitchen. But he liked to eat breakfast at the kitchen table, because it afforded him a view of the cupboards so that while he ate he could plan what he was going to eat the following day and determine if he needed to pick up anything for it. And in the spring the sunrise aligned with the little kitchen window, providing a bit of light in the morning.

But Sye's chair was between Ryan and the window. His vaporous form was dense enough that, while technically Ryan could see the sunrise through him, Sye diffused all the morning brilliance right out of it. It made Ryan resent Sye even more in the spring.

Plus Ryan couldn't take Sye staring at him. Sye never spoke, and had one look: an accusing one. Ryan guessed that Sye was mad at him for moving into what Sye probably still considered his home. But Ryan wasn't moving out over an angry old man, dead for nearly a century. He also wasn't about to move the chair, since that would likely only make Sye angrier.

So for a while Ryan regularly took his cereal bowl to the sofa and ate breakfast in front of the TV even though he didn't want to. And Sye would stay where he was, staring at Ryan's empty chair as though furious at how Ryan wasn't in it to be stared at.

Those were dark days. Holding his bowl in his lap inevitably meant drops of milk falling onto the cushions and soaking in, and sometimes bits of cereal would tumble out into recesses of the sofa where they could never be recovered except by vacuum. Sometimes his mood was so dark that he wouldn't even finish.

After a few weeks of that, Ryan decided he was giving Sye too much power. He was going to eat at the table and pretend Sye wasn't there. That's what people did post-Blackout: carry on like the ghosts weren't there. It felt rude at first but constant interaction with them just wasn't possible. There were too many of them.

Besides which, Ryan reasoned, this was *his* place now. Maybe Sye had lived there in the distant past. But his time was done. Just because he was physically constrained to this place forever by some cosmic rule didn't mean he paid rent. If one of the two of them was an intruder or a squatter, it wasn't Ryan.

Emboldened by that, and also by the sour milk smell the couch was taking on, Ryan embarked on a show of territorial strength.

He started eating breakfast at the table. He half-expected Sye to protest, to angrily overturn the table and demand that Ryan leave. But Sye didn't react at all. He just stared at Ryan with that seething soup of hate behind his vaporous eyes. Ryan ate in silence and pretended Sye wasn't there, feeling the old man's semi-translucent anger directed at him the whole time.

He kept it up for nearly two years. Eating his breakfast quietly at the table, thinking about tomorrow's breakfast, glancing up occasionally at Sye and looking quickly away. Neither of them saying anything.

Two years. And then Sye's chair fell over, and everything changed.

Ryan did not kick it on purpose, or at least not completely on purpose. But it was an early morning and Ryan was off to a bad start after trying to get through a bowl of Frosted Flakes without taking notice of Sye's simmering rage. He had planned Frosted Flakes for this morning because A) it was autumn, B) the forecast called for rain, and C) he had to get up while it was still dark out if he was going to walk to the bus in time. Golden flakes of corn lovingly factory-drenched in sugar could have eased him gently into a miserable day like that. But because of Sye and his relentless eye-hate, the day now promised to be cold and wet and hopeless. When he left the table to get dressed, he passed too close to Sye's chair and caught the leg with one foot. Almost sort of not on purpose.

But he completely forgot that Sye had no weight, so he was essentially kicking an empty chair. He had almost sort of not intended to shift it an inch at most, but instead it pivoted a half turn, caught on a protruding floorboard, and tipped. Reflexively, Ryan grabbed the back of the chair to keep it from falling, and his hand passed inadvertently into the substance of Sye's back.

Ryan felt a surge of electricity flow upwards through his hand. The hairs on his arm stood on end.

He had passed through ghosts before, felt that tingle and experienced flashes of foreign emotions and thoughts as their being passed through his. Everyone had. Since the Blackout, it was impossible to walk a block without passing through a dozen of them. People had been doing it even before the ghosts were obvious, only without realizing it.

This was vastly more powerful. He was blasted by a jolt of sadness-contentment-love-loneliness-joy-humanity-frustration-anger-longing. Ryan thought that it might be everything Sye had ever felt in his entire existence, all compressed into one moment. Its intensity stunned Ryan, and the sheer volume of emotions was staggering, especially given that he had always thought Sye's emotional range went from rage to smoldering disdain, and nowhere else.

Ryan jerked his hand back. The chair followed it and toppled backwards, hitting the hardwood with a loud *crack* as the backrest snapped in half down a jagged diagonal line.

Sye hadn't moved. He was still sitting in the chair in stubborn defiance of physics, lying on his back on the floor and aiming his resentment at the ceiling. He seemed to have no awareness that his vertical alignment had changed so radically.

Still reeling from the rush of emotions that weren't his, Ryan delicately lifted the chair onto its legs, holding the two halves of the back, each dangling by a single rusted screw, so they wouldn't come off. He slid the chair back to its spot at the table, and Sye moved with it like he was an immutable, massless part of the chair's construction. The two disconnected halves of the chair back wouldn't take any weight, but Sye had no weight and didn't seem to notice.

Forgetting the time, Ryan sat across from Sye and studied him for the first time ever. Really *looked* at him. Sye's expression hadn't changed. He looked like he would dive across the table and choke Ryan if he could.

But Ryan understood now. He had felt Sye's entire emotional life in fast-forward and first-person, and he knew Sye's anger had a specific focus. It wasn't directed at Ryan at all. He had been wrong this whole time.

It was the chair. Sye wanted out of the chair.

The chair, wherever it had come from, was his prison. He

was doomed to haunt it forever, and it was keeping him from doing… something.

Despite ruined Frosted Flakes, Ryan's day was looking up. Because he now understood that he and Sye had something in common.

They both wanted Sye gone from the breakfast table.

THREE

The day after Ryan kicked over Sye's chair, he arrived home from work to find Benny the Poltergeist trying to push a nearly empty water glass off the kitchen counter. It sat right on the edge, and Benny kept sweeping his hand through it like he was trying to waft away a foul odor, but the glass was refusing to move. Despite the possibility of having to clean up broken glass later, Ryan was glad to find Benny at home because he had spent the entire day at work thinking about asking him a question. He couldn't even remember having done any actual work, though there must have been some in there somewhere.

"Benny, can I talk to you for a second?"

"Why? Are you scared?" Benny dropped his voice a few octaves and dragged out the word "scared" like a taunt. "Things moving on their own? Noises in the night? Things going missing without explanation?"

"Are you saying you hid something?"

"No."

"What did you hide?"

"Nothing. Would you be scared if this glass fell off the counter all by itself?" He swept his hand through it again, evidently hoping that it would finally topple with impeccable dramatic timing. It didn't. He sagged.

"I'll let you keep trying to do that if you answer a question for me."

Benny shrugged. "Fair enough." He hoisted himself onto the counter to listen. Ryan wondered at the contradiction of Benny sitting like that. One minute he could sweep his hand through a glass like it wasn't there, and the next he could sit on the counter like he was still made of something. How did that work?

"I've seen you leave the apartment," Ryan said. "You can come and go all you want, right?"

"Yep. I'm a free spirit! Literally."

"How did you get to be that? I heard ghosts have to stay pretty much in one place."

"Not all. Some people get lucky. Like me."

"How does that work?"

"I'm not sure. Something about strong emotional attachments at the moment you die. I heard it on a talk show. I guess I didn't love anyplace when my ticker exploded."

"But you're here most of the time. Did you die here?"

"Pfft, no. I never even lived here."

"So… why are you…" Ryan decided halfway through his question that asking it might lead down a whole tangential road. Benny's history wasn't why he had entered this conversation. "What about Sye?"

Benny looked over at Sye, who was in his broken chair staring indignantly across the table at nothing. "That guy? He's always been here. Never leaves the chair."

"So he's haunting the chair."

"Probably. Poor guy. Can you imagine that? Having to sit forever in a chair from, like, Gilligan's Island?"

"Is there any way to break them up? Let him go? Like, can I exorcise the chair or something?"

Benny snorted derisively. "I've been exorcised like five times and it never did anything to me. I mean, I did leave the place after, but only because I wanted to. When a priest tells you to go to Hell, he means it literally. I gotta tell you, it makes you feel pretty unwelcome." He hopped off the counter and turned his attention back to the water glass. "But if you really want to help him, you could try the Clinic. They do that kind of thing."

"What Clinic?"

"The Post-Mortal Services Clinic. Been open about a year and a half, someplace here in Cambridge I think. Ghosts go there when they need stuff done. If they're haunting something they don't want to be haunting, the Clinic can take care of that. I have this buddy, died of a stroke at a McDonald's and got stuck haunting a Filet-o-Fish. He must've really liked Filet-o-Fish, I guess. Anyway, after a couple of years the thing was really starting to stink. He got his brother to carry it to the Clinic. Pow, no more Filet. He still hangs around that McDonald's a lot, but I think that's by choice."

Ryan nodded. He had never heard of a Post-Mortal Services Clinic, or known that any such place might exist, but it sounded perfect. He searched around for his tablet to look up the address. "Thanks, Benny. I'll look into that."

"No problem. Now prepare to be terrified." Benny went back to trying to shove the water glass off the counter. "The secret is, you don't move the glass. You move the air *around* the glass."

"And that works?"

"Almost never."

A few minutes later when Ryan was dialing the Clinic, he heard the sharp crack of the glass shattering on the floor behind him. And he had to admit that it scared him a little.

The Post-Mortal Services Clinic turned out to be only a ten-minute walk from Ryan's apartment, on a drab and busy section of Massachusetts Avenue near Davis Square otherwise populated by banks, convenience stores, and bland four-story apartment boxes.

Ryan managed to get an appointment on a Saturday morning, early enough that the streets and sidewalks were still quiet. He walked the whole distance with Sye's chair slung over his shoulder, Sye himself glued resolutely to it and apparently oblivious to the rocking motion of Ryan's walk.

Ryan had refused to consider a later appointment. Every city in the world was thick with ghosts since the Blackout, but the older a city was, the worse they had it. On Saturday afternoons, Boston's streets were typically bustling with a million or so living people out doing their weekend things. But their numbers were dwarfed by the billion or more ghosts crammed onto every sidewalk and meandering the streets as far as their hauntings would allow them. There was barely a square inch of space in the city not occupied by numerous roaming ghosts. If they weren't immaterial it would have been impossible for the still-living to move.

But Ryan was out early, and it was sunny. The living were still asleep, and the ghosts were hard to see. On cloudy days they were practically solid, like the city was submerged in a thick fog with faces. But on a bright day like this their shimmering outlines had no detail, like he was walking through a sea of human-sized soap bubbles. He much preferred these days. It gave the illusion that the street was emptier than it really was. And seeing the details on unfamiliar ghosts was frequently disturbing. Many times he had made accidental eye contact with someone only to realize a second too late that they must have been flattened by a dump truck or fallen off of something high. A semi-translucent gaping head wound is still a gaping head wound. And flat is never a good look, alive or dead.

The Clinic itself was a monolithic slab of dark brown brick. It was a decade old at most but sported white columns framing the front door in an attempt at classical austerity. It possessed all the "I should whisper when I'm here" somberness of an old church without the stained-glass holiness.

Ryan couldn't think why he recognized the building. It wasn't until he stepped through the front entrance that he figured it out. He'd been here once before, in pre-Blackout days. For a funeral.

The funeral business had been one of the hardest hit by the effects of the Blackout. With the dead never actually going anywhere, there didn't seem much point in having a funeral anymore. If you wanted to have a gathering to tell affectionate stories about someone after they died, you were likely to invite them along to join in. So funerals were rare, and funeral homes went out of business almost literally overnight.

So it wasn't surprising that the building had been re-purposed. Ryan just felt like they could have tried harder. The inside of the building, though it had clearly been remodeled quite recently, still retained a lot of the same funereal atmosphere it had needed before the Blackout. Except that the waiting room with piped-in classic pop and inspirational fitness magazines would have seemed inappropriate to anyone waiting to put a loved one to rest. *Dancing Queen* isn't funeral music.

If funeral homes had any advantage over other common buildings, it was that they tended not to be overly haunted. While lots of dead people passed through funeral homes, very few of them stayed there. So the waiting room had only current clients in it, one alive and one dead. The ghost was an ancient woman in a hospital gown. She looked old-lady-sweet, almost pixie-ish, except for the wide gash on her abdomen. From his one quick glance Ryan had already surmised that the wound was oozing. It confused him. What could a ghost possibly have inside it that could ooze? He guessed that she must have died in surgery, but that did little to explain the ghostly seepage. The other one waiting was not a ghost but a living man, very slight and balding, with a prodigious mustache. He fidgeted the whole time he waited. Ryan wondered idly what he was there for. Perhaps he had brought a ghost relative in to have something done, and was waiting for them to come out. He was eventually called in by name, leaving Ryan alone with Sye and the ghostly surgery victim.

Sye sat in his chair, staring straight ahead exactly as he had always done at home. Ryan had positioned Sye's chair slightly offset from his so they wouldn't be staring at each other for the entire wait.

There was a simple form to fill out for the visit, but Ryan was tripped up by several of the necessary fields. He had no idea what Sye's last name was, or whether he was a citizen, or his marital status, or indeed anything at all about him. He wasn't even completely convinced that his first name was Sye. But he didn't want to risk delaying the appointment, so he just filled it all in with his own name and stats, and hoped nobody would ask. Then he leaned so Sye could see him.

"Sye, you know why we're here, right?"

Sye stared ahead, looking as choleric as ever. Ryan had never received even the slightest hint that Sye comprehended anything. Perhaps he didn't speak English. Perhaps he couldn't hear. There was no way to tell.

Ryan pressed on anyway. "I'm going to get you out of that chair so you can go do... whatever it is you want to do. Forever. Do you understand? No more breakfasts."

Still nothing. They sat in silence. Ryan skimmed a pamphlet of the Clinic's services that he found mixed in with the magazines. "Unhaunting" seemed to be the most prominent one, and the one he had brought Sye in for. But there were others he would never have thought of. Ghosts could have their density adjusted to be more visible, or more invisible. If they were trapped in an infinite loop of repetitive action, they could have the loop broken. Other services he had to read about twice and still couldn't understand what they meant.

Ryan didn't make it to the end of the pamphlet before the man with the mustache returned.

Ryan sensed right away that something was different

about the man. But he was slow to figure out what it was. When he finally put it together, he couldn't believe it had taken him so long.

The man with the mustache was dead.

He had gone in alive, and half an hour later he came out dead.

And he looked delighted about it.

Ryan knew that he was staring at the man, wide-eyed and agape. But the now-ghostly mustache man ignored him. He drifted languidly through the waiting room to the exit. And missed the exit door by a foot or so in his reverie, passing right through the wall instead.

Ryan struggled to explain what had happened. Unless the man had been murdered during his appointment—which seemed unlikely given how happy he appeared—how had this happened?

Ryan didn't have long to wonder, because seconds after the man departed, Ryan's name was called.

He quickly pulled himself together, delicately picked up Sye's chair by the two halves of its back, and carried Sye with it into the appointment.

FOUR

The fluorescent lights in the examination room buzzed like surgical saws.

Ryan suspected this room had been used for embalming in the funeral home days. It was in the basement, and had a corresponding damp chill. But at some point since the demise of the funeral business it had been dressed up in a simulation of comfort. The slab table was covered with a thin cushion and a fitted sheet, and the walls were painted a pale blue that, beneath the incessant lights, was more blinding than soothing. Whatever instruments of horror he imagined had once been down here were mercifully gone, although he could still see the drain set into the tile floor where God-knows-what used to sluice down.

He wished Sye would say something. Or at least move. But the old ghost sat with his chair propped against the exam table, staring hatefully at the wall as though robin's-egg blue was a mortal offense to him.

A lab-coated woman strode in. She went right past Ryan like he wasn't there and gave Sye a clinical smile. "Hello," she said coolly.

Sye, unsurprisingly, didn't respond.

Ryan guessed that the doctor was probably only recently into her 30's, but it was hard to tell anything about her because under the merciless lights she just looked, as anyone would, sallow and green. All he could see for sure was that her hair was tied up tightly, she wore glasses, and she seemed utterly unwilling to acknowledge his presence in the room.

She sat on a wheeled stool and rolled it close to Sye. "Just need to scan your SES, don't move please." She dipped the end of a hand-held scanner into Sye's side and held a button down for several seconds. That done, she pushed her glasses up her nose and studied him intently. "At least a seventy percent particulate density, resolved down to the millimeter or less." Ryan didn't know why she was saying this out loud. It seemed like the sort of information that would normally be noted on a chart. Did she expect him to know what she was talking about? He was relieved when she pulled a chart from a drawer nearby, and noted things on it.

She leaned in close to study the old chair where Sye's form touched it. "And you're looking for an unhaunting?"

No answer from Sye, so Ryan piped in. "I think so."

The doctor looked at Ryan for the first time and pushed her glasses up her nose as she studied him. The way her gaze scanned over him made him feel like she was precisely calculating his surface area. "You're family?"

"Well, no, not family." He fumbled for a way to explain the situation. "We eat breakfast."

She sighed. "So I presume he haunts where you live?"

"Yes."

She lost interest in him right away and spoke closely to Sye. "Mr. Matney…"

"Um… *I'm* Mr. Matney," Ryan interrupted. "I don't know Sye's last name, so I just filled in the form with my name. Sorry."

She glanced at him again, and he felt like in that moment of eye contact she was breaking down his chemical composition component by component. But she said nothing and returned her attention to Sye. "You want to not be in the chair anymore. Is that right?"

"Yes. Please," Ryan said.

"Sye?" she said, pointedly ignoring Ryan.

Sye stared straight ahead, giving her only what he ever gave Ryan. Ryan let the silence drag out for a few seconds before venturing another try. "He doesn't say… or do… anything. Ever."

"Then how do you know he wants out of the chair?"

"It's a guess. I mean, why wouldn't he?"

She let out an exasperated snort. "Let me guess. You want him out of your house."

"Well, yeah, but..."

She stood up from her stool and emphatically closed her file. "I'm not an exorcist, Mr. Matney. Who are you to say what this man wants or doesn't want?"

"I think I..." Ryan didn't know what he was going to say, but she wasn't interested anyway.

"I get people like you in here all the time. We all have ghosts in our homes. They are people. People do not stop being people just because their bodies are gone. They have rights. They..."

"Touch him," Ryan interrupted her as calmly as he could muster.

"Excuse me?"

"Touch him. Please."

"We are not allowed to..."

"You want to know what he wants or doesn't want, just touch him. I have. By accident. I would be happy to have him out of my house, that's true, but believe me, there is nobody who has ever wanted out of anything as much as this man wants out of this chair."

She hesitated, studying Sye's face again, maybe hoping for some sign that he was listening to them.

Finally, like she was poking an avocado on the shelf to test for squishiness, she let her finger deftly dart out and poke into Sye's torso. Only for a second.

Ryan heard her breath catch in her throat. She shivered. Her face transformed and softened in an instant as a wave went through her. Ryan knew exactly what she was feeling because he had felt it.

She hovered for a moment, looking deep into Sye's eyes. Her eyes were wide, and he thought perhaps teary.

Finally she said "This should take about five minutes."

The doctor rolled something out from its hiding place behind a counter. It was an electronic box riding on the top shelf of a wheeled metal cart. The box itself was as utilitarian and nondescript as it could be. It was gray, about the size of a microwave, with a simple LCD display embedded on the front. It had various knobs and buttons whose purpose he couldn't guess. On the cart's lower shelf was a power supply brick the size of a cinder block, which struck Ryan as probably being dangerously high-voltage for something riding on an eight dollar craft-store cart. Attached to the main box by a baffling spiderweb of wires was a collection of things that late-night vacuum infomercials refer to as "optional attachments". Some were shiny steel prods, some were paddles, others looked like spatulas and old radio microphones. He counted eight different inscrutable accessories, two hanging on each of the cart's four sides. The whole assembly gave the distinct impression of having been cobbled together from kitchen appliances and jumper cables.

The doctor flipped the biggest switch on the box, a rocker that took up an entire edge of the front console. Even from where he sat, Ryan could see that it was labeled "Master Power" with a plastic strip printed out of a label maker.

"This will just take a minute to charge up," the doctor said. She directed all her attention to writing on her chart, evidently to shut down any attempt he might make at conversation.

Ryan was desperately curious about the box, with its array of inexplicable lights and its various tentacle-like appendages. But she already seemed annoyed, and the fear of annoying her even more overruled everything else. He stayed silent.

The metal box made a steady, pulsating drone that rose in pitch as a progress bar on the LCD display inched from left to right.

Ryan's curiosity tugged at him. Attempting to look like he was casually passing the time, he strolled around the exam table. He pretended to study the paintings hung on the walls, all the while seeing if he could get close enough to the box to read the other labels stuck to the front of it.

"Stand back, please," she said without looking up.

He obediently took a few steps back. "Sorry, I was…" He didn't have an actual excuse and she didn't appear to want one. So he stopped speaking.

He waited.

When she still hadn't looked up after another twenty seconds he tried a different tack, leaning towards the box but moving no closer to it. He leaned as far as his balance allowed, but he still couldn't read the small text on any of the knobs and dials. He squinted and held his pose, hoping that she'd look up and notice that he was curious.

Out of the corner of his squint he caught a flicker of movement. She had glanced at him.

"Sorry," he said, "I was just trying to read the…" he flicked his finger in a circle, vaguely pointing at the box.

She finally spoke again, still writing on her chart. "If you have a specific question…"

"How does it work?"

She grunted irritably. "That question is the opposite of specific."

"Sorry."

She stopped writing. "Strong emotional attachment in life creates a molecular bond between the ghost and an object or a place."

"How?"

"We don't know."

"Okay."

"This appliance breaks the molecular bond with directed electrical charge."

"And that works?"

"We wouldn't be in business if it didn't."

Ryan obligingly went silent.

He considered asking about the mustache man from the waiting room, but he let the box get to half charge before he dared speak again. "Oh, doctor… I meant to ask…"

"I'm not a doctor." The words were icy enough to chill the air.

"Oh. Sorry. But I meant to ask…"

"Mm hmm," she said, while clearly implying "shut up".

"Before us there was a guy who came in. He was alive when he came in, but when he left…"

"Mm hmm," she said again. Still not looking at him.

"Why…" Ryan started. He wasn't sure how to phrase the question. "I mean… what happened there?"

"I can't discuss other clients."

"No, of course not." He let the box's pitch climb another octave or so. "But hypothetically…"

"Extraction," she said curtly. She glanced at the machine, most likely hoping it was done charging so she could end this conversation now. But it wasn't.

Ryan pressed on, fascinated. "Extraction? Extracting what?"

"We don't do teeth here, Mr. Matney."

It sounded ridiculous in his head but he said it anyway. "You extracted his ghost?"

"Correct."

"Why?"

"He was not my client, but I assume that he requested it. It is one of the services we provide."

"But why would he want that?"

"You'd have to ask him, wouldn't you?"

"Okay. Put it this way: why would *anyone* want that?"

She looked at the ceiling. "If you want to discuss the possibilities, you need to speak with…" She chewed on the name like a sharp bone found in her chicken. "…Roger. The owner. Upstairs."

As if it had been listening to her and wanted to hit its cue, the box's drone reached a crescendo and overlaid that with a tinny *ping*. She failed to conceal her relief. "Please stand back," she said.

Ryan obediently took a step backwards. He watched as the not-a-doctor lifted two horseshoe-shaped paddles off the cart and uncoiled the long wires connecting them to the box. She leaned in close to Sye, holding them in front of her. Sye still showed no awareness of anything happening.

"What are you doing?" Ryan couldn't resist asking.

"What you came in for," she replied unhelpfully. She positioned one paddle beneath the seat of the chair and the other behind the backrest. He was impressed with how steady she was able to hold them, not touching the chair or Sye, but perfectly still in what seemed precisely calculated spots. She was good at this.

She pressed gently with one foot on a pedal wired to the bottom of the cart. She did it so exactingly that the rest of her body stayed motionless. The paddles in her hands still didn't move at all. They seemed locked rigidly in space. Ryan wondered how she did it.

The machine made a heavy *pop* like a giant flashbulb.

The paddles in her hands ignited with bursts of blue energy that crackled for only a fraction of a second, but were powerful enough to jolt the chair violently. Half of the broken back came loose and dangled by the one screw holding it on.

The drone from the box dropped to silence, then immediately began rising through the octaves again, much more quickly this time. Another burst was coming.

Ryan sprang forward, grabbed the dangling half of the chair back and swiveled it into place. He didn't know if the broken back would affect the procedure, but he thought it better to be safe. The technician, or whatever she was, ignored or didn't notice him. She kept the paddles rock steady as another *pop* rattled the cart. Ryan jumped back, barely getting out of the way of the burst of crackling energy. He felt it tug at the hair on his arms.

She held the paddles steady for another few seconds, and then took her foot off the pedal and withdrew the paddles, careful not to let them touch the chair.

The box's drone descended fast to nothing. A fan on the back switched on.

She relaxed. "That's it," she said.

Nothing appeared to be different. Sye sat in the chair, staring angrily straight ahead. Ryan had expected him to leap triumphantly out of the chair, and perhaps to shower Ryan with gratitude. In some of Ryan's more optimistic imaginings of this moment, Sye even started to break-dance. But none of that happened. He didn't move at all.

"Did it work?" Ryan asked.

He was surprised to find the technician smiling softly, watching Sye with what appeared to be wide-eyed wonder. Ryan warmed up to her a little. "It worked," she said. "Give him a second."

Sye remained seated and still for what felt like minutes.

And then Ryan was astonished to see the anger on Sye's face melt away, replaced with an expression of curiosity and puzzlement. Ryan had never seen any expression other than anger on Sye's face, so although he had been expecting a change, the transformation still took him by surprise.

Sye shifted in his seat and looked down at his chair quizzically, like it wasn't the color he remembered it to be.

"He feels it," the technician said. "He's figuring out that he's not haunting it anymore." She looked like she might cry. Like someone who had just set a rescued fawn loose in the wild.

Ryan held his breath. He still held out some small hope for the break-dancing.

Sye—perhaps for the first time since his death—stood up.

He bounced tentatively, testing the unfamiliar weight on his legs. But right away he stooped, holding his back. He stumbled backwards and sat in the chair again. He immediately looked relieved to be off his feet.

Ryan was immeasurably disappointed. "What's happening? Why is he sitting again?"

Sye shifted his weight backwards in the chair and closed his eyes. Like he needed a nap already.

The technician, too, seemed let down. "Give him time," she said. "He obviously wants to get up. But he's old."

"He's a ghost!"

"He's a man who died old. And surely you've heard, whatever your state at the time of death, that's the state of your ghost. If he had problems getting around before he died, then he's going to have problems now."

"That's not fair."

"That's life. And death." She closed her file and stood. "Take him home. Give him a little time." The chill returned to her voice. "You don't have to kick him out today, you know."

Ryan was slightly offended that she thought so little of him when he felt like he was being heroically considerate.

Sye's eyes were still closed and he hadn't moved, aside from clutching his knees with both hands. It seemed cosmically unjust to Ryan that Sye would be like this forever. It was hard, he was sure, to spend a few years alive in that state. But to spend the rest of time enfeebled? It almost seemed worth getting your ghost out before—

Something clicked in Ryan's head. The mustache man. "This is why people do it," he said. "Extraction. They get out of their body early, while they're young, so they get a good ghost. So they don't have to spend forever like Sye."

"Yes. That is why they do it. More often than not."

Ryan let the idea meander around in his head. He waited

for it to settle. Wondered if it might stay for a chat. "It kind of makes sense," he said. "Doesn't it?"

She paused on her way past and looked at him. She seemed to want to answer. But she struggled with it, and finally just said "Will you let me know what happens with Sye? If he goes anywhere?"

Ryan could tell by her voice that this wasn't professional interest. She cared.

"Sure," he said.

The technician-who-was-not-a-doctor nodded and disappeared into the corridor, leaving Ryan alone with Sye.

Still in his chair.

Ryan carried Sye's chair home from the Clinic the same way he had carried it there: over his shoulder, with Sye glued to it like it wasn't moving at all.

The street was already far more populous than it had been just over an hour earlier when he arrived. The ghosts were dense enough now to give him the sense of walking through foam with thousands of eyes floating in it. He tried to ignore their stares and their occasional pleas for conversation. He ducked off Mass Ave. as soon as he could, and into the relatively less-dense side streets. It would take him longer to get home, but it would be worth it.

He thought about dropping the chair on the sidewalk and leaving it. Sye could leave it at will. Why should Ryan be forced to take him home?

He didn't have an answer aside from his nagging conscience. So he brought Sye and the chair home.

He placed the chair back in its usual spot next to the table. He expected to see relief or satisfaction on Sye's face. Or, less likely, gratitude. But Sye's face betrayed nothing.

Ryan checked on him several times through the course of Saturday and never saw him move. Never saw his expression change. Ryan had already amended his plans for Sunday because they relied on Sye not being there. Breakfast was high on the list. As was buying a whole set of new chairs for the kitchen.

Late Saturday night—late enough that it might have been Sunday morning—Ryan woke to see a figure standing in his bedroom door. He had to blink the sleep and surprise from his eyes to make out details.

Sye stood in the doorway, peering in at Ryan. His face was expressionless. Not angry anymore, but not happy either. Not anything other than serious and hard.

They stared at each other for half a minute or so, neither saying anything.

Ryan finally broke the silence. "Sye?"

Sye betrayed no hint of having heard him. Just stared. Ryan felt cold.

Without a sound or a flicker, Sye shuffled his feet and stepped out of sight.

Ryan waited to see if he would reappear. Within a few minutes, Ryan nodded off again.

When he woke on Sunday, the chair was empty. Sye was not in it, nor was he anywhere in the apartment.

Ryan poured a giant bowl of Cocoa Puffs because he felt both good and guilty and wasn't sure why he felt either one. Cocoa Puffs were a solid choice for both.

He ate them alone at the table, watching the sun come up unobstructed through the little window behind Sye's empty chair.

A thought crept into his mind, and it conjured up both excitement and worry in equal measures.

Cocoa Puffs were a solid choice for both of those too.

FIVE

When Ryan called for an appointment the day after Sye's procedure, he wasn't sure why he was doing it. He told himself it was just to gather information. He had not decided anything, and he was not going to decide anything. He was going to get a brochure, ask questions, and then leave and stop thinking about it. If he forgot about it, no harm done. If the idea stayed in his head—

He refused to contemplate that. That was getting ahead of himself. *Gather information. That's all.*

Roger Foster, the Director of the Post-Mortal Services Clinic, was a towering, spidery man well into his fifties, with a close-cropped silver beard and frosty gray eyes above which hovered eyebrows that could curl into a hundred different variations of sympathetic expression. Ryan could imagine him as a funeral director, which was no doubt what he had once been. Ryan could imagine him even more as a funeral director in Victorian times. His spindly form and pale, sharp features would have looked like death itself clad in a black suit and top hat. Instead, in defiance of the sombre funeral parlor office he worked in, he wore a lab coat with sleeves far too short for him. They probably didn't come in his size. People shaped like him were more likely to be the subjects of experiments rather than the ones performing them.

"It's an important distinction," Roger was saying. "We are not talking about 'killing' you."

"Well what do you call it then?" Ryan expected him to have a euphemism for this kind of thing, something equal parts science and bureaucracy. "Artificially Induced Life Cessation", or something equally clinical. But he wasn't falling for that. They were still talking about killing him. He wanted them to be upfront about it.

"Killing you would be illegal," Roger went on, in a speech he had clearly given a thousand times to a thousand people just like Ryan. He picked up one of many odd souvenir-shop trinkets from his desk and fiddled with it as he talked. "Murder is still a crime, though the courts remain tied up deciding exactly what constitutes a murder in these haunted times. Ending a mortal life is no longer a capital crime anywhere, and in some states is barely worse than credit card fraud. But it remains a crime nonetheless. So we can't do that."

Ryan found himself weirdly trusting this man. He knew it was because Roger talked in a warm, soothing, funeral director voice, the one he had undoubtedly used to convince people, at the worst time in their lives, to spend extra thousands on felt casket interiors. But he was good at it. The voice worked. If somebody was going to kill him, Ryan kind of wanted it to be Roger.

He had to remind himself again. *But you haven't decided to do that. You're staying alive for now.* Why was it so hard to stay in that frame of mind?

"What we do," Roger continued, "is simply to extract your ghost from your body. With your consent, obviously. Your body goes right on living. Entirely unconscious, of course, but with all its biological functions intact. There's certainly nothing illegal about that yet."

Ryan barely caught the last word. "Sorry, did you say 'yet'?"

"I don't think I did. Any other questions?"

Ryan was almost certain he had heard "yet", but he didn't feel like pressing the issue. "What happens to my body? After I'm... you know, 'out'?"

"We keep it in a secure storage facility here. Hence the monthly fee." Roger tapped the brochure on the desk between them, which laid out all the costs of the procedure.

"That covers keeping your body warm and clean and intravenously fed until it expires naturally. You may rest assured that once you have left your body, it will be comfortable and well maintained for as long as it continues to live. If it happens to become terminally ill and expire prematurely, well that's just savings for you. Your monthly fee is terminated, and our business is done."

Ryan didn't like the idea of his body being terminally ill and him not being there to help it. But he supposed if he was going to suffer from a terminal illness, better to skip out and let his body do the suffering without him.

There remained one thing, the thing that scared him most, and he had to ask. "How do you actually... do... it?" *If it hurts,* he thought, *there's no way I'm doing it.*

"The extraction?" Roger smiled. He set down the trinket he had been fiddling with. It was a snow globe with a little model of Myrtle Beach in it. Ryan could tell it was Myrtle Beach because most of the actual beach was taken up by the words "Myrtle Beach" in big black plastic letters. He wondered in passing if it ever actually snowed in Myrtle Beach, or if that was just the fantasy of some over-zealous snow globe designer. "Ah, now the extraction is something you needn't worry about either," Roger went on. "There's nothing to it, really. Science has known for years how to create what they called an 'out-of-body experience' by stimulating certain areas of the brain with targeted electrical impulses. They assumed this to be evidence that such experiences were not actually a departure from the body, but merely a trick of the brain. But of course we now know that science was wrong."

"So this is all totally scientific?"

"Oh heavens no. According to science none of this should work at all. But according to science there shouldn't be any such thing as ghosts. And yet look out the window. There are a hundred billion of them out there. That's why nobody listens to science anymore."

Ryan found that hard to argue with. "Huh," was all he got out.

Roger went on: "And the procedure is, of course, fully guaranteed."

"Guaranteed?"

"If you're not completely satisfied with your ghostly existence, the process is fully refundable and reversible for ten days."

Ryan felt his eyebrows shoot up. "Reversible? I can get back into my body?"

"That's right. For ten days. After that, the body stops being receptive to the ghost."

"Why ten days?"

"I've no idea."

"Huh." *Shouldn't he know something like that?*

"Of course you need time to think. Take all the time you need. This is, after all, quite possibly the most important life decision you will ever make."

"More of a 'death' decision," Ryan said with a chuckle. He instantly regretted it because surely Roger had heard that one a million times.

Roger smiled wanly. "Once again, Mr. Matney, you are not dying. Nobody is killing you. Both you and your body will be just as much alive after the procedure as before it. You might even say you'll be more alive than you've ever been, completely unshackled from your mortal limitations."

He made it sound, just with the tone of his voice, like Ryan would be a fool to decide against it. Yet still, Ryan was battling his own survival instinct. *This doesn't feel right,* he kept thinking. *This man wants to kill me. He wants me to pay him to do it. I shouldn't want this.*

Roger stood up and moved around Ryan to the door. "You've got a lot to think about. It's understandable. You don't have to make up your mind right now."

"If I decide I want to do it," Ryan said, "and I'm not saying I will. But if I do, do I need an appointment, or…"

"You can call at any time and we can generally accommodate you within six months. The procedure takes about thirty minutes, and then you're off on your new postmortal life." He opened the door a crack and called through it, "Trudy? Would you show this gentleman out, please."

Before Trudy could arrive, Roger shook Ryan's hand. "Think about it, Mr. Matney. How many years do you have left to live? Forty? Fifty? Compared to the eternity that comes after, it is a drop in the bucket. Not even a drop. A single *atom* in a single drop in the largest bucket you can possibly imagine. Such a small sacrifice to ensure an optimal eternity, don't you think? Ah, but it's up to you, of course."

Trudy, a ghost whom Ryan guessed to be Roger's personal assistant, pushed through the opening in the door. It wasn't quite wide enough so she had to dissolve partially through the door frame. She wore a neat, casual sweater and skirt of indeterminate fashion era. When Ryan couldn't guess a ghost's time period from their clothes he would usually turn to their hair for clues. But in Trudy's case, looking at her hair was futile.

Because Trudy didn't have hair. Or, indeed, a head. There was only a ragged, meaty stump.

Ryan had to look away and suppress the urge to vomit.

Roger patted him on the back. "It's all right. She gets that a lot."

Ryan couldn't look at her beyond a second or two. He felt rude, insensitive. But he also wasn't sure she could see or hear him at all. He didn't know if ghosts needed eyes and ears. Why would they? Why would they need heads? If they were made entirely of gas or energy or whatever elemental particle it was they were made of, what difference would a head-shaped part make?

"Poor Trudy," Roger said, reaching out and pretending to

pat her shoulder. His hand aimed a little low and passed right through her arm instead. "You know those boats people drive around the Everglades in, with the large fan on the back? Those are not as safe as they are made out to be. Here stands the proof! Well, most of it."

Her shoulders pivoted towards Roger a little. Was she looking at him? Her silence made him uncomfortable. Without a head she felt like an unfinished, animated mannequin.

Ryan saw what Roger was doing. *You're a sly one,* he thought. *You're trying to make my mind up for me. Decide to become a ghost now, and avoid Trudy's fate. That's what you're saying.*

Roger pulled the door open wider and Trudy stood aside, holding up an arm to usher Ryan out. Ryan still couldn't look at her.

"You have our number," Roger said, giving Ryan a business card and his best funeral-director smile. "And we have a special discount on for the rest of the month, so I do recommend acting soon. But take all the time you need."

Ryan followed Trudy back down the hall to the waiting room with his eyes on everything but her.

He didn't want Roger's tactic to work. He wanted to be the guy who could see right through sleazy sales tactics, wagging his finger and saying "you're not fooling me".

But as Trudy waved goodbye to him in the waiting room and Ryan thanked her with his eyes fixed on the exit sign over her shoulder, all he could think was: *that could be me. I could step out this door and get hit by a bus, and then I'd have to spend the rest of eternity with tire tracks across my flat head. I could fall down an elevator shaft and spend forever with a broken spine. Best case, I die of old age and spend eternity stooped over like Sye, barely able to take two steps. This life is another few years. That one never, ever ends.*

As he stepped out onto the street and turned towards home, he was already memorizing the number on the business card.

SIX

Congratulations Matney, Ryan on
your decision! Your appointment
is scheduled for Friday, June 10
at 9:30 AM. Please arrive at
least 30 minutes prior to your
scheduled time. Do not park your
vehicle in the Clinic parking
lot, as you will not be alive
afterward to drive it home.

Roger had told Ryan to expect an appointment within six
months. The appointment he got was in three days. It
shocked him at first, and he didn't know whether to be
pleased or scared. He decided to be excited. Get it over with.
What would he do with extra months anyway?

Now that you have taken the
first step to ensure the best
possible post-mortal existence
for yourself, it is time to make
sure you are properly prepared.
We have included a helpful
checklist of practical items
that should be addressed while
you still have a body.

1. Notify your employer of your
decision, and be sure you have
made arrangements to continue
your employment as a ghost,
should you wish to do so.

Ryan quickly discovered that preparations for death, like
death itself, were not as complicated as they had been before

the Blackout, because you would still be around after. If you had living family to provide for, you could likely go right on providing for them after you died. Depending on what your job was, of course. If you worked in construction, you'd probably have to look for a more suitable post-death career because, with rare exceptions, ghosts can't swing hammers. But ghosts could do many jobs just as well as the living. Some they could do better. Ryan's job answering tech support calls for electric razors would be easy to keep doing. There were a few ghosts working in the call center with voice-activated phones, but they weren't any better or worse at it than the living ones.

So it was a decision he could make. Keep the job, or leave it. He didn't have a family to provide for. He didn't even have a pet. And his one potted plant had long since shriveled. So why earn a living? They call it a "living" for a reason. If you're not living, you don't need to earn one.

So the first thing he did on the morning after booking his appointment was quit his job. It took him four tries to get through, which he thought didn't reflect well on the call center. And when he told Dave that he was leaving, they let him go right then, over the phone, without two weeks notice. He suspected they would have his position filled by someone better before lunch.

> 2. Make any necessary
> arrangements to keep your
> present home, or to continue
> haunting it after it is re-sold.

Ryan thought about where he would live. Or rather, he corrected himself, where he would spend his time *not* living. (He was realizing he'd need to get used to a whole new vocabulary. He made a mental note that after the extraction whenever somebody asked him where he lived, he would say "I don't". It might be funny for a while.)

The real estate by-laws concerning ghosts were relatively new, but he knew them because he had been on the other side of them when he rented his apartment. Ghosts were allowed to keep staying where they had lived. Much of the time they were constrained to haunt there anyway so they didn't have much choice in the matter. But the law at least stipulated that, in those cases, they didn't have to pay rent. There were virtually no apartments or houses left anywhere that didn't already have ghosts in them, so what was one more? An apartment could be rented out to someone living without evicting any ghostly former occupants. The deceased occupant was free to stay and haunt all they liked. In the early days after the Blackout this seemed like something of an affront to privacy and property rights. But the fact was that ghosts had been haunting the homes of the living since the dawn of time anyway and nobody had ever tried to sue over it. In a strictly legal sense, nothing much had changed. The courts were effectively saying to ghosts "Keep doing what you've been doing. It's all good."

Ryan decided that he'd stay in his apartment for the time being. It was as unpleasant as ever, but it was at least familiar. And both Benny the Poltergeist and the refrigerated Algonquian seemed at least indifferent to him. Later he would move somewhere more interesting. A bit longer in the apartment wouldn't be a big deal while he figured things out. But he didn't want anybody else moving in and crowding him during that time. So he renewed his lease for another year, and in return Gabriel dimly wished him luck. Ryan felt like they should say goodbye. But it seemed ridiculous because he wasn't going anywhere. So he handed over the check and they were done.

> **3. Take a day to notify your friends and loved ones so that they are not surprised to find that you're a ghost the next**

> time they see you. Consider
> throwing a "GhostDay Party"
> after the procedure to unveil
> the true you!

A day seemed like overkill. Ryan set aside two hours to call friends. And he stopped after thirty minutes because the friends he had called weren't particularly interested. He briefly considered letting his parents know. But he worried that they would try to talk him out of it. Like many of the older generation, they were conditioned to see dying as a major event. They'd probably tell him he had too much to live for, and that sort of thing. As if he was actually talking about ending his life. He didn't need it. He finally decided to not call them at all. As long as he kept showing up for Thanksgiving, what would they have to complain about?

There were more items on the list, but that seemed like enough for day one. For an hour or so he filled out the information forms that were attached to the confirmation email. They were what you would expect when going to a new dentist, or skydiving lessons. Health issues, allergies, family history, and so forth. He emailed them back early so they'd be one less thing to worry about.

When night fell he considered ordering his last pizza ever. He didn't need to look after his body anymore because he would not be in it. But he was nervy so he spent the evening walking in circles around his apartment trying to think of things he would do when he was dead.

He could do anything. Literally *anything* that didn't need a body.

He couldn't think of anything yet. But he was confident that he would.

> 4. Secure your finances, and
> make sure they will still be
> available to you after the
> procedure by registering your

```
Spiritual Energy Signature with
the bank of your choice. Ensure
that   you   have   arranged   for
monthly fees to be automatically
withdrawn by the Clinic.
```

Ryan had already put the procedure itself on his credit card. And he never went on vacations or bought anything, so he had enough in savings to pay the monthly fee for a little more than nine years. After that, he'd need a plan. But he had nine years to think of one. He didn't know what the Clinic would do with his body if he stopped paying. Perhaps, if he was lucky, his body would have died by then. Banks had, wisely and necessarily, adjusted to post-Blackout society very quickly. Early on, there had been a cataclysmic shift in the financial markets as everyone tried to figure out how to handle the sudden strain of people returning from the dead. But with the usual financial voodoo, they figured it out within weeks. Maybe because they liked that billions of lost customers were suddenly back again. Some had outstanding investments the banks could now resume capitalizing on, and some had outstanding debts the banks could now collect. The Blackout was a positive boon for bankers.

All they needed was a way to carry out transactions with ghosts. It was difficult to do securely because ghosts could neither sign a form nor carry identification. Banks needed to conclusively verify the identity of a ghost in a way that was both easy and legal. Or if not both, then one or the other. Eventually they settled on a method of sampling a ghost's energy and identifying characteristics of it that were, as far as anyone could tell, unique by individual. It was akin to ghost DNA, though they settled on the acronym SES, for "Spiritual Energy Signature". Which sounded just scientific enough to satisfy the security concerns of most clients. Once you had it done, your ghost could transfer cash, take out a mortgage, even use certain voice-activated ATM's to perform basic banking. As long as you didn't have to carry anything.

The SES identification could be done before death with an electronic meter, if the customer had the considerable foresight to get it done. Ryan possessed that foresight and then some, so he had had it done years ago. The very first day the process was first offered, in fact. He skipped his parents' 40th anniversary party to get it done. So all he had to do now in anticipation of the procedure was let the bank know he was dead. So he did so, one day in advance of his death, to the bored surprise of the teller.

On his way out of the bank he received a complimentary embossed pencil. Which, after his appointment at the Clinic the next day, he would never be able to use.

> **5. Cancel any utilities that you won't need after the procedure, such as heat and cellphone service.**

Since his landlord Gabriel took care of all the utilities, Ryan had only his cellphone to worry about. It was fairly new and he sort of wanted to keep it. But he knew there would be no way for a ghost to carry it around. So he bit the bullet and canceled the service, effective Friday. And he reflected, after making the call, that the cellphone company had sounded more upset by his news than any of the friends he had notified.

> **6. Install voice-activated controls on any utilities and appliances you wish to continue using, such as light switches and televisions. There are many products on the market made specifically for use by ghosts.**

Since the Blackout, technology companies had raced to the finish line on every voice-activation technology they had already been working on. There were suddenly a lot of ghosts who would love to be able to change the TV channel or dial a phone. So now, seven years later, there was hardly a gadget or gizmo out there that couldn't be controlled exclusively through voice.

Ryan had never shopped for them before, and he was surprised how expensive they were. But he finally settled on a minimally-featured universal home automation system. The box featured a cartoon of a ghost surrounded by enough TV's, lamps, and computers to overstuff a black market warehouse. He was speaking into a microphone and looking seriously pleased with his choice of remotes. Ryan spent most of the afternoon plugging in and configuring it. And the rest of the afternoon playing with it, because it was novel to tell the lights to do things and have them listen.

He spent the evening pacing. Nerves were taking over. He found it difficult to imagine that in two days, he wouldn't have a body anymore. Once it got dark he spent hours just gazing out the window at the countless milling spirits glowing softly in the street below. He wondered how it would feel to be one of them, insubstantial and luminous.

He wound up finally ordering his last-ever pizza, loaded with everything he liked. But he ate only half. He put the rest in the fridge for tomorrow. Last-ever leftovers.

> **7. Your ghost will be a snapshot of yourself at the moment it leaves your body, and it cannot change. So wear your favorite clothes because you will be wearing them forever.**

On Thursday, the day before his appointment, Ryan's nerves had fashioned his stomach into the kind of knot sailors use to tie aircraft carriers up to piers. He wondered if he might be having second thoughts. He decided, at least for now, to assume he was going to do it. Still a whole day left to reconsider.

He spent a good portion of the day going through his closet. This was by far the longest he had ever spent choosing clothes, including for weddings and funerals. He discovered quickly that choosing an outfit is a decision on a whole new level when you know you will never change out of it. It would define him. It would establish when he had died, and what kind of person he was. Or at least how stylish of a person he was, which was not at all.

He laid out everything he owned on his bed, and immediately ruled out ninety percent of it. The ten percent that remained consisted of several nearly identical shirts, and a few pairs of exactly identical jeans.

He thought about shopping for something new. But he feared shopping for clothes quite literally more than death. So finally, in mid-afternoon, he picked the jeans that looked newest and matched them with a comfortable sweater that dwelled somewhere on the hotly contested border between dressy and casual. He decided that the sweater needed something under it, but he had already put away most of his T-shirts. So he dug out from the already discarded stuff the first shirt he could find and folded it on top of the sweater. He set this outfit aside. Everything else he dropped into a donation bin.

> 8. If you wish your ghost to retain any possessions, prepare them and bring them with you to the procedure. If you possess them during the procedure, your ghost will possess them. But make sure they are things you really want, because you will never be able to discard them.

Ryan couldn't imagine anything he'd want to carry forever. He guessed that a smoker might decide to have a lit cigarette in their hand during the procedure which they would then be able to puff on for eternity. Some people might want a favorite book, or a picture of a loved one, or a Rubik's Cube to keep busy. But he didn't want any of that. He wanted his hands free for whatever it was that he would be doing.

9. Do not eat or drink anything for four hours before the procedure.

This was the last day of his mortal life, and he was having Lucky Charms for dinner.

He did have some justification for his choice of last meal. If he went with the four-hour rule, he could have no breakfast the next morning unless he got up before 5:30. So he decided that he might as well have breakfast now. He couldn't really taste it, though, because in his mind it was already 9:30 the next morning, and he was dead.

Congratulations again! And we will see you at your appointment. You are about to stop living in the mortal sense. But in the immortal sense, you are just about to start!

That was the whole point, he kept telling himself. It would be the beginning of an eternity with all mortal concerns stripped away. He could do anything, with no limitations. And he could spend all of it without ever leaving his prime.

He fell asleep wondering if Sye was having fun somewhere. He hoped he was.

SEVEN

"How are we feeling?" Roger asked as he spidered into the exam room. He went straight to the sink and vigorously washed his hands.

"Nervous, I guess," Ryan replied. It wasn't a guess at all.

The doctor/technician/whatever who had performed Sye's procedure shuffled in after Roger and plunged onto her stool. If she remembered Ryan from Sye's appointment, she gave no indication of it. She rolled her stool up behind him and scrutinized his head.

Ryan couldn't help feeling like he was about to undergo an intentionally lethal tonsillectomy. He was lying on the slab bed. Flat on his back, there was no escaping the lights. They buzzed and pierced like a swarm of insects burrowing through his eyes and straight out the back of his head.

"Mr. Foster?" another voice said. Ryan hadn't seen this man come in. Which was surprising because he was enormous, the kind of man you see on TV dragging a truck by a rope held in his teeth. And he was rendered even more intimidating by the fact that there were two of him, and they were identical. The only discernible difference was that the first was alive while the second, judging by his translucency, was not. Ryan tried to puzzle out how this man could be simultaneously alive and dead.

"Yes, Ethan," Roger said, finishing washing his hands. "We'll be done here in a few minutes. You may prepare the storage unit."

"I'm off in half an hour, Mr. Foster," Ethan said. "Ewan will do this one." He jabbed a thumb back at his transparent clone.

"That's fine, Ethan. Thank you Ewan. We'll see you in a

few minutes."

Both looked at Ryan again like they were considering whether his body was the right size to play catch with. They turned and squeezed themselves back out into the hall.

Roger dried his hands with paper towel. "Twins," he explained, anticipating Ryan's question. "Our orderlies. Ewan obviously can't do the job anymore, given that he's dead. Couldn't lift a feather. But Ewan covers for him, and we pretend not to notice. Don't want to hurt his feelings, I suppose. And they get to keep drawing two paychecks." He tossed the paper towel into the wastebasket. "Almost ready!" he added cheerily.

"Slide back please," the technician said from behind his head. "We need several inches of your head off the end of the table."

Ryan squirmed until he could feel open space beneath the back of his skull. It gave him a faint sense of vertigo. "Hi again," he said lamely. He wondered what you're supposed to say to someone who is about to kill you.

She looked at his face for the first time, and he caught a flash of recognition. "Weren't you just here?"

"Yeah, I was in a few days ago with…"

Her eyes lit up as she remembered. "Did he go?" There was genuine interest in her voice. Excitement, even.

Ryan smiled and nodded. "He's gone. No idea where, but he's gone."

She nodded before going back to poking at his head, pulling his hairs apart like she was hunting for lice.

"Margie, one-twenty A-two?" Roger asked.

"Mm hmm," the technician replied. She drew her handheld scanner out of her lab coat pocket. "I'm going to scan your SES," she said to Ryan. "This might be a little cold."

"I've had it done before," Ryan replied.

Her name is Margie? I'm about to be sort-of-killed by

somebody named Margie.

She touched the metal edge of the scanner to his neck and held the button down. It was indeed cold, and had a tingle like touching your lips to the contacts of a nine-volt battery. After a few seconds she pulled the scanner off, rolled her stool away and made a note on his chart.

"Is this your current address?" Margie asked. He twisted his head around to see her.

"Yeah, I filled it in."

"Nice place?"

"Not really."

Without any follow-up to that she wheeled her stool back over to Ryan. He felt her fingers on his scalp. Her glasses went past his line of sight every once in a while, and her nearly pointed chin, and her sanitary shower cap. He was glad for the lab coats and the caps. It gave him the feeling that at least some part of this was either scientific or hygienic. It was a feeling that the table, and the weird box with all the wires, and virtually everything else about this procedure totally failed to inspire.

"Margie," Roger said, "can you finish the prep, please? I will be back in a moment."

Ryan snapped his head around. "Is something wrong?" he asked.

Roger enhanced his smile with a few extra units of reassurance. "Everything is fine," he said. "I just have something to attend to. Relax, Mr. Matney. You're in good hands." He slipped out the door.

"You'll have to remove that," Margie said coolly after Roger had gone.

"Remove what?"

"The sweater."

"Why?"

She tapped one of the buttons near his collar with her pen. "Metal buttons."

"That's bad?"

"You're familiar with electricity?"

He hadn't even considered electricity when selecting his outfit, but he did vaguely recall something in the confirmation email about buttons. He could see there was no point in protesting, so he undid the two buttons at the top of the sweater and started to pull it over his head.

He stopped halfway when he remembered what he was wearing underneath. It was the shirt that he had counted on nobody ever seeing under his sweater. The shirt he had barely glanced at. He couldn't remember where it had happened, or when, or how, but somewhere in hazy decades long past he had come into possession of a Float Beer T-shirt. It was emblazoned with the logo of a soda from the mid 90's that had attempted to simulate the flavor and texture of a root beer float, without the need to use actual ice cream. It was an exceptionally poor simulation, and its poor sales and quick demise had reflected that. Yet somehow Ryan had the shirt. It had been worn mostly for sleeping, and had been washed countless times. Though it had once been loose and comfortable it now stretched snugly over his abdomen. Even with the sweater on he could feel cool air through the shirt's many rips and holes. It had stains that entire forensic teams would need to work long nights with electron microscopes to identify. It was, in short, the worst possible thing he could be wearing.

He didn't want her to see it. And he certainly didn't want to be wearing it forever without something to cover it up. "I can't," he blurted. "I mean, this is what I'm wearing."

"If you'd like to go home and change, we can reschedule."

"For when?"

"Probably six months."

"But I only made this appointment three days ago!"

Margie looked surprised. "Really?"

Ryan balled his fists and weighed his options. Another six

months. He was ready now. He was excited now. He had already shut off all his services, prepared, set everything up.

Just get it done, he thought. *The shirt isn't that bad.*

He sat up, self-consciously pulled the sweater off, and tossed it onto an empty plastic chair in the corner. He lay back down. *Doesn't matter,* he thought. *Nobody cares.*

Margie did nothing for a few long seconds. Ryan glanced back at her. She was staring at the shirt.

"You know," she said, "we have some clothes here from when this place was a funeral home. You could go through them."

Wearing a corpse's clothes was worse than wearing the Float Beer shirt. Only by a little, but still worse. "No thanks," he said. "I'm good."

Margie resumed prodding Ryan's head, not saying anything for an uncomfortably long time.

"So how does this work?" he asked her finally when he couldn't take the silence anymore. She had two fingers about an inch apart halfway up the right side of his scalp, pressing there for about a minute. Maybe she had found what she was looking for.

"We're going to stimulate a part of your brain with an electrical pulse," she said casually, like she was fitting his cerebral cortex for comfy new slippers.

"Which part?" he asked, trying to sound as if he know the names of all the brain parts.

"To be perfectly frank," she said, "virtually all of it. This thing is quite powerful."

He felt a cold and damp point touch his scalp. Was she making a dot with a permanent marker? For some reason he wanted to know what color.

"Is this safe? Can't it, like, cause heart failure or something?"

"You don't need your body anymore. What do you care?"

Ryan supposed that was true. Somebody could stab him

in the stomach right now and it would just save him years of monthly fees.

Margie wheeled the cart with the scary gray box on it over to his table. It was the same one she had used on Sye. Only this time she left the horseshoe paddles where they were and instead lifted another attachment from behind the box. It looked to Ryan like a horrific monster spider, the kind that attacks and eats birds in South America. And he reflexively squirmed when she tried to put it on his head.

"You need to stay still," she scolded.

Ryan tried not to think about spiders and let her affix the device to his skull. Its long spider legs clutched almost around to his cheeks. *She's the expert,* he thought. And then he wondered how he could possibly know that. She could be making this up as she went along.

"It's tight," Ryan said.

"It's supposed to be."

"It hurts."

"That's because it's tight."

He could hear her fiddling with things on the cart. He was afraid to move. "Hey, can I ask you something?"

She sighed. But she stopped what she was doing. He took that as a sign she was listening.

"You've done this to a lot of people, right?" he asked. "What do they say?"

"You won't feel anything other than a soft tingling and a sense of…"

"No," he interrupted her. "I don't mean that. I mean what do they usually say about it? Do they freak out after? Or are they, like, happy?"

She wheeled her chair around so he could see her. She was studying his face again, just like she had done when he asked about the procedure days ago. He felt like she was measuring the distance between his eyes, the angle of his eyebrows, the percentage of worry evident in his brow.

"It will be disorienting," she said. She had softened a bit. She seemed to actually want to comfort him. "You will find yourself without your sensory organs, for example. And weightless. But you will adjust quickly. Your mind is used to accepting sensory input so it will learn quickly how to form the same impressions from the new kinds of inputs it's receiving."

She glanced around the room. Ryan felt like she was checking that nobody else was there, but she could just as well have been looking for a pencil.

She leaned in close to him and, to Ryan's surprise, whispered in his ear.

"Be sure you want this," she whispered.

Ryan was frozen for a second. He risked a head twist to look at her, wanting to see her expression.

But she wheeled her chair away again and went back to her well-practiced speeches. "Your mind is also used to gravity, solid objects, that sort of thing, and it will adjust to the lack of those quickly as well. Generally it will construct a familiar experience because that's what it wants."

He was still thinking about the whispered warning. "What did you just say?" he squeaked.

"Once you get past the first few minutes of disorientation you will be just fine." She grabbed his head and wrenched it back where it was supposed to be. "Keep your head still," she said firmly.

Her whispered question circled around in his mind like a disoriented housefly. Did he really want this? He had gone over the logic so many times, done the math from every conceivable angle. And it always gave him the same conclusion. This was the way to optimize the biggest portion of his existence. It made perfect sense. But did he really want it?

She interrupted his line of thinking. "I am going to charge the capacitor now. Everything is going to be fine. We should be ready in a few minutes."

She emphasized the last sentence so it sounded like a warning. *She's not allowed to talk me out of it,* he thought. *It's probably against the rules to tell customers they don't want the service. But she's letting me know this is my last chance to make up my mind.*

He heard the thump of her flipping the master power switch, and the piercing drone began its steady rise, vibrating the table he was on.

"How is everything going?" Roger said brightly as he ducked into the room, his long legs carrying him like a robotic war machine out of H.G. Wells. "Are we ready?" Ryan caught the exact moment when Roger's eyes locked onto the T-shirt and a look of disbelief intruded on his usually well-maintained smile. "You know we have a selection of clothing here that you can…"

"Roger, um, sorry," Ryan interrupted. "Can I have a few minutes?"

"Margie, is everything ready?" Roger said, pointedly ignoring Ryan's question.

"Almost," Margie said. "One minute." He couldn't see her face, but he thought he caught something in the tone of her voice. Like she was saying to him "you have one minute. Decide now."

"Roger," Ryan whimpered, "I need some time. Please." He just had to think. He was almost certain he'd still go through with it. But he had to think. Just for a minute.

Roger leaned over him and aimed the lighthouse beam of his smile right into Ryan's eyes. "It's natural to be nervous. Everyone is nervous at this point. Everyone has second thoughts."

"Just a minute to think, that's all."

"We are on a schedule here, Mr. Matney," Roger said. "If, however, you would like to reschedule, I'm sure it wouldn't be more than a few months. Are we ready now,

Margie?"

"Roger," Ryan demanded, "I want to reschedule!" *What am I doing? No I don't! Do I?*

"Cold feet, Mr. Matney, that's all it is. Cold feet. You're making the right choice."

Ryan tried to sit up, but was concerned that the metal spider might rip his scalp off if he did it too quickly. He struggled against it, testing how long its wires were.

He felt a soft pressure on his sternum that intensified quickly, pressing him down to the table. Ryan strained to see where it was coming from.

It was Roger, with one arm outstretched, his hand pressing into Ryan's chest.

"Proceed, Margie," Roger said firmly.

"No! Margie, no!"

Margie was behind him where he couldn't see her face, but he could hear the tension in her voice. "Roger," she said, "He doesn't want…"

"This happens every time, Mr. Matney," Roger said coolly. "We see this every day."

The box made its bright "fully charged" *ping*, the drone of its capacitor steady now at its highest pitch.

"Go ahead, Margie. Proceed." Roger's calm was breaking. It was not a request. It was a command.

But nothing happened. *She's not doing it,* Ryan thought, relief and gratitude flooding through him. *She's refusing.*

Still keeping his hand on Ryan's sternum, Roger stepped around the table. His long arm stretched all the way to the box without him having to lift the other off Ryan's chest.

Ryan heard the wheels on the cart squeak. Roger was pulling it closer to him so he could step on the pedal. *He's going to do it himself.*

"That's alright, Margie," Roger said. "You may go."

"Roger, stop!" Margie said.

"Yes!" Ryan whimpered, nodding as wildly as the giant

metal spider clutched to his skull would let him. "What she said!"

There was a deep *thump*.

Ryan had barely a microsecond to register what it meant.

Roger had activated the box.

There was a piercing jet-engine whine as power surged out of the box and into the spider on the back of Ryan's skull.

Ryan felt the hairs on his head and down both of his arms stand up rigid like cactus spines. A jolt gripped his skull, all the way down his neck and shoulders and into his heart. He wondered if it would stop his heart beating, but his heart kept pounding violently, accelerating.

As his entire body seized, a warmth washed over him. He felt his eyes close.

Electricity was the only sensation he was aware of. He thought he could hear Margie saying something loudly to Roger but he couldn't tell what it was. Power surged down his spine, inundating every tributary of his nervous system. His toes twitched. His hands balled into fists.

He had a profound sense of vertigo, dizziness, like the table was tumbling out from under him and he was rolling in the air, tumbling infinitely. He didn't know if he was falling or being lifted. But he was spinning and he couldn't stop it or get his bearings. He was nothing but electricity and he didn't know anything but that.

And then, although he was certain he hadn't been asleep, he woke up.

EIGHT

"You're the one who finds missing ghosts, right?"

"That's what it says on my business card! 'I find ghosts!'" Lowell Mahaffey answered with a grin that he always assumed came off as winning. He laced his fingers behind his head and leaned back in his chair so far that his knuckles pressed into the window blinds and wrinkled them out of shape. His chair made a tightly coiled spring noise that threatened to snap any second and topple him out the window into the street six floors below.

The client scanned his desk with a perplexed expression. "You didn't give me a business card."

"I don't actually have any right now. But that's what it says on them. And there's an exclamation mark."

The client flicked her eyes around his office as though wondering if she had somehow overlooked part of it. It was an impressive size—luxuriously spacious, even—but most of the furniture had been removed long ago, so the emptiness of it had a presence, like a five-hundred-square-foot stalker looking over your shoulder. But on the positive side, it was devoid of ghosts, which made it feel nice and private. He had bargained with the ghosts years ago to take off during the day when he was with clients, and they were mostly sticking to their end.

And he still had his desk. The desk made this room an office. The desk gave clients confidence. It said, "Here is a man who needs a surface to write on. Here is a man who has office supplies that need to be in drawers that might even be locked." Aside from the desk there was only his own leather desk chair, and the plastic folding chair he kept across from him for clients. But the desk, Lowell thought, was undoubtedly the most significant feature of the decor.

"Is that a dentist's chair?" the client asked, staring.

The desk, Lowell thought, was undoubtedly the most significant feature of the decor—aside from the large, disconnected dentist's chair balanced on its single metal leg in the corner.

"It is."

"Why is it here?"

"Because I don't have room for it in my condo." That was true, especially given that he didn't have the condo anymore.

The client shifted in her chair, trying to get comfortable. Lowell felt sorry for her. He knew for certain that it was impossible to be comfortable in that chair. The guy at Staples had practically admitted it.

The client was in her mid 30's, he guessed, with a professional look. Some kind of junior-level executive, probably. He sized her up, noted her makeup, her nails, her shoes, her cellphone, the way she sat, the way she spoke, the way she kept her hair wound like a cobra sleeping on her head. It all came together in his mind, a swirl of facts unifying into a single, crystalline impression. *Human resources, probably tech sector, low six figures. Unhappily married, at least one child. She had breakfast less than an hour ago, bran muffin and coffee.*

"May I ask what you do, Mrs. Nichols?"

"It's *Miss*. And it's Nicholl, not Nichols. I'm a graphic designer."

"What did you have for breakfast?" he pressed, hopefully.

"I don't eat breakfast. Does that matter?"

"Never mind." *Wrong on all counts.* Regardless, she was potentially a paying client and that made her rare and precious, like an endangered bird with a credit card.

Don't let her go. Impress her.

He leaned across his desk, grateful once again that it was there to be leaned across. Leaning across open space would just have been awkward. "Why don't you tell me who you're looking for? Let's start with that."

"My father," she said. "My *biological* father." She fished around in her handbag and produced two photocopies. She slid them across the desk to him, and again he thought, *if I didn't have the desk, what would she slide those across?*

The pictures were obviously terrible quality even before they were photocopied. These copies showed little more than vaguely human-shaped clumps of photocopier toner. He guessed that each picture had three people in it, but for all he could tell, they could have been three vaguely human-shaped potted ficus trees. "Which one is he?"

"In the middle. Those are the only pictures of him I could find anywhere."

"What was his name?"

"Leonard Nicholl. Two L's."

Lowell nodded, studying the pictures expertly. Or rather, in a manner meant to suggest expertise.

"You've got them upside down," she said.

He decided to just push through that. "How do you know he's dead?"

"Because I found his obituary. He died of a heart attack in 1993. In his sleep."

"Did you know him when he was alive?"

"No, I didn't. They—my biological parents—couldn't afford to keep me. They gave me up right after I was born."

Bingo. It would be a bit of a hassle to find those adoption records, but he could do it and that would lead to where her parents lived. Where they would likely still be haunting.

"I tracked down the adoption records and found out their names and where they lived, in Somerville."

Dammit. She did that already.

"But I looked, and he's not haunting there. Isn't it true that ghosts have to haunt where they died? They don't have a choice, right?"

"That's exactly right." It was mostly wrong. But if she knew that, she'd never pay him to do things.

"So if he died at home," she asked, "why isn't he in the house?"

This is perfect. She has no idea. Reel her in.

"How much do you know about him?"

"Not very much. I found out he worked for the railroad, in Beacon Park Yard. He was a yard crew foreman."

Beacon Park Yard. First place to check.

"What about your biological mother?"

"She was at the house, but she drowned in the bathtub in 1996, so she has water in her mouth and can't speak. It makes it hard for her to tell me anything."

Lowell leaned back in his chair again. The back of his head pressed into the blinds and he could feel warm, thin patches of sunlight on his scalp. He wondered why, with all this space, he kept his desk so close to the window. "Is there anything else you know? What were his interests? What did he do when he wasn't working?" *Careful, now, don't give it away.*

"Only one thing. When I was at the house, the new owners said they found this." She dunked into her handbag again and came out with a small trophy, barely eight inches tall, with a three-inch figure of a bowler perched on the base. The tiny plastic man was painted to look like bronze, and frozen forever in mid-throw. Engraved into the base was "1984 Division Champions". She slid it across the desk to Lowell .

He picked it up and turned it over and over in his hands, pretending to study all of it. But he was only interested in the bottom. There it was: the name of the bowling alley. "Pin Drop Bowlounge". It even had the address. This would be too easy.

"There were six trophies like that. I guess he was good at it," the client said. "Oh, and a bowling ball. I didn't bring that. It's heavy."

Lowell nodded sagely and took a deep breath, trying to look like he was carefully considering the evidence and even now devising an investigation plan involving lots of fingerprints, stakeouts, and assistants poring over public records on microfiche. What he was actually thinking about was when he could send her the first invoice.

"I'm not going to lie to you," he finally said, lying to her. "Cases like yours are very difficult. When the ghost isn't haunting the place where it died, it's almost impossible to track it down."

Heartbreak flooded over her face. He almost felt bad. For a second.

But he hurried into his reassuring smile. "But you did the right thing coming to me. Nobody's better at this than I am." Happy lies made him feel better.

She looked at him with fresh hope in her eyes. "That's why I chose you. It said on your website you have a one hundred percent success rate."

"That was true!"

"Was?"

"Now, I'm not going to say this will be easy. It's not going to happen overnight. But if you stay committed—and I mean that in the financial sense too—for as many weeks or months as it takes, I promise you, we'll find him."

She nodded vigorously. "I'm committed. Just find him!"

He smiled approvingly, as though she had just decided to go to college and make something of herself. "Good. Good. You saw the fees on the web site?"

"Yes."

He did the smile again. "Good. Good. Well, I have one... two other big cases to clear off my desk first but I'm pretty sure I can start, let's say, next Monday."

He caught a flash of disappointment on her face. But he couldn't have her knowing that he would start, and probably finish, well before lunch.

She leaned forward seriously. "Where will you start?"

"At the house, obviously, since that's where he died. But if, as you say, he's not there, it may take a little digging to find out why. There are any number of factors, both natural and supernatural, that can lead to a ghost being displaced from its point of death."

"And why did you ask about things he liked to do? Is that important?"

Lowell froze. *Don't say anything. Nothing. Don't speak.*

"Mr. Mahaffey? You haven't said anything for a few seconds."

He waved as though brushing an irritating thought away. "Oh that was… I was just curious. What kind of guy he was, you know."

"Is it possible he could be haunting someplace he was interested in? Instead of the house where he died?"

Lowell pretended to carefully consider the possibility. "I doubt it."

"Does that ever happen? Do ghosts get to haunt places they liked instead of where they died?"

Lowell shrugged dismissively. "It's very rare."

"But would it make sense just to look there? Maybe you could find out where this trophy came from!" She reached for the trophy. He slid it backwards away from her.

"That might factor into my investigation, but it will take some time. This is an old trophy. I need to find out where it was made, who it was sold to, that kind of stuff. But don't worry, I've got… connections." He wondered what kind of connections he could possibly be referring to. Trophy makers? Bowlers? Had anyone ever referred to such people as "connections" before?

But if she wondered about it, she certainly didn't show it. She just nodded and lowered her voice as though they were discussing the Bowling Trophy Illuminati. "Of course."

Lowell stood and reached out a hand to her. "Leave it with me, Miss Nichols."

"Nicholl." She pushed the chair back and shook his hand.

"I'm not gonna say this'll be easy. But I've been doing it a long time. I'll find him, I promise."

"I'm so glad I came to you," she said, smiling and maybe even a little teary-eyed.

"Me too," he said.

And he was. Because he found her father two hours later at the Pin Drop Bowlounge, the first place he looked. The place was teeming with ghosts, which surprised him a little. He had no idea so many people were that attached to bowling. He identified her father by asking around, but didn't introduce himself yet. He did, however, stay to bowl a few frames and eat some onion rings, and added both the bowling and the rings to his expenses as "miscellaneous". And he thought he might come back and bowl some more over the next two weeks, after which he would finally bring the client in to meet her father. Two weeks was generally how long he could pretend these cases took. Not too easy, not too hard.

He just needed more cases like this. Lots more. And everything would be fine.

NINE

Ryan drifted nebulously, unable to lock his attention onto anything. He couldn't even lock onto the concept of himself.

What am I? Am I anything?

He decided that he must be something because he could remember his cellphone number, and they don't give you a cellphone if you're not something.

Amorphous blurs that surrounded him took on hazy definition like emerging Polaroid images. He could recognize them, eventually assigning them words that seemed to match their concepts. Light. Dark. Floor. Table. Person.

His awareness was emerging, a different awareness that had been buried beneath his senses the whole time. A broader, deeper perception of things, unobstructed. He recalled a day when he had forgotten he was wearing sunglasses and had kept them on well into the night without realizing it. When he finally removed them long after dark, it was like seeing for the first time. This was a similar revelation, except it encompassed all his senses and made no fashion statement.

He recognized in a dizzying rush that this new awareness extended in all directions at once. It was overwhelming, impossible to process. He needed to narrow it, get his perception directed into one specific arc the way he was used to.

Eyes. He struggled to figure out which way his eyes were pointed. After a quick attempt to blink he concluded that he didn't have any eyes. So he decided he would simply choose a direction to be looking.

He attempted to block out anything that wasn't in the direction he had selected to be forwards. It was like forcing himself to listen only to voices coming from behind him in a crowd. It could be done, but it took concentration. It made resolving the shapes in that one direction easier, and they came into focus more quickly. He could concentrate on details.

Table. Shadow. Person. That's what that was. A human person.

Once he figured out what it was, he could discern details. He willed the face to make sense, all the parts arranged where he expected face parts to be. And he recognized it. He had seen that face before. Just a few hours ago.

In a mirror.

That didn't seem right. He shouldn't see himself. Especially not from above. And yet there he was beneath himself, lying on his back, his eyes closed and not seeing anything at all, his mouth open slightly like he was taking a breath to say something. His hair was standing on end like clumpy dry grass. There was an undulating tendril of smoke curling around the side of his head from somewhere behind his ear. And something with long legs was gripping his head like an enormous, head-sized spider.

He decided that his awareness was too high up. He wasn't as tall as that, so it made him feel like he was standing on a step ladder. He attempted to force himself down to where he thought his eye-level should be. There was a weightless, vertiginous feeling as his consciousness descended abruptly. Or rather, it descended *instantly*, like it never passed through the intervening space at all. He found himself at a more familiar height. But he gave himself an extra inch because he always wanted to be taller.

Now he felt like he was at the right height for standing, but he could sense no weight on his legs. He looked down and was stunned to discover that he had no legs. And then he did. Hazily translucent ones, like his expecting them to be there had caused them to materialize out of nothing.

He looked over at his legs on the table for comparison, at his jeans and his shoes. When he looked back at his shimmering new legs, there were those jeans and shoes.

He was intrigued. *So that's how that works,* he thought. He had assumed it was just an automatic thing the universe did to you, rather than conscious, willful construction of your own ghostly figure.

Stop, he thought urgently. He shifted his focus upwards, backwards, anywhere but down at himself. *Don't look at your shirt,* he commanded himself. *This is your one chance. Don't look at your shirt. If you don't look at your shirt maybe you can give yourself a better one.*

He struggled to visualize what he'd rather be wearing. The sweater. Where was the sweater? He scanned the room for it, trying to keep his eyes off himself.

But as he was scanning, his perception flickered over his own ghostly torso. He was mortified to find that the shirt was already in place. There it was in all its ridiculous, ill-fitting, Float Beer glory. Just as horrible immaterial as it was material.

He tried to transform it, mold it into something else. But he didn't know how.

He tried to move his legs, and they moved but he didn't feel it. No muscles, no skin, no force. There was a strange fluid sensation and his consciousness drifted forward as though carried along by the force of his legs. He was somehow simulating the act of walking because it felt familiar. He thought he could probably advance without moving his legs at all, but he didn't want to. It would feel strange. There were enough strange things going on without adding another.

A form shifted of its own accord into his path and he called it a person because it was shaped like one. Person. Female person. Not a doctor. Margie. He recognized her and assigned her the Margie concept, and then all her details snapped clear like pressing the auto-focus button on a camera.

He could see she was talking. She was looking straight at him and her mouth was moving, and he vaguely recalled that when that makes noise it is called talking. Talking, he recalled, was basically a good thing.

But she wasn't making noise. The silence, now that he was aware of it, felt overpoweringly oppressive. There was literally no sound at all, and it pressed in on him from all sides like a smothering blanket.

He tried to focus on sounds. But he wasn't completely sure he could remember what sound was.

He recalled something about it being vibrations in the air. So he focused on trying to detect vibrations. He became aware that he was indeed sensing vibrations, though not through anything like his ears. They were detected throughout his being. He felt like a subwoofer, a wholly vibrating object. He assigned those vibrations to the movements her mouth was making, and again he felt clarity snap in, and he could hear her.

"Mr. Matney?" she was saying. "How do you feel?"

He let those words ricochet around in his consciousness for a while until he figured out what they meant. And then he struggled to produce a coherent answer. How, in fact, did he feel?

He had no sense of smell, taste, or temperature. That was troubling enough, but even more disturbing somehow was the realization that he also had no *negative* feelings. It had never occurred to him before, but when you're alive you always have some measure of discomfort and you just get used to it. Your shoes aren't fitting right or your hair is tickling your forehead just a tiny bit or you need to scratch your arm or there's a bit of chicken stuck between your teeth. It's not enough to stop you from doing anything, not even enough to spur you into doing anything about it. You just navigate your awareness around it and carry on. But you can always find it if you look.

So he went looking for it. And he couldn't find any. A total absence of discomfort, coupled with a total absence of comfort. And he didn't know if that was good or bad. It was neither and both.

"Good," he said.

Or rather, he *didn't* say. He didn't have a mouth, or vocal cords or lungs. He wondered how ghosts speak. How did they make sound at all? But they did, and they even sounded like themselves. He had heard Elvis's ghost give a concert just a few months earlier, and while it was not up to his early stuff, he still sounded great. So it could be done.

He could feel vibrating air, so maybe he could vibrate it.

He focused on his atoms somewhere just below the level of his awareness, about where his mouth would be. And he willed the atoms to move just as he had done with his legs, only on a much smaller scale. He moved them faster and faster like he was strumming a guitar string. He felt sound waves rippling out from him. A horrifying, tortured sound, like a cello played exactly, precisely wrong. Nothing resembling a voice, but unquestionably a sound.

Margie looked at him with a puzzled expression, trying to decode what he was attempting to say. That demented noise he had made did not communicate much.

He spent a few seconds trying to shape the sound, to control the vibrations in a way that would allow speech. Finally he managed a kind of sing-songy up-and-down pitching of the tone. *Close enough,* he thought. *Try some words now.*

"I feel good, I think."

The first couple of words barely sounded like him at all. But by the time he hit the last one, he remembered what he sounded like and managed a reasonable simulation. He even made it a bit deeper than it had been, because it sounded cool.

She nodded with a look of relief. "You're adjusting," she said. "Good. Mr. Matney, I'm sorry, this shouldn't have happened. Roger is not supposed to force his patients like that."

Ryan shifted his consciousness around the room. Where was Roger?

Margie stepped into the cone of his vision. "If you want the procedure reversed, I can do it right now. Just tell me. Is that what you want?"

He examined his new ghost hands. He noticed that a little mole he had on his right hand was missing. And then it wasn't missing anymore. The more he could remember about himself, the more he looked like himself.

"No," he said, uncertain but too intrigued by his new state to care. "I think... I think I'm okay."

"Because if you feel like you were coerced—"

Roger lanked back into the room, staring at Ryan with keen interest. Where had he gone?

As soon as Roger came in, Margie was all business. "Forty percent particulate density," she said, studying Ryan. "Fifty. Resolution no more than five millimeters but improving. Everything seems normal."

"How long does it take to get used to this?" Ryan asked, assuming that she'd seen countless others like him in their first dead moments, so she must know.

"Well," she said, looking at the clock.

Before she could answer, Roger cut in. "Prep the body please, Margie. I'm very sorry, Mr. Matney, but we have another appointment in three minutes."

"But how long does it take to adjust...?"

"Right now, it takes three minutes. Thank you."

Ryan felt like it should be longer. Like there should be a whole orientation training program, or at least a book, or a brochure. It should be called "So You've Decided to Sort-of-

Die". There should be a counselor here. Or some kind of buddy program. He'd made the most significant life change he could ever possibly make, and nobody was going to help him through it? He had three minutes. Three minutes, and then he'd be completely on his own, literally for eternity.

After thirty seconds he realized he hadn't said anything, and nothing much was changing. Margie was busy detaching the spider from his body's head, and Roger was impatiently watching the clock and reading a chart.

So Ryan asked, "Do I have to stay for the three minutes?"

A minute later he was out on Mass Ave., his first public appearance as a ghost. He tried to approximate a strut and a smile.

There were hundreds of ghosts in the street. He flowed among them, smiling and nodding at each one he passed. *I'm one of you now.*

Not one of them took notice of him. Not for a second.

It reminded him of all the times he'd had a haircut when he really, really needed one. He would come out feeling transformed, a new and fresher and less hairy version of himself. And he expected that everyone he passed would notice it and they would turn their heads and look, and point his hair out to their friends as they whispered "You should get yours done like that". But he never got that reaction. Nobody knew he'd had a haircut. They didn't see the "before" so they didn't notice the "after". He was inevitably disappointed.

And this was no different. These people had no idea that he'd been alive half an hour ago. He wanted to flash a secret hand signal to other ghosts as he passed, like he'd just joined their exclusive club. But he began to realize that all he'd done is what every single person who existed before him had also done. It was the least exclusive club in the world, because literally everybody gets in.

He amused himself as he walked by doing little experiments. He wondered if he closed his eyes, would he be able to see through his eyelids? They were, after all, translucent. So he tried it.

Nope. His awareness went dark when his eyelids dropped. But he felt like he had *willed* it to go dark, simply because that was what he expected to happen. Like his consciousness was keeping things working in familiar ways. He tried covering his eyes with his hands. And sure enough his hands, though transparent, blocked his view. It made no sense, but it worked every time. Ryan was fascinated.

Or at least, he was fascinated for about two blocks. After that he was crowded and bored, and thinking about going home.

He shook that off. If he was bored today, how would he feel in a billion years? He reminded himself that this was a completely different existence, and he could do literally anything he wanted. *This,* he told himself, *is the beginning of your eternity. Start big. Start* really *big.*

Four days later, he was standing at the summit of Everest.

TEN

The mountain cast a long evening shadow that stretched for hundreds of miles into, Ryan supposed, China. But Ryan had no shadow. He didn't even make footprints in the snow.

He had been at the bottom that morning, and now he was at the top. During the climb he fell into a crevasse. There were two frozen climbers at the bottom, but fortunately their ghosts had long since departed so he didn't have to chat. He climbed out and the whole mishap only slowed him down by an hour or so. Climbing isn't that big of a deal when you can't get tired or hurt.

There were nine other ghosts at the summit when he arrived, waiting their turn. One of them was in a SCUBA wetsuit and flippers and had half his torso bitten out in a rough semicircle. The combination of shark bite and flippers must have made scaling the north face a challenge, even for a ghost. Near the front of the line were three men who might have been Vikings, sporting several impressive ax- or sword-inflicted wounds. They stood at the peak and whooped Nordic things at the sun, then stepped politely back in line to let an elderly Asian woman go next.

As Ryan waited his turn he contemplated what route he would take down, and what he would do when he got home. He felt like once you've scaled Everest, most other things are going to be kind of a let-down. He wondered if he should have saved this for much later in his post-mortal life.

He glanced at the man behind him. He was hunched, avoiding Ryan's gaze and keeping his head down. It hid his face but made the ragged wet hole in his right temple all the more prominent. Ryan could recognize a guy who didn't want to chat when he saw one, so he said nothing.

Finally the old Asian woman came down the slope grinning and pumping her arms triumphantly. Evidently Everest was a high point for her, figuratively and literally. It was Ryan's turn. He walked up and stood at the peak and watched the brown crags to the west suck down the sun, and he wondered how cold the wind was. He was pretty sure it was deadly. No doubt it would at least hurt.

I guess that's it, he thought. *I've done that.*

He stepped off the peak and the man behind him moved forward. They passed each other halfway, and Ryan caught the man's face. It was round, and stern, and had a short, dark toothbrush mustache. He avoided Ryan's gaze as he passed.

Ryan said nothing, but he was fairly certain it was Hitler.

Ryan had encountered celebrities before, both living and dead. Once the guy who played Victor Newman on *The Young and the Restless* had asked him where the nearest bathroom was. But Hitler was a celebrity on a whole different level.

There was no way Ryan could prevent his face from betraying his considerable surprise. And when Hitler, if indeed he was Hitler, saw that he had been recognized, he hunched again and turned his face away.

As they passed, Hitler snickered softly and muttered something, and Ryan barely picked it up. And he was so stunned by what he heard that he stopped dead, frozen in place. It was several seconds before he turned to watch Hitler, if indeed it was Hitler, walking away from him.

The Hitler-resembling man didn't look back at him. He slumped the rest of the way up to the peak and stood there silently contemplating the twilight vista.

Ryan remained frozen in disbelief. He spoke no German at all, but it wasn't hard to guess what had just been said to him.

What Hitler had said was: "*Schickes* T-Shirt."

Hitler had dissed his Float Beer shirt.

Well, that's it then. His mind was made up. Hitler was the deciding factor. Somebody on the plane had made a remark about his shirt too, but somehow it hurt more coming from someone evil.

Ryan didn't regret his decision to leave his body. Not at all. This new existence would just take some getting used to. But he knew now, for a fact, that he needed to find a way to change his shirt. Or he would be hearing for all eternity what he had just heard from Hitler.

He thought if he jumped, slid, and rolled he could probably be at the bottom before it got completely dark.

ELEVEN

Even before the Blackout, Lowell Mahaffey had hated police stations. The feeling always started as soon as he got within a block of a station and started to see the flow of police cruisers like ant scouts swarming to and from their hill. He'd freeze up in fear that every black-and-white that passed him was going to suddenly veer onto the sidewalk and block his path. He worried that SWAT cops might materialize out of mailboxes and sewer grates to encircle him. He felt that way even when he hadn't done anything obviously illegal, which was usually.

Not always, but usually.

Piled on top of that anxiety were whole other big, fat, supernatural reasons for avoiding the police station. And he was feeling that tension now as he turned down Rogers Street and the office of the Cambridge Police Department drifted into view ahead.

It was still two blocks away, and already the ghosts were filling the street between him and it. He flicked on his headlights as the car plunged into them.

The popular theory before the Blackout had been that ghosts were the spirits of dead people with unfinished business. Vengeances, vendettas, injustices, and so forth. And while the theory may have been correct in spirit, it ignored one crucial fact: *everybody* who dies has unfinished business. Every single person. The occasional 107-year-old on their deathbed might think they've led a full life and done everything they wanted to do and closed off every dangling subplot. But there's always something left undone. Like maybe they forgot to clean out the pan under the fridge before they kicked off. It's still unfinished business, albeit unfinished business that doesn't seem worth hanging around eternally for. Many others, though, find themselves stuck with full-on vengeance quests: murder victims wanting to implicate their killer, parking ticket victims wanting to implicate their meter maids, and so forth. That's a lot of ghosts looking for justice. And many of them, once the Blackout afforded them the opportunity, turned to the police. Six years later, the police were still struggling to deal with them. They had barely even begun to make a dent in the case load. Hence the human soul pea soup that now made Lowell almost rear-end a parked U-haul.

He couldn't begin to guess the number of ghosts. Tens of thousands, maybe. They swarmed the place, as they did virtually every police station and public services building in Boston, and likely in every other city on Earth. They were a constant billowing cloud around the station, pressing in from all sides down every artery. Almost all sense of individual ghosts was lost. They were just fog filled with voices.

But unlike actual fog, the ghosts were not held at bay by the windshield of the car. You didn't get to drive through them in a fog-free bubble. Lowell's wobbling little 1990-something Cavalier, which was well past its prime and the primes of cars half its age, wasn't good at keeping even actual fog out. So it stood little chance against such a relentless press of spiritual smog. The car filled up with the stuff as he pushed down Rogers St., and he felt the chill electricity of hundreds of ghosts passing through him. Too many foreign emotions to process and too many voices to single out any one.

He had planned to try parking in one of the spots reserved for police cruisers along the Bent Street side of the building. Technically he could be assured of being towed away for parking there. But tow truck drivers didn't like coming down here any more than he did, so he was prepared to risk it. But the density of the human cloud proved too much for him to drive through even before he got within a block of the station. So he cut left down 5th street, aiming for the parking structure on Cambridge Center where visitors to the station were supposed to park. Walking back to the station through ghost vapor chilled him nearly as much as the parking fee.

"Lowell, not that it's not good seeing you, but get out."

Lowell hadn't even made it halfway across the office, and already Detective Blair was yelling at him. But Lowell had expected that Blair would stop him in the lobby well before he even got into the elevator, so he had surpassed his own modest expectations.

Lowell was always disappointed by the office of the Criminal Investigation Unit. Bad movies had conditioned him to expect, even *want*, a police station to be a bustling hive. Sweaty detectives with rolled-up sleeves barking into phones. Arrested prostitutes and handcuffed bikers spitting threats at each other. The Chief in his adjacent office demanding that some loose cannon turn in his badge. Instead, the place looked like the sales department of a moderately successful insurance company.

Blair seemed to have second thoughts about kicking him out. "Wait, first tell me how you got in here. Then get out."

"It's no big deal," Lowell said. "The Desk Sergeant knows me."

"He knows you because I told him not to let you in here. He has a picture of you taped to his desk."

"See? He knows me."

Blair sat down and rubbed his temples. "You still got a working card, don't you?"

"Come on. Do you think they'd let me keep a working security card?" They had, in fact. By mistake. And it had continued working even despite him having dropped it in the toilet twice.

"Give it to me." Blair held out his hand and motioned with his fingers.

Lowell sat across from him and glanced around the office. It was quiet and nearly unpopulated. Two other detectives at their desks paid him no attention, but that was it. The place was, compared to the ghost-infested nightmare he had come through in the street and the lobby, an absolute oasis. "This is nice, Blair. I never seen it like this! How'd you get all the ghosts out?"

Blair sighed and pointed up to the corner of the office. A white hemisphere about the size of half a softball was affixed to the wall near the ceiling. Its perimeter was dotted with dark circles and a red LED glowed softly at its apex. Lowell checked the other corners and, sure enough, each corner had an identical device.

"Ghost Wall?" he asked, genuinely surprised. The devices, which generated some kind of electrical field he didn't understand that somehow prevented ghosts from passing through, were generally considered an expensive luxury that billionaires installed on their yachts. "Is that in the department budget?"

"It's why we don't have a coffee machine anymore. Now give me the card, Lowell, and get out of here."

"I need cases. As many as you've got."

Blair sighed again. "I told you on the phone. I'm not giving you any more cases."

"Why not?"

"Because I'm tired of people coming back to the department complaining that we sent them to a con man."

"It never used to bother you."

Blair flinched and glanced around at the other detectives, too far away to be listening. He lowered his voice. "That wasn't a con. That was a non-traditional avenue of investigation. And it was helping people. Remember when you used to help people?"

"So if you're not going to give me a case, pay the rent on my office."

"Why would I do that? It has nothing to do with me."

"*Somebody* has to. And the way things are going, it's not going to be me."

Blair cocked an eyebrow. "It's that bad?"

Lowell caught a softening of his expression. Blair had always been a softy, not really the hard-boiled detective he tried to project. *Okay, so, pity is the play of the day,* Lowell thought. *I can do pity.* He looked down and shifted in his chair, trying to appear humiliated. He knew if he hit the right notes, Blair would fold like he had done so many times before. But Lowell realized partway through his performance that he actually *was* kind of humiliated. Things were tough. The more people learned about ghosts, the harder it was for him to convince them they needed him. He was a specialist in doing things people could easily do themselves, and the market for those was small and shrinking. He had been forced to sell most of his office furniture. The bowling dad case wasn't nearly enough to turn the corner. But he was adamantly opposed to displaying *actual* humility, especially since he was so much better at feigning it.

"It's worse than that, Blair, I need cases. Big ones. You gotta have something."

"What am I supposed to give you?"

"I don't know, something easy."

"If it's easy, they don't bring it to the police. We are here specifically to handle stuff that is hard." Blair was sounding annoyed now. The pity play hadn't worked. "There's a bazillion ghosts downstairs. Go ask them. Gotta be a case for you down there somewhere."

Lowell shivered. "I can't find a case for me in that pea soup. Come on, Blair. You owe me." Lowell hadn't planned on dropping the "you owe me" bomb so early in the conversation, and so casually. But there it was. It had slipped out. And the hardening of Blair's face made Lowell instantly regret it.

"No, Lowell. I *owed* you."

"You wouldn't be sitting here if it wasn't for me."

"I've repaid that debt fifty times already. It's paid."

Pity had failed. Guilt had failed. Blair was proving to be made of harder stuff than Lowell had ever suspected. Lowell sat back in his chair and tried to look angry, which was hard because he *was* angry and it was messing up his performance.

Blair shook his head, whether from annoyance or pity Lowell couldn't decide. "Have you ever thought about finding another line of work?"

"This is the only thing I've ever been good at."

"But you're not good at it."

"Well then this is the only thing I've ever been able to pretend to be good at."

Blair checked to make sure nobody was listening. "You know I appreciate all you did for me. But the fact is, Lowell, you're not much good to me anymore. I'm sorry. I got nothing for you."

Lowell stepped out of the elevator and into the chill, electrically-charged ghost fog of the lobby. He was so consumed with his frustration and annoyance at Blair that he hardly noticed the countless souls passing through him as he trudged across the lobby. Or the thousands of insistent voices pleading with him that they needed his help, that their problem was more important than all these other people's. There were so many voices it became a white noise as thick as the soul fog.

He couldn't see more than a foot or so through the thronging, grasping mist, so he aimed himself generally towards where he thought the door was and hoped for the best. A couple of times he passed sweating, befuddled-looking cops with clipboards. Probably rookies being hazed with the unenviable task of trying to take statements from fifty thousand ghosts a day. It was impossible and everybody knew it, but they had to put on a show of serving and protecting.

The silhouette of the information desk loomed up out of the seething, grasping cloud and Lowell realized he had aimed too far to the right. He adjusted his course, squinting through a hundred semi-translucent faces to see if he could spot daylight anywhere.

What he spotted, instead, was a surprisingly solid form, a dark mass like a rock that the river of ghosts flowed around. An actual living person, he thought. The only one here other than Lowell and the few pitiable cops. Whoever it was, they were standing at the information desk and as he passed he discerned a woman's voice.

"I don't know where he is," she was saying. "That's why I need to talk to someone."

Lowell couldn't make out what the desk minder's reply was, but he had heard all he needed to hear. It was a gamble, to be sure. There was no guarantee it would be easy. But she was alive, she was missing someone, and he needed cases. Badly.

He doubled-back and pushed through the glowing mass towards her, fishing around in his raincoat pockets in the vain hope that he might come across a stray business card.

TWELVE

Ryan couldn't judge the reaction on Trudy's face, given that she lacked one. He found it impossible to tell if he she had heard him at all. He tried to watch for body language but his gaze kept drifting back to the ragged stump of her neck, which displayed little if any emotion. She just sat behind her desk, doing nothing at all. Headlessly.

"Trudy," he tried again, "I need to talk to Roger about the guarantee."

He thought he saw her shoulders swivel towards him slightly, a degree or two, and then swivel back. He didn't know what that meant.

He decided to try asking one last time, and if it failed he was going to go find a living employee, preferably one with a head. "Trudy, I need an appointment with…"

He stopped mid-sentence, because his very next word was walking across the foyer.

"Roger!" Ryan called out, dashing around Trudy's desk to catch up to him.

Roger didn't stop but turned to him irritably.

Ryan fully expected Roger not to recognize him. He assumed that Roger saw ten clients like him every day, and that he wouldn't have made much of an impression. So he expected that he would be forced to re-introduce himself. He did not expect Roger to even remember his name. And he certainly did not expect Roger to look astonished at the sight of him, immediately lose his grip on the paper coffee cup in his hand, and drop said cup onto the carpet, splattering his socks with coffee foam. But that is what happened. Twice, because he was carrying two of them.

"Sorry," Ryan said, jumping back to avoid the coffee spill

that couldn't stain him if it wanted to. "I don't know if you remember me, I'm…"

"Mr. Matney," Roger said immediately. He was staring at Ryan with what looked like a mixture of shock and bewilderment. Ryan couldn't explain either one.

"That's right," Ryan said, surprised. "I wanted to talk to you about the guarantee."

"The guarantee?" Roger didn't seem to recognize it as an English word. He looked, as the old expression would have gone, like he had seen a ghost.

"The guarantee? Getting my body back?" He only wanted it temporarily. Long enough to change his shirt. And then he'd be asking for another rushed appointment to get back out again and get on with whatever-it-was-he-was-going-to-do-forever. But he wasn't sure he wanted to mention that. Not yet.

Roger took a long time to respond. He seemed to be waging a war with his composure. Finally he won it, and that funeral-director calm emerged mildly triumphant. "Of course. The guarantee. Come in, please!"

He led Ryan down the short hall to his office, his legs twisting around each other even more quickly than they usually did, and stood aside to let Ryan enter first.

"You said the guarantee is ten days, right?" Ryan asked.

"Ten days is the time during which the procedure may be safely reversed, yes."

"Yeah, I need to do that."

Roger circled around his desk and sat down. Ryan could have sworn Roger still looked a little nervous. He seemed to be thinking about something else entirely. "Ah, I see. May I ask why? Are you unhappy with the service? Is there a problem?"

"No, everything worked fine. I just…" Ryan sighed and sucked up his humiliation. He felt like he was asking for extra-strength hemorrhoid cream at the pharmacy counter.

Just tell him. "I need to change my shirt. And then we can re-do everything and take me out again. That's it."

Roger cocked his head, like what Ryan had said was pushing it off balance. "You want back in your body. And then out again."

"Just long enough to change my shirt. Otherwise I'm totally happy. Totally. It's just the shirt. The shirt is kind of... well, it's ruining everything."

"Well, that is certainly..." Roger looked disdainfully at Ryan's shirt. "...understandable."

Ryan folded his arms over the Float Beer logo.

Roger stared at him for too long. Ryan started to get uncomfortable.

Finally Roger just broadened his smile and leaned forward to his laptop keyboard. "Alright then. You're a decisive man who knows what he wants. Or at least, a decisive man who knows he doesn't want anymore what he wanted a few days ago. Let's make you an appointment."

Roger clicked his mouse a few times and typed an M. He clicked through a few pages before finding what he was looking for. "There we are. You do understand you will have to pay for the procedure again. It's really rather expensive."

"That's fine."

"And there will be an extra cancellation fee if you change your mind again."

"That's okay."

Roger clenched his jaw. "Excellent. Let me just..." He clicked a few more times. And then he stopped. He stared at the screen. For a few seconds he didn't click. "Oh dear," he said.

"What is it?"

He was silent for several more seconds. Ryan could see his eyes scanning the screen as he read something. Finally he turned to Ryan and folded his hands on the desk. "I'm afraid we have a bit of a difficult situation," he said in a sympathetic voice that Ryan imagined he had once reserved for widows with bad credit.

"I paid the full fee," Ryan said quickly. "I'm sure it cleared."

"Indeed it did. That is not the problem. Do you recall when you first applied for the procedure you were required to fill out several legal forms. Releases, declarations, that sort of thing."

"Yeah, I did them all. I got them in early."

"Yes. But you see, the problem is that you failed to report your condition. A rather significant condition, I'm sure you'll agree, with an obvious impact on procedures such as those offered by this Clinic. And that, I'm afraid, is a violation of the Terms of Service."

"Condition? What condition?"

"I think you know, Mr. Matney."

"I think I really, really don't." Ryan struggled to recall if he had lied about anything on the forms. He was certain that he hadn't. He had even listed his dislike of goat cheese under the Chronic Disorders heading. "I put everything on there."

"You mean to tell me that you don't know that you have, or rather your *body* has, Wedell-Gunderson Syndrome?"

"I don't even know what that is!"

"Oh dear. Oh dear oh dear. You were never diagnosed?"

"Diagnosed with what?!" If he had a stomach, it would have been knotting up. He felt something similar but it was probably his molecules bunching up into a tight ball somewhere in his center. He wondered if it was visible, a big glowing grapefruit of anxiety.

"Wedell-Gunderson," Roger explained, "is a degenerative condition of the para-central lobule. In ten or fifteen years, as the condition advanced, you would gradually become unable to distinguish between things that are light yellow, and things that are slightly darker yellow. In very advanced cases, patients have reported a tingling sensation in the middle toe of their right foot. And in extreme cases, the left. There is no cure."

Ryan blinked, only partially aware that there was no physical reason why he needed to ever blink again. "What does that mean?"

"It means you are not eligible to claim the guarantee."

"But it's a guarantee. That means it's guaranteed."

"Terms and conditions, as such things are prone to doing, apply."

"You don't understand. I can't spend forever in this shirt. There has to be some way."

Roger separated his hands and turned them palms-up in the universal gesture of *it's-not-up-to-me.* "This is not just a formality. Your... 'irregularity' is a degenerative condition of the brain. It makes it impossible to return you to your body. To even attempt it would likely kill your body and obliterate you. Permanently."

"Obliterate? Like, not existing anymore? That happens?"

"It happens. Though obviously we do try to avoid it. For insurance reasons."

Ryan felt desperation seizing him.

"I do sympathize, Mr. Matney. It is an unfortunate position we find ourselves in." He shook his head a little at the injustice of it all. "But may I suggest you attempt instead to make the most of your post-mortal existence?"

Exactly what I'm trying to do, Ryan thought.

THIRTEEN

Ryan crept along the side of the Clinic, uncertain why he was creeping. There were dozens of ghosts in the street and it was broad daylight. Creeping would not make any difference. If anything, he'd be more conspicuous creeping than strolling. But he crept anyway because he was about to sneak into a place and you're suppose to creep when you do that.

He spent a few minutes hunting for an inconspicuous back entrance before finally deciding to bite the bullet and go through the wall. He'd been trying to avoid passing through solid objects since his extraction, intimidated at the idea. Everything else he had done was more or less in line with the laws of physics as he understood them. His natural instinct still informed him that walking straight into a wall on purpose would hurt. But necessity gave him courage. With a quick scan of the street to make sure nobody was looking—uselessly, since dozens of ghosts were looking—he stepped up to the wall near the back corner. He steeled himself, balled his fists, and pushed himself into the wall.

The wall pushed back at first. Then something gave way, like he was breaking through a membrane. And then he was inside the wall.

It was quite similar to the sensation of passing through a ghost when he was alive. Except instead of getting a flood of emotion and humanity, he got a profoundly intimate sense of brick.

And then he was through and he found himself with a metal shelving unit inside his torso and the wet end of a mop poking into his head. He took a few rapid steps forward to get clear, and found that he was in a dark supply closet. The only light was the soft glow coming from himself. Seeing in the dark was a nice perk he hadn't anticipated.

He steeled himself again and forced his head through the closet door, hoping to locate himself. On the other side was a familiar clinical/funereal corridor, and the basement stairs to his left. The basement had been his target, so he congratulated himself on picking a good spot to enter. A couple of ghosts milled around but nobody he needed to worry about. So he forced himself through the door and darted into the stairwell.

At the bottom, identical duct-lined corridors led off in two directions, both passages long enough that they vanished into vague dim. He had been here twice before, for Sye's appointment and for his, but he was struck again by how un-clinical this part of the Clinic was. It was cavernous and dim, like a channel of a dried-up underground river. He felt like he should be wearing a helmet with a light on it.

He took the right passage, towards the exam room where he had been extracted. At least that way was familiar.

As he passed the door to the exam room, someone coughed inside. He ducked out of sight. When there was no reaction from inside he ventured a peek.

It was Margie. She had her back to him but he recognized her hair protruding from under the sanitary shower cap. She was reclining on the little wheeled stool with her back against the side of the table and her feet pressed against a wall cabinet. She was eating a sandwich and reading a paperback.

It would have been easy to sneak past, but he hesitated. Even if he located his body down in this basement somewhere, what could he possibly hope to do with it? If Roger was right about his bizarre brain condition, getting back into his body was impossible. And even if Roger was wrong, Ryan didn't know how to reverse the extraction anyway. He would need Margie. Running into her like this, he decided, was an opportunity. He would make friends with her.

He stepped into the room, expecting that to be enough for her to notice him. Be he forgot that his footsteps made no noise at all, so of course she didn't hear him. He attempted to approximate the noise of clearing his throat. Poorly, because what he produced was the sharp, guttural growl of some hell-beast.

Margie was so startled that she shrieked and jerked backwards. The stool flipped and she was on her back on the floor. The paperback and various bits of her sandwich rained down on her.

She leapt up again, wild-eyed.

"Sorry!" Ryan said, "I'm so sorry!" He jumped forward, trying to help her. But of course he couldn't, and she stumbled backwards away from him anyway.

"What do you want?! You're not allowed down here!" Once she recovered from the surprise he was relieved to see recognition in her eyes. She relaxed a little. "Oh. You again. Well you're still not supposed to be down here." She bent to pick up her book and the pieces of her sandwich. It was well beyond repair so she tossed it in the garbage and scowled at Ryan for it.

"I was just upstairs talking to Roger. He sent me down." Ryan struggled not to give away the lie. He worried that some part of him might light up specially or blink when he lied, like a spectral Pinocchio nose.

She retrieved her glasses from the floor and studied him. He couldn't help feeling like he had just been laser scanned in full 3D. "Sent you down for what?"

"Um, the guarantee. Reversing the procedure. Whatever you call it."

She made an exasperated noise. This wasn't going well. "Right after the extraction, I asked you and you said you were... 'good'."

He suspected that if he admitted he only wanted his body

back for a few hours, it wouldn't win her to his side. So he attempted a lie. "Yeah, well... now I'm... not... because..." It was such a dismally transparent attempt at a lie that he stopped halfway through it. Even he didn't want to hear the rest.

"It was totally inappropriate for Roger to force you to go through with the procedure like that when you were clearly not comfortable with it."

Ryan latched onto that. It was better than a lie. It was true. "Yes! And I intend to complain."

She cocked an eyebrow. "You said you were just talking to Roger upstairs. You didn't complain?"

"I'll do that in an e-mail."

She sighed again. "Well the simple fact is that I'm not permitted to perform either an extraction or a reversal without Roger's consent, and in your case possibly even his presence. You need to make an appointment."

"I tried, but Roger said you might have an opening right now and I should come straight down."

She guffawed. "No he didn't."

"Yeah, he did!"

"You don't know Roger. Nobody passes gas in this building without an appointment."

"I can say from personal experience that's not true."

She was seeing right through him, both literally and figuratively, so he decided to be honest about the present situation and let the chips fall where they may. "Okay, look, I talked to Roger but he wouldn't make me an appointment. Something about a brain condition."

He saw her forehead crease into a puzzled expression. "What brain condition?"

Ryan scanned his memory and drew a blank. "Somebody-somebody syndrome."

"You didn't think a brain condition was important enough for you to take note of the name?"

"Something about the color yellow. He said my body has it and that means I can't get back into it."

She folded her arms. She was disapproving of something and he couldn't tell if it was him or somebody else. "Roger said that?"

Ryan shrugged. "Is it true?"

She didn't answer. She was staring at him hard in a way that he utterly failed to interpret.

"If it's not true," Ryan pressed on, "then why would he say it?"

Again she didn't answer. She pursed her lips and he could hear her teeth grinding. "Let's go upstairs and talk to him."

She tried to step around Ryan to get to the door, but he moved into her path. "Please... I don't want to get into a whole thing with him. And I don't want to wait for an appointment. Can't we just do it now? I'll pay you. Under the table."

She tried to step around him the other way, but he moved to block her again. "Please," he said, more desperate-sounding than he wanted to be.

Fed up with him blocking her, she charged straight ahead right through him, aiming for the stairs. It was the first time anyone living had gone through him. He was surprised to find that he felt nothing at all beyond a slight pressure like a strong gust of wind he had to lean into.

As soon as she was through him she stopped. He saw her shiver a little, and he remembered the chill of passing through a ghost, the surge of compressed, encapsulated emotion. He wondered what she had just felt from him as she passed through. Everything he had ever felt in his entire life, blasted at her all at once. What would that feel like? Would it overwhelm her?

She turned back to him, one eyebrow much higher and more crooked than the other.

"That's it?" she said, like she had just come off a roller

coaster that had no hills.

He couldn't help but be a little offended. "Why? What?" was all he managed to say.

She shook her head in apparent disbelief.

"Follow me," she said finally. "This way."

She headed down the corridor away from the stairs. Deeper into the basement.

Margie's footfalls echoed off the ductwork while Ryan's made no sound at all. They passed in and out of buzzing puddles of light that stained his translucent form green. A few more doors drifted past, some closed, some open onto other embalming rooms, one stacked with cardboard boxes and plastic bins.

He wondered what it would be like getting back into his body. He hoped he wouldn't have a bad taste in his mouth from whatever they were feeding it. He already couldn't clearly remember what tasting things felt like. Except for Froot Loops. He would definitely have some Froot Loops after he got back into his body.

There was a brighter light ahead. They rounded the next corner into a long, tiled room with a high concrete ceiling. The walls were lined with what looked like oversize filing cabinet drawers, he guessed a hundred at least, stacked six high to the ceiling in every row.

"Morgue?" he blurted.

"The same idea," she said, "except the bodies aren't dead."

"I'm in here?" He looked along the rows of drawers, thinking that he must be cold in there. It couldn't be comfortable.

"Somewhere," Margie said. She moved to an alcove set in amongst the drawers where there was a thin desk with a computer monitor. She brought up a touchscreen keyboard. "Matney?" she asked. She was already typing it.

Ryan stepped along the cabinets, wondering if maybe

he'd sense a cosmic connection and be able to tell which one he was in. But he felt nothing.

"You're in seven-seven-one," she said. "We're lucky. You're close to the floor."

He couldn't make sense of the numbers pasted to the front of each cabinet, but she seemed to know what she was doing. A gurney sat loose by itself and she snagged it and wheeled it with her as she moved about a third of the way down the room. "Here."

He drifted beside her, but she didn't open the cabinet right away. "Just so you know," she said, "I could get in a lot of trouble for this."

"Then why are you doing it?"

She shook her head, grabbed the handle on the second drawer up, and leaned her whole weight into pulling it open. The drawer scraped open like a knife edge dragged across a cinder block, the grind reverberating thunderously through the morgue.

Ryan leaned in to look.

He felt his anxiety grapefruit re-form in an instant, intensely clenched and so bright that he thought it might be illuminating Margie's astonished face.

A few IV tubes ran down both sides of the cabinet, presumably carrying vitamins and water and whatever else kept Ryan's body alive. But the ends of them dangled free, one of them hanging over a puddle of fluid already dried to a yellowish crust in the corner of the cabinet. It was apparent that the tubes had recently been plugged into a body. But the body wasn't there now.

Ryan's body was gone.

FOURTEEN

Margie half-closed the cabinet so she could check the label on it. "Hold on," she said, and hurried back to the computer.

"Where's my body?" Ryan asked feebly, still staring at the empty drawer.

She tapped on the computer screen a few times and studied it gravely. "Well it has to be a typo. You'll be one drawer up or one down or something."

She marched back to him and unlatched the cabinet above his. But Ryan took the faster route and shoved his head through the front of it into the empty space beyond. It was dim inside, his own glow the only illumination, but he could see a woman's feet. Definitely not his. He crouched to check the lowest drawer, and all the drawers in a square around the one they had opened. Of the eight, two were empty, two were women, one was a man much hairier than he remembered himself to be, and three he had to check their faces because he wasn't convinced of his ability to recognize the bottom of his own feet. None of the drawers were empty, and none were him.

He emerged from the wall of drawers shaking his head. "No."

"Well you're here somewhere," she said. "You were probably just misfiled. Ethan would have processed your body after the extraction, and he's not the brightest."

He thought she meant it to be reassuring, but it didn't prevent a sense of dread from seeping in around the fringes of him. What if his body had already been immolated? Or buried? He'd be stuck with the shirt forever. The thought was too much to take.

Margie studied the rows of cabinets. "I'm going to ask

Ethan if he remembers anything." She caught the worried look on his face. "I won't tell him you're here. I'll make something up. I'm the one who can get in trouble here, remember?" She was already striding back to the end of the morgue and the passage out. "Just stay here and stay quiet!"

Left alone, Ryan couldn't stay still. He had to keep looking. He pressed himself through the cabinet wall, feeling that membrane pop as he cleared the surface, and adjusted himself until his head was inside a cabinet. From there he walked the length of the room, bending and straightening to see inside the bottom three rows of drawers as fast as he could. Pairs of feet whipped past him one after another. It took effort, like walking through deep water, but he moved at a good clip.

He froze.

Were those voices? In the morgue?

One sounded like Margie. Her voice was muffled by the thick walls of the drawer he was in, which barely managed to contain the body of a very tall and overweight man. He had trouble hearing her at all over the big man's slow, labored breathing.

He was uneasy being so close to a body that didn't have a person in it, especially one that filled up so much of the available space. So he shifted positions to another drawer and another until he found an empty one.

He could hear another voice with Margie's. A male, muffled and too distant to understand. Roger? Maybe. Ryan strained to distinguish his words, but they were crushed by the structure of the cabinet.

Oh God, Ryan thought, *she's in trouble. Roger caught her and she's in trouble and it's my fault.* He considered stepping out of the wall to take responsibility, but decided to wait and see how she handled it. Maybe she could still salvage the situation, and if he revealed himself he'd ruin her chances.

Another few words from the man. A response from Margie. None of it intelligible.

And then silence. A long, agonizing silence. He could hear nothing, see nothing but the pale bluish glow from himself reflecting off the inside of the cabinet.

Were they gone? Or were they waiting? He had to risk a look.

He leaned forward, shuffling his feet until he was close to the front of the drawer. And then he forced his head slowly through into the open space beyond, allowing as little of his face to pop through as possible.

The morgue was empty. The gurney Margie had retrieved was against the wall across from Ryan, but Margie herself, and whoever she had been talking to, were gone. The silence was total, a pressure that engulfed him on all sides.

Ryan shrank back into the drawer. If Roger had caught Margie, she had probably just made some excuse and covered up. Surely she'd come looking for Ryan when she could.

But he didn't want to wait. What if she needed him right now? If Roger was firing her, there might still be a chance for Ryan to stop it.

He pushed himself through the wall into the open space of the morgue and crept back into the hall. It stretched infinitely, flooded with subterranean silence. The light spilling in from the few open doors ahead made pulsating green trapezoids on the floor.

Ryan crept forward, wishing his footsteps would make a sound, anything to break the silence. His soft glow made dim moving shadows behind the pipes that lined the walls as he slid along the tunnel.

He dashed through a pool of light from an open door, though he realized right away that this was pointless. If anything, light hid him better than darkness. Still, he tried to press himself against the wall as he moved.

As he neared the stairs he detected a sound from further

up the corridor. The unmistakable rising electrical drone of the gray box.

Somebody in the exam room ahead was charging it.

He crept forward towards the exam room door. He hoped he might see a shadow of Margie moving inside, or hear her wheeling around on her stool, but there was nothing. The hum of the box, which had already cleared the lower octaves, was the only thing he could sense. The sound was a presence, a warning voice, an alarm.

Just as he was about to peek in, there was movement in the stairs. Through the spaces between stairs he saw a pair of feet descending with an oddly robotic deliberation, making no sound at all. Not a living person. They were ghost feet.

Ryan sank back into the ducts. He kept pushing backwards until he was fairly certain no part of him was exposed. But it was too far. He was all the way inside the exam room.

The room was empty, everything exactly where they had left it. There was even still a leaf of lettuce from Margie's sandwich wilting pathetically under the table. The gray box sat on its cart in the corner. It was powered on, and passing through the mid range of tones now. The progress bar on the display was past fifty percent.

Through the door he saw the ghost, whoever it was, emerge from the stairwell into the hall. Ryan pressed himself against the wall next to the door, then forced himself to sink into the wall. Not too far this time. He struggled to ignore the concrete wall's profound loneliness as he disappeared into it.

He waited, holding his breath for no actual reason other than it made him feel more like he was hiding.

Nothing happened for a very long time.

The ping from the box reaching peak charge startled him. The piercing pitch of its capacitor saturated the exam room.

Finally he dared a look, pushing his face out of the wall.

The room was still empty. The ghost was nowhere in sight.

He emerged again and risked a look into the hall. Nobody was in the stairs to the right. But when he looked left, down the long hall towards the morgue, he caught sight of a familiar figure drifting away from him.

A familiar *headless* figure. Trudy.

Just as he looked, she stopped moving. Her shoulders swiveled a few degrees, back towards him. Had she sensed him there? If she had a head, would it be looking at him?

He ducked into the room. Pressed himself backwards to hide in the wall again.

Before he could reach the wall, a shadow shifted across the floor at his feet. It couldn't be his. He didn't make a shadow anymore. Somebody was behind him.

He spun around.

A figure was coming at him fast. Dark. Alive.

Rapid footfalls as the form lunged at him.

Horseshoe-shaped paddles flashed into the light, long wires snapping taut as the figure leapt.

He heard the *pop-sizzle* of the box discharging. The room lit up blue.

A force seized him. He felt again that vertiginous roll that wouldn't stop, like falling in all directions. He lost all sense of up, down, even of himself as his energy was compressed, kneaded, and finally locked in place, frozen by an irresistible force.

It would have been agonizing if he could feel pain. He could see only smears of color, hear only a static sizzle close enough to be inside his head.

He struggled to refocus his consciousness in one direction where he could see light. *You're dead,* he thought as dread crushed him. *Actually dead this time. Go into the light. That's what you're supposed to do, isn't it?*

But as the light came into focus he saw that it was a bare, dangling fluorescent light, flickering. Not the kind of light anybody wants to go into.

A human form blocked the light, looking down at him. He couldn't see features. He tried to call out but his molecules were locked in place.

The figure cocked its head, studying him. And then it reached for something he couldn't see.

Another *pop-sizzle*. Another spark of blue.

The world pitched around Ryan, pulled out of shape, twisted out of focus, drained of light. And he finally lost all sense of everything.

FIFTEEN

"Is that a dentist chair?"

"It was here when I moved in," Lowell said, forcing a smile.

As soon as Lucinda and Rufus Flowers stepped into his office, Lowell knew he had made a mistake. When he ran into Lucinda in the lobby of the police station it had seemed like a calculated risk to offer her his services. There was no telling how complicated her case was going to be. And now that she was here, he had premonitions of expenses and research and lots and lots of difficult actual detective work. As a detective, he hated that. But he had to hear her out and look for his angle. Maybe there would be something.

"Please, sit down." He clutched a pen with the sincere intention of taking notes on the napkin he had saved from lunch.

Lucinda Flowers was a thin, slight woman in her mid-to-late-forties. She carried herself as if shouldering the weight of a fifty-pound sack of corn. Her husband Rufus, on the other hand, was well over six feet and enormous in girth, and yet seemed almost to glide. Though the fact that he was a ghost might have contributed to the illusion.

Lucinda went for the folding chair and her ghost husband Rufus scanned the spacious office for where he was supposed to sit. Lowell took the moment of confusion to size them both up. He studied Rufus first, taking in his crisp but ill-fitting suit, his scalp that was ungracefully balding in two separate spots on front and back, his nails that, even as a ghost, clearly needed trimming, the wrinkles around his eyes, the mole on his cheek that his ghost form rendered as a distracting bright spot. Lowell compiled a total mental picture. Rufus, he deduced, had been a mid-level executive in an investment firm, though he had lost his job shortly before his death and bought the new suit—the best he could afford with his severance pay—for interviews. Lucinda was undoubtedly a teacher, possibly pre-school though more likely kindergarten or first grade, and he was fairly certain she had two older sisters that she resented for their success. She was also, he quickly surmised, allergic to milk.

"May I ask what you do, or did, Rufus?"

"I sold toilet parts."

"And you, Lucinda?"

"I'm an assistant at a litigation management firm."

Dammit.

Hoping for a win on at least one point, Lowell tried: "Something to drink? Some milk maybe?"

"If you have some."

"Never mind." *Wrong on all counts.* Lowell had long ago learned never to say his deductions out loud, and he was grateful for that habit once again. He pretended to make note of their vocations on his napkin, though what he actually wrote was "don't deduce anymore".

Rufus finally resolved to just stand next to his wife rather than continuing the quest for a seat. Lowell considered acknowledging his lack of furniture, but it was a discussion he didn't feel like getting into again so he left it alone.

Lowell dreaded the answer but managed finally to choke out the question anyway. "How can I help you?"

"We need you to find Rufus," Lucinda said.

Lowell glanced over at Rufus, standing next to her with his arms folded, and he wondered if maybe this case might be easier than he thought. *Does she not know he's there?* "Um… case closed, then." He laughed, pointing at Rufus. The joke didn't go over well. Both of them were looking at him like he'd scribbled obscenities on their living room wall in permanent marker. He forced himself to turn serious. "I don't think I follow."

"Not his ghost," she said. "We need you to find the rest of him."

"You mean his body?"

The word seemed to push her to the brink of tears. Rufus tried to put a hand on her shoulder for comfort but it went right through.

"You do know," Lowell said, "that I specialize in locating missing ghosts, not bodies? Have you seen my business card?"

"No."

"Well if you had, you'd know that it says 'I find ghosts'." *What are you doing,* he thought, angry at himself. *Why are you talking them out of this? You need it.*

"You came to me," Lucinda said.

Lowell had to admit that she had him there. "Okay, what's the story?"

In contrast to his broad and towering form, Rufus's voice was whiny and nasal, like he had kazoos jammed high in his nostrils. "I'm not dead," he said.

Lowell stared at them, flicking his eyes from one to the other, waiting for somebody to elaborate. "I actually think you might be," he tried.

"No, see, I worked late, closed up the store. What is it now, Lucinda, a week ago?"

She nodded.

"I remember walking across the parking lot to my car. Must've been eight, nine o'clock. And then, boom, it's like I blink and next thing I know, I got no body anymore."

Lowell still couldn't see the mystery in this. Lots of people reported dropping dead with no warning whatsoever. "Unh huh," he said, pretending to make careful notes. But what he wrote this time was 'I am making notes'. "No offense, Rufus, but you look like a man who... let's put it this way, you're probably in the high risk bracket for just about every heart disease on the market, am I right?"

Rufus frowned. "I heard about when people die, they can feel themselves leaving their body. And they can look down on themselves and see how they died."

"I've heard that too."

"Well that never happened. When I figured out I was a ghost, I was fifty miles outside the city, and my body wasn't anywhere around. I looked for it."

"As soon as Rufus came home," Lucinda said, dabbing at the corner of her eye with a tissue "we went back to the parking lot at the store to check. The car was still there, but his body wasn't. And nobody ever found it. We asked everyone. It could be anywhere. It could be..." Her voice cracked and faded out.

Rufus nodded and leaned into her. She seemed comforted by him overlapping her. "We thought maybe I got mugged or something, and my body would turn up in a hospital or a morgue." He shook his head. "A week, and still nothing."

Lowell was now, he had to admit, somewhat intrigued. "If you got murdered, you'd remember it. And you'd definitely have seen your body after you left it."

Both of them nodded in reply.

"So where's my body?" Rufus asked, like Lowell should already know.

Every ghost Lowell had ever talked to could describe in great detail exactly how they died, and how their body had looked as they floated above it. Every single one. Even ones that died in their sleep. It was the ghost equivalent of talking about the weather. If you sat on the bus next to a chatty one, that's what they'd be yakking about for the whole ride—how they had fallen off a building or choked on gum, how their body was lying face-down in the toilet or had the dumbest look on its face. How did Rufus Flowers get out of his body and fifty miles away, without remembering dying or seeing his body at all?

Lowell leaned back in his chair. He felt the blinds cut into his fingers. "Okay, so yeah, there's a case here. Not something I'd usually be into, but you know, a case. And don't get me wrong, because whatever happened to you definitely sucks... but why not just be a ghost and, like, move on? Why do you need the body so badly?"

The couple glanced at each other. A silent, awkward communication.

"It's not so much the body," Lucinda said. "It's something that's... on it."

"My wedding ring," Rufus said. He held up his hand so Lowell could see the ghost version of the ring. It looked painfully snug on his thick finger. "It has..." He glanced at his wife again, and she caught his eye and then looked at the floor. Struggling with her composure. "...sentimental value."

It looked to Lowell like a plain metal band. And a problem. "Somebody could have just taken it off the body," he said.

Rufus yanked on the ring a few times. It didn't slide at all. "It doesn't come off anymore. I've gained some weight since we got married. So it'll be with my body, unless somebody took extreme measures."

And if I find it, what extreme measures will you use to get it off? Lowell wondered, but didn't ask.

Lucinda's eyes welled up again, and she buried her nose in the tissue. "It's not fair," she said, sobbing.

"I'm still here, Lucinda," Rufus said gently.

"He made my coffee every day," Lucinda said to Lowell. She was imploring. As if there was something he could do about it. "He drove me to work. He was warm. He never even died, and now..."

Rufus reached down to take her hand. But of course he couldn't. She stared forlornly at his hand floating halfway through hers.

Lowell shifted in his chair. He wasn't buying the

sympathy act. He judged that they were probably fishing for a discount, which only made him want to bill more. He twiddled his thumbs while Lucinda composed herself.

"What do you think, Mr. Mahaffey?" Rufus asked.

Lowell had a mental air-raid siren that went off anytime a case was likely to be too complicated for him to solve. It was the only instinct he had that was ever actually right, and he trusted it implicitly. At this moment it was blasting at such mental volume that he feared it might form a tumor in his brain.

The well-practiced, easily-delivered words "I'm not going to take your case" were lined up and ready to march. But he swallowed them. Forcing a smile onto his face was like trying to make a hand impression in cement that was already mostly dry. But he managed it. He made a careful note on the napkin that said 'do it'. "My rate is three hundred a day plus expenses," he said. *Lots and lots of expenses.* "And I can start today."

Lucinda's face didn't change. She continued staring at her hands. But Rufus, at least, looked relieved. "Where will you start?" he asked.

Lowell wasn't at all sure. There had to be a way around this. They had already searched the parking lot, the last place Rufus could remember being alive. And there seemed to be virtually nothing else to go on. He had one hope. One avenue he could go down. And if it turned up nothing, he would be forced to walk away from these people and watch his batting average go down. Again. But he needed a case. He needed to try.

Show confidence, he thought. *Let them know you do this every day, and you have a plan.*

"Let's start with this… when I realized you were a ghost, you said you were fifty miles outside the city? Where, exactly, were you?"

SIXTEEN

Consciousness slapped Ryan hard across the face.

He could see, and that seemed new. But he couldn't remember ever not seeing. He must have been seeing without realizing it, and now he realized it.

Raindrops pelted him and he felt them burrowing through him like voracious termites. The world was made of wet gray and he suspected it was cold.

He limited his vision to a specific cone, as he had become accustomed to doing, but he couldn't get it into focus. There was a lighter gray area that must be the sky, though even it was murky and the only way to distinguish it from the ground was that the rain wasn't coming out of the ground.

He struggled to focus. He saw what looked like a mountain far across a plain. The plain was blanketed in lumpy dark gray-green boulders with a sheen like packed garbage bags, and around the boulders the ground was thick with mud and criss-crossed with trenches full of slow-flowing sludge. The sky dragged low over the mountain, roiling and sagging. It was like no landscape he had ever seen on Earth.

I'm truly dead now.

He guessed that he must have passed into another plane of existence. And from the looks of it, not one of the good ones. He could not sense temperature but a chill rippled through him and his soul shivered.

I am doomed to spend eternity here. Banished from my world.

His despair at that thought was diminished slightly when a bulldozer trundled past, narrowly missing running over his feet.

He re-focused his vision sense as best he could and studied the plain that extended between him and the mountain. He blinked several times, to the extent that a ghost can blink at all. And it became clear, the rocks that looked like garbage bags weren't rocks that looked like garbage bags.

They were garbage bags.

The mountain itself was less a mountain and more a towering heap of trash, which the bulldozer was buzzing around trying to keep somehow organized.

It's a landfill.

This was only slightly better than the alien dimension he had thought himself to be imprisoned in. But better. He was glad he hadn't figured out yet how to detect smells.

Ryan struggled to remember how he had arrived here. But he had no recollection at all. It was as though he had ceased to exist for a span of time. But how much time? He could only dimly recall even what had happened in the embalming room at the Clinic.

He was fairly certain somebody had attacked him. With the same box Roger had used to extract him from his body. He remembered the pull of it, the seizing, the static charge, exactly like when he had first been extracted. Somebody must have used the box to grab hold of him, and then they had somehow brought him here and left him. But who? Roger? Why would Roger do that?

The bulldozer was coming back towards him so he decided it was time to move. And to find a way out of this place.

He moved across the trash-strewn field away from the mountainous heap of garbage and towards the sound of traffic he could faintly hear in the distance. If there was a road that way, he hoped he might recognize it and be able to figure out where he was.

He passed other ghosts on the way. A whole family of

what he took to be 17th century settlers huddled near a pile of wet, flattened cardboard boxes. They ignored him as he hurried past. Further along he passed a couple lying together on a half-burnt mattress propped against the side of a trash mound. He guessed that they had burned to death in their bed because both of them were little more than horrific clumps of ash in roughly human form. They watched him as he drifted past, and he waved politely, trying not to stare.

As he trudged through the insistent rain, he thought about Roger. In particular, he recalled the expression of surprise on Roger's face when Ryan had shown up at the Clinic to ask for his body back. What was that look about? And why was his body not where it should be?

He halted at that thought, his feet embedded in the mud up to his calves. His body was gone. He had a total of ten days to get back into it and change his shirt, and he didn't know where it was. Nor did he know how long he had been here in this landfill, or how many days it had been since he first left his body. Three days to Everest, three days back, and then whatever time had passed between there and here.

What if it's too late?

The thought gripped him hard and squeezed.

He spotted a middle-aged ghost in a distressed business suit searching through trash nearby as though he had lost something in it. Ryan sprinted to him.

"Hey," Ryan called to the ghost who was struggling over a refrigerator box, "do you know what the date is?"

If the man heard him, he showed no sign. He dove into the trash bags like a snorkeler diving off the side of a boat and disappeared beneath the surface of the garbage.

Ryan looked around wildly. The bulldozer swung into view, coming back from the mountain. Ryan ran towards it, waving his arms above his head. When he caught up, the driver didn't stop. So Ryan jogged alongside, keeping pace with him.

"Hey, what's the date?!" He yelled over the growl of the engine. "Do you know the date?!"

Ryan could tell that the driver saw him, but he likely got pestered by a hundred ghosts a day in this place, and he was well practiced at ignoring them. He pressed hard on the gas and the bulldozer pulled away.

Ryan yelled the best obscenity he could think of at the driver's back. And he could tell the driver heard it, because he turned his head and threw Ryan a murderous glare. Ryan ducked behind a mound of compressed cardboard boxes and listened until the bulldozer had trundled a safe distance away from him.

Ryan stood, uselessly brushing himself off. He aimed himself at the traffic sound and strode off through the trash. He had no idea how long he had been here, and had no way to find out. He had to get out of here and back to the city.

If it was not already too late, it soon would be.

At a desperate pace he jogged across the debris-strewn plain, which might have been a quarter mile or more.

As he went on, a strange reluctance began to nag at him. Like he was a child leaving home for the first time. Twice he considered turning back, but didn't.

He finally passed through a high temporary fence wallpapered with bits of loose trash held pressed against it by the wind and rain. Beyond it he caught sight of the entrance to the landfill. A mud road led out through a wide gate into rolling grassy hills, and a long line of garbage trucks idled at a weigh station outside the gate. Two more bulldozers criss-crossed the open area at the entrance, forcing stray trash into some kind of order.

He realized that the trucks arriving and departing must have been the traffic noise he heard. But still, this was the way out and it had to connect to a major road somewhere. So he walked alongside the dirt track, staying out of the way of the trucks. The drivers ignored him as he passed.

As he put distance between himself and the landfill, his anxiety intensified and started to slow him down. Since the procedure, walking had always felt like moving through fluid. But the fluid now seemed to be getting denser. He had no trouble moving his legs, yet he struggled to actually keep moving forwards.

He fought against it, forcing himself to go on, but the further he got, the stronger the pull became. He sensed bits of his energy tearing off of him, yanked backwards like someone was holding onto the back of his shirt and it was stretching out behind him with increasing tension. There was no sensation like what he remembered pain to be, but it was uncomfortable and after another twenty yards he couldn't take it anymore. He gave in to the pull and, without him having to move at all, it yanked him backwards. A hundred yards flashed past instantaneously, effortlessly, like he was being snapped back on a bungee cord.

He was halfway back to the landfill before he could even stop to think this through. And even then he had to *force* himself to stop. The instinct to run back towards the trash heap was all-consuming. *Is there something about this place that traps ghosts inside? Is it a ghost Alcatraz?*

It hit him.

He was bound here. Like Sye to the chair. That had to be it.

But how? The Clinic could un-haunt an object, like releasing Sye from his chair, but could they create a haunting that wasn't there before? And if so, how could they create a haunting when the equipment was all back at the Clinic? There was no way anybody dragged that box and its power supply out to this landfill.

So whatever he was attached to, it had to be a thing, not a place. They must have forced him to haunt an object, and then brought it here just as he had carried Sye's chair into the Clinic. And they left it here so that he wouldn't be able to leave.

Ever.

He passed the line of trucks and arrived again at the weigh station and the gate. The rain pelted through him as he stopped himself and stared at the landfill. There were acres of trash and junk and detritus, some in bags, some loose, tons of it heaped into the mountain he could still see in the distance with bulldozers swarming around it.

My God, he thought, the slow leak of dread intensifying into a fast, relentless gush. The object could be anything. Anywhere in this place. And he had heard that landfills were relentlessly efficient about compressing the trash and burying it. They had to be. Whatever was keeping him here, it would soon be buried forever. Whoever had put him here had planned the perfect way to trap him.

I am never leaving this place.

SEVENTEEN

About half an hour after he walked back into the landfill, Ryan had come up with something resembling a plan. It resembled a plan in the way that a heavy rock resembles a parachute: it gives you something to hold onto on the way to your doom, but it's almost certainly not going to help.

The first part of his plan was to retrace his steps and find the spot where he had regained awareness. Perhaps that would give him some hint about where the mystery object was buried. It was at least a place to start looking.

The second part of his plan remained vague, in that there wasn't yet a second part. Finding the object was nearly impossible. And even if he managed to find it, there wasn't anything he could do about it. It wasn't like he could pick it up and carry it somewhere.

But for now he would try to find it. That was somewhere to start.

A new worry tugged at him. He had no idea where his body had gone or why. What if it was having unthinkable things done to it? Could it feel those things? Could *he*? He realized that, besides changing his shirt, he kind of wanted to make sure his body was okay and back in its comfortable drawer having tubes provide for its every need. He was surprised at the concern he felt for something he had so readily abandoned. And it confused him to think of it as though it were another person, and one that required his protection. *It's not a person,* he had to keep telling himself. *I'm the person it was. It's nothing anymore. Whoever's got it, for whatever reason, it doesn't matter as long as I can get into it for an hour and change that shirt. Focus. Gotta find where I landed in this place.*

The first problem was that he hadn't paid attention to his surroundings on his way out, because he had not expected to come back in. He concentrated hard, trying to remember if he had passed any landmarks during his exit. There weren't any trees or other features of the natural terrain. The only features he could hope to make use of would have to be part of the trash. And those features seemed to be in a constant state of flux. Even now he could see the bulldozer far across the field shoving a huge pile of debris into a new resting place. It seemed nothing here stayed where it was for long. At least until it was buried.

He suppressed all thoughts of the utter impossibility of what he was trying to do—and there were lots of those thoughts—and kept walking.

He arrived back at the main heap, which more bulldozers had begun to chip away at. In walking the entire length of the landfill he hadn't seen a single familiar thing. Or rather, everything he had seen had looked familiar, but exactly as familiar as everything else.

He turned around and walked back towards the gate. The low-hanging clouds pressed closer to the ground and the rain got thicker, threatening to disintegrate him with machine gun droplets as he walked. He wondered if it was possible for a ghost to be ripped apart utterly by rain. It didn't feel good. But he kept walking.

There had to be something he had seen, a unique trash object perhaps, or…

Not an object, he thought. Ghosts. He had seen ghosts. And no doubt they were haunting objects that couldn't have moved far. They would be near where they had been when he passed them before.

He quickened his steps and paid closer attention to the ghosts he passed. There were dozens of them, and he had barely noticed any of them during his walk in the opposite direction. He was amazed how easily he had ignored them.

He had thought, especially now that he was one of them, that he was more aware than that.

He clearly remembered the pioneer family, the couple on the mattress, the suit-wearing-trash-snorkeler. But he couldn't see any of those. He passed four marching soldiers in Union uniforms, their bodies riddled with wounds and one missing a shoulder, no doubt from a cannonball in flight. He passed a relatively contemporary man in a bathrobe, pacing. He passed a jogger in a tracksuit running literally in place as though on a treadmill, though no such thing was beneath him. He passed half a dozen more at least, but nobody he recognized, and already he was getting close to the gate again.

He decided that he was too far to the left of the main heap, so he turned around, walked about a hundred yards to the right, and then started towards the mountain again.

A thick gloom had settled in, even thicker than the gloom that had preceded it, but it helped to make the ghosts stand out. He counted fifteen or more, glowing brilliantly like gas lanterns spread out along the whole length of the field. He hurried towards the closest ones, running as fast as he could remember ever being able to run.

He didn't know the first few, but he quickened his step even more when he finally saw someone he recognized. The charcoal couple on the mattress, still lying propped up against a small mound.

They had the same offended expression on their ash faces as the last time he had seen them. Still, he was happy to see them and wanted to tell them so. "Am I glad to see you guys!"

"Get lost!" the male of the two barked at him.

"Sorry! I'm not weird or anything, I just…"

He was cut off by a blast of engine noise from an enormous vehicle thundering past him. It was like a bulldozer but three times as large, and in place of the usual tank tracks, it rolled on enormous steel wheels with thick, protruding spikes like rows of pyramids around their circumference. As the machine blasted on, the giant wheels crushed and compressed the trash beneath it. One wheel caught the bottom edge of the couple's mattress, and Ryan had to reel in horror as the machine crushed the foot of the mattress into the trash and kicked the head vertical. The mattress flipped and folded in half beneath the weight of the behemoth. The couple remained glued to the surface of the mattress the whole time, showing no awareness of the horrific thing that was happening to them.

As their mattress mashed into the ground under the bulk of the compactor, Ryan's instinct was to run up and help. But there was nothing he could do. and the couple seemed unperturbed, so he just stood and stared. In seconds, they disappeared completely, crushed beneath several feet of garbage.

The compactor backed away past Ryan and he threw a scowl at the driver. The driver gave no hint of having noticed Ryan, though, and a few seconds later he was rumbling away down the valley.

Ryan stayed at the spot for several minutes, wondering if the ghost couple might emerge. But there was no sign of them, and he couldn't think of anything to do. He could only hope they were comfortable in there.

Whatever object Ryan was haunting, he worried it might already have been shoved down into the earth like the mattress. There might already be no way to reach it. In that case, living with the Float Beer shirt would be the least of his worries. No, not the least. It would be the *second biggest* of his worries. The *biggest* of his worries would be living in a landfill forever. Being old and stooped for eternity seemed like a cakewalk compared to spending all of infinite time wandering around a dump wearing a Float Beer T-shirt with holes in it. It wasn't like he would just have to tolerate it for a while on his way to something better. No, this was forever. There was nothing at the other end of it, no better set of future circumstances he could look forward to. The thought was terrifying.

He stretched the frayed hem of the T-shirt down so it would cover his belt for at least a few minutes until it gradually shrunk back to belly-button height. And he hurried on, trying to outrun his despair.

He came upon the pioneer family next. Studying them more closely this time, he saw that they all had frost on their faces and clumps of snow and ice in their hair. There were icicles dangling from the tip of the father's nose. It was easy to guess how they had all died here together, hundreds of years ago.

As he ran past them he knew he was getting close. He could *sense* he was close. The drag from his haunting was almost imperceptible here. He had almost forgotten about it as he approached, but now he was keenly aware of its absence. The farther away he was, the more it pulled. So here, where it was hardly pulling at all, he must be close.

He stopped and turned in a circle, scanning the ground. The scan felt futile, since he had no idea what he was looking for. He hoped he would know it when he saw it. But the gloom was so deep, and the rain was falling in such dense curtains, that it was difficult to discern anything at all in the field of trash. And for all he knew, the object wasn't on the surface at all. It could be thirty feet deep already.

Despair nagged at him again. But he had a flash memory of the empty body drawer at the Clinic, those dangling tubes that were supposed to be jabbed into his body and keeping it alive. What was keeping it alive now?

He approached a nearby mound and scanned it up close. Some of the trash was bagged, some of it loose and sopping wet. If only he could dig through it. But the best he could do was meticulously inspect the outer surface and look for anything familiar.

For hours he searched like that, leaning in close to the trash mounds so the soft glow from his vaporous form illuminated them slightly. The rain stopped after an hour or two, and he was relieved for that at least. He felt like he could keep his structure together with less effort, and his glow was stronger when he wasn't being ripped apart by raindrops.

Once in a while a shimmering form would meander past, reflected in the dark wrinkles of countless garbage bags. And sometimes he'd hear distant conversations. But the other ghosts took little notice of him. He kept looking. There was nothing else he could do.

He was sure it was late in the day by the time he gave up. Frustration overcame him. He kicked at the nearest trash pile, and his foot passed through it with no resistance at all. That just made him angrier. So he punched at it and found that equally unsatisfying.

He lay down on his back in the muck and closed his eyes, not even caring that a bulldozer rolled right over and through him.

He lay there for a long time. It might have been an hour. It might have been a day. He didn't know. He didn't care. He had an eternity to feel sorry for himself, so he might as well start now.

But he stopped doing that when he became aware that somebody was standing over him.

Ryan waited, annoyed, hoping that whoever stood over him would stop doing that. When they didn't, he opened his eyes.

The Trash Diver. The middle-aged man in the dark suit whom Ryan had seen diving head-first into one of the trash piles. Ryan had never seen him up close. And now that he did, he didn't gain any new information. The Trash Diver was a middle-aged ghost in a business suit. He had a hard-set expression of rage, and it annoyed Ryan that his gaze was affixed not on Ryan's face, but several inches lower. On his shirt.

"I know," Ryan groaned.

"Get out of here," the Diver snarled.

Ryan was stunned at the vehemence of the man's tone. What had he done to deserve this anger? Ryan studied his surroundings. Was this the man's territory somehow?

The Diver advanced another step closer to him. There was a seething behind his eyes that Ryan had seen before. It was the same focused anger he had endured from Sye, every morning for years at breakfast. "I'm sorry," Ryan said, "is this your..."

"Get away from there. Right now," the Diver snapped. "It doesn't work anyway. There's no power, and the CD tray is stuck out. So forget it."

Although he had no idea what this man was talking about, Ryan sprang to his feet and sidestepped away from the spot. He didn't know why he should feel intimidated. It wasn't like the guy could hit him. But instinctively, he didn't want to pick a fight.

"Don't let me catch you back here," the Diver huffed, jabbing a finger an inch into Ryan's chest. "You don't even know how to use it right."

"Okay," Ryan said, wishing he was the kind of person who had cool rejoinders ready, even for crazy people.

The Diver stepped up to where Ryan had been lying in the trash. He closed his eyes and seemed to drift for a moment, turning in place. He stopped his turn, adjusted a few degrees back. Took a half step forward.

And then he dove head-first into the garbage bags. He kicked his feet like a swimmer as he forced himself deep below the surface.

Ryan inspected the spot where the Diver had

disappeared. Partly he wanted to watch for any trace of him coming back up. But he also wanted to figure out how the Diver had known so precisely where he wanted to dive. It didn't appear any different from any other spot on the hill. None of the garbage bags were distinctive.

He had mentioned a CD tray. Was the guy haunting a piece of stereo equipment? Ryan wondered why anybody would love their stereo so much that they'd stick to it forever.

Whatever it was, it had to be buried below the surface here. The guy had known the exact spot, within inches.

And if Ryan could determine how the Diver knew that, maybe he could locate his mystery object too.

The Diver reappeared at Ryan's feet, only his head poking out of the trash like he was treading water. "I said get out of here!" He seemed to have picked up a few degrees more rage while under the surface.

"Look," Ryan pleaded, "I don't want your... whatever it is."

"Everybody wants it! It's a Sanyo!"

"No, I don't! I just want to know how you..."

"Sanyo!" the man roared, and disappeared again beneath the surface.

The guy was haunting his stereo *hard*.

Ryan stepped back, chasing a thought. The haunting. That had to be it. The guy was following the pull of his cosmic attachment to a stereo. Ryan had lost track of his own pull, but maybe there was a way to detect it and trace it back to the source.

He probed his awareness for it, and discovered it lurking somewhere just left of center in his abdomen. It was faint, but present, like a persistent itch he had put out of his mind. As he turned in a slow circle he could feel it grow marginally stronger, then weaker again. Maybe he just needed to hone it. Pay closer attention to it. Use it as a compass. This was his only hope. He had to try.

And then he spotted the dump trucks.

There were four of them, far off at the edge of the field, with several bulldozers clustered around them like scavenging rodents. The first truck had already begun emptying its contents onto the field of trash.

It was full of soil.

They were going to bury the field.

EIGHTEEN

He needed to start with distance. The further from the object he travelled, the stronger the pull got. To follow it, he had to start from far away.

He jogged towards the gate. As he drew near he dodged between the dump trucks full of soil. He studied each driver as he passed, considering whether they might listen to him. Most didn't even glance his direction. Two were already ignoring the pleas of several other ghosts swarming around them. So he gave up that hope and continued running.

By the time he reached the gate the tug of his haunting became pronounced. He focused on it, surprised at how it manifested not only as a physical pull but also a desire. He *wanted* to go back. He concentrated on the feeling as he turned and started back. *Don't look,* he kept telling himself. *Feel it. Just go where it pulls you.* He even allowed himself to close his eyes. Why not? He couldn't get hurt.

The pull lost strength as he covered more and more distance, but he kept his focus on it. He refused to let go of it. Like fastening his gaze on a single letter in a page of text, or locking onto one particular voice in a crowd. He blocked out every other sensation, allowing only awareness of the pull.

After a while he sensed himself losing track of it. He knew he was close, but that wasn't enough. He shifted his attention away from the pull and focused on the desire. *Which way do I* want *to go? Where will I be most comfortable? Where do I belong?* He kept walking, not questioning his direction.

His sense of the physical force became thin, faint, and disappeared completely. The desire was all he had left. But it was powerful, and he continued to let it guide him.

Another few dozen steps, and he stopped. He felt a gentle sense of comfort, of satisfaction. Like he could live here on this exact spot and be happy. This, right here, was a perfect spot where everything would be fine forever and maybe he should lie down and have a snooze.

He opened his eyes. He was standing knee-deep in diapers spilling out of a garbage bag. It did little to diminish his warm sense of contentment. Although he felt like it should.

Please, he begged nobody in particular, *if it's a diaper I'm haunting, let it be a clean one.*

And then he saw something. Mercifully, it was not amongst the diapers. Rather, it was beneath the diaper bag, half covered by it, poking half an inch into the air. The corner of an envelope on the top of a stack of other envelopes, wet and stained with mud.

Printed on it was the logo of the Post-Mortal Services Clinic.

Ryan's heart would have skipped a beat, except that it was miles away somewhere having bad things done to it. Maybe.

He kneeled, scrutinizing the envelope and everything around it. Was he haunting the envelope? It seemed like a strange choice. Perhaps the object he sought was mixed in with other trash from the Clinic. He wished that he could dig under the envelopes. There had to be more.

Fighting back revulsion, he pushed his face through the surface near the envelope. But he couldn't see anything clearly and he pulled back when he got a sudden, depressing sense of how diapers feel about their lot in life.

As he was pondering his next move he noticed a vibration in the air. He translated it into a sound, the low rumble of a compactor trundling across the field towards him. Final compression of the trash, he guessed, before the soil was spread on top of it.

He tensed as the compactor crushed garbage beneath its massive spiked rollers like a gigantic medieval war machine. It would miss him. But not by much.

He stood up, clenching his fists. *Please don't turn this way, please don't turn this way.*

The compactor paused, backed up a few feet, paused again. Ryan watched the driver looking around for spots that needed more compressing. He recognized too late that it was the same driver he had yelled at shortly after waking up in the landfill. As soon as he realized it, Ryan turned away to hide his face.

When he risked a glance back, the driver was staring at him. Ryan had been recognized.

The driver was evidently determined to live up to the names Ryan had called him. He hauled the compactor around in a turn as tight as the lumbering monolith could muster.

It came straight at Ryan.

Although he knew it wouldn't help, Ryan waved his arms above his head, crossing them repeatedly into an X. "Stop!" he yelled. "Don't!"

He immediately wished he hadn't, because the driver treated it as a bulls-eye to aim for. Like he had just seen a fly in the toilet bowl and couldn't resist aiming his stream at it. He accelerated. And it was hard to tell, but Ryan suspected he was grinning.

Ryan stopped waving and took a fearful step backwards. The compactor could crush all of this trash so far below the surface that he'd never find it again. He watched the machine's immense wheels annihilating everything they contacted. They tore boxes apart, exploded garbage bags like ripe grapes. And the beast was still steering directly towards him.

Ryan took a step forward again, determined to make a courageous stand.

Uselessly, as it turned out.

The compactor rumbled right through him. He despaired as the pile of envelopes disappeared beneath the roiling chaos of plastic, paper, and mud. The driver looked at Ryan and Ryan thought he saw him do a little victorious eyebrow raise.

Just beyond Ryan, the compactor stopped. It paused. And then reversed through Ryan again, pounding the diaper bag deeper. It kept going in reverse away from him, the driver apparently satisfied that he had tormented Ryan enough.

The trash settled into its new compressed position around him. The envelopes were gone. Lost in the crush. Impossible to find.

But he saw something else, exposed by the compactor's passage. The sun glinted off glass or plastic, and he had a flash of recognition. He kneeled again to look.

There it was.

A hemisphere of shattered clear plastic, half of it broken off and gone. The liquid and sparkling snow had drained away. But the words "Myrtle Beach" were still printed across the plastic sand. And as Ryan pressed his face near it, he felt a surge of utter contentment. This destroyed, nonsensical souvenir was, to him, the single best thing in the universe. He was near it, and that was in every way good.

Roger had forced him to haunt the snow globe.

He didn't have long to enjoy the triumph of having found it. He sensed again the rumble of the compactor. Seagulls that had settled to the ground took flight again with panicked squawks. Ryan turned to look behind him.

The compactor was coming back. Fast.

This guy was not going to stop.

The maniacal driver gunned the engine, announcing his malign intent. Ryan could see plumes of black smoke spitting from the twin exhausts on either side of the driver. He could see the ground deforming beneath the beast as it pulverized everything in its path.

Ryan lay down on his stomach and put a hand on each side of the snow globe. He struggled to focus his energy.

What was it Benny had said? Don't move the thing. Focus on moving the air *around* the thing.

He focused all his being into his hands, formed them into a kind of sail to catch the air. And he thrust them both forwards into the snow globe.

They went right through. The snow globe defied him.

Behind him he heard the rumble of the compactor intensify to a roar as it closed the distance. Ryan thought he could hear the driver laughing. It was only a matter of seconds before the compactor would reach him. He didn't know what would happen to him if it shattered the snow globe altogether. Would he shatter too? Was his link to it so strong that he would cease to exist, obliterated like Roger had talked about? Was that Roger's plan all along?

He tried again, cupping his hands over the snow globe. He waved them through it a few times trying to sense any resistance, some indication of contact. But it felt like air.

He blocked out everything else, trying to forget that there was a massive machine thundering towards him. Again he directed every ounce of his energy all the way down his arms and into his fingers. He circled them around the snow globe and pushed with everything he had. "Come on," he heard himself muttering. Still the globe didn't move. But this time he thought he felt that faint membrane pop, the sensation of knowing he was passing through something. It was progress. But it wasn't progressing fast enough.

He dared to look behind him. The compactor was almost upon him. The driver blasted the horn. A war cry.

Ryan had one more chance. He lined up both hands, palms-out in front of the snow globe like a plow. He closed his eyes and summoned up everything that he was made of. Every particle of him that he could spare he gathered up and concentrated into the plow shape he was making with his hands. He converted himself into pure kinetic force.

Move the air.

The compactor gave one last roar and he felt the air shatter around him as its titanic wheels bore down.

He thrust his hands forward. *Move the air, move the air, move the air.*

Nothing moved.

Ryan roared, a frustrated animal noise. He couldn't do it. He had lost.

And then something moved. But not because of him.

A shadow shifted in front of him and a hand—a *living* hand—reached in out of nowhere, easily hooked the snow globe by its shattered edge, and lifted it clear.

The compactor plowed straight through Ryan, and for a few seconds all he saw was metal and smoke, rubber and fire.

And then it was past him, blasting away across the field, the driver throwing a hand up in a mocking wave.

Ryan didn't care. He was staring at a man. A man standing in the muck and holding the broken snow globe.

The man was pushing 40, and entirely unkempt in various ways that conflicted even with each other. He was dressed in a long raincoat and threadbare loafers entirely unsuited to walking through a dump. And he was looking at Ryan with mild interest, as though he was curious what Ryan would do next.

Ryan watched him back. They considered each other for silent seconds while the compactor noise faded enough for them to speak.

Ryan asked the most obvious question.

"Who are you?"

"Lowell Mahaffey," the man replied. "I'm looking for a body."

Ryan stared and wondered why this man holding the snow globe enraged him.

"So am I," Ryan said.

NINETEEN

A dense rain sloshed against the windshield of Lowell's alarmingly shimmying Cavalier as they sped along the Mass Pike towards the city. Ryan found it hard to tell where they were. Veils of rain obscured any landmarks they passed. And Lowell's car had no windshield wipers at all, so the glass was a steady inch-thick waterfall plunging through their line of sight. It was inconceivable that Lowell could see well enough to drive safely. Ryan might have feared for his life if he still had a life to fear for. But they had been driving for a half hour, so the landfill must have been twenty or thirty miles outside the city at least.

"So," Lowell said, "you got your ghost pulled out. On purpose?"

"Yes." Ryan had explained his situation as they pulled away from the landfill with the snow globe balanced precariously on the console between them. Unburdening himself had been a relief, though he wished Lowell hadn't laughed. Mostly at the shirt.

"Why would you do that?" Lowell asked.

"Because it makes sense."

"Does it, though?"

Ryan fought annoyance. He'd gone through this with himself so many times, it bothered him to have to explain it to somebody else. "Because I'm good now. Good health, no big problems. I want my forever to be good."

"I guess," Lowell grunted.

Ryan felt like turning it back on him. "Why *wouldn't* you do it?"

Lowell snorted. He glanced down at himself. "I'm not sure this is who I wanna be forever, you know?"

Ryan threw the subject away, trying to force Lowell back on track. "So how did you end up back there?"

"Just so we understand each other," Lowell said, "by law I'm not allowed to tell you the details of the case I'm working on. But I kinda really want to."

"Then tell me. I told you everything about me."

"I can't tell you anything," Lowell said. "It's a law. Probably. I mean, that sounds right, doesn't it?"

"I have no idea. So why not just tell me? You said you were looking for a body. Whose body?"

"You're falling behind."

"What did I miss?"

"No, I mean you're falling behind." Lowell pointed at Ryan's seat.

Ryan realized that his body was sinking backwards through the upholstery. He was halfway into the padding of the passenger seat, his torso hidden inside the backrest and his face sticking out of the headrest. He had taken a few taxis and airplanes traveling to Everest, but still struggled with having no inertia. Having to work consciously to match speed with a vehicle took effort. It didn't help that Lowell's driving was worryingly erratic. Ryan wondered how complete Lowell's understanding of the concept of a steering wheel was.

He squirmed himself forward. "Okay, so, you think I'm connected to your case?"

"Let's just say that my client, whose name I'm not gonna say, finds himself in a... condition—"

"He's dead."

"I'm not gonna say. But yeah, he's dead. But the thing is, he doesn't remember how he got in this... 'condition'."

"I know what the condition is. You already said he's dead."

"I'm not gonna say. I'll just say this: do you think it's a coincidence that two ghosts who lost their bodies turn up in the exact same landfill just a couple of days apart?"

"Hmm," Ryan said.

"Do you?" Lowell asked again. "I'm seriously asking. I mean, it seems weird to me, but does it to you?"

"I don't know."

Lowell looked crestfallen. "You don't?"

"I have no idea. Maybe it happens all the time."

"Really? I thought I was onto something there."

"Well, maybe you are. I mean, I just don't know."

"But it's worth looking into, right? Like, investigating deeper?"

Ryan stared at him, trying and failing to spot sarcasm or insincerity. "You said you're a professional detective, right?"

Truck taillights loomed out of the mist of spray ahead, and Lowell jammed on the brakes. Ryan hurtled forward and found himself with his lower body in the engine block of the car, the rain and road spray blasting through his torso and the engine thrumming inside his legs. His thinking got hazy, disconnected, as the raindrops carved ant tunnels through his being. He struggled to keep his shape.

He forced himself backwards through the windshield to his seat, and his mind cleared as he got cohesion back. "Warn me next time," he said.

"Next time what?"

Ryan settled into his seat. "So your client…"

"Rufus."

"You said you weren't going to say his name."

"I'm not."

"How much does Rufus remember?"

"Nothing."

"Nothing?"

"What's the first thing *you* remember seeing after you got ghosted?"

Ryan vividly recalled that disconcerting sight of his own body from above. The closed eyes, the hair standing on end.

"Myself," he replied finally, chilled at the memory. The shirt, oh God, the shirt. He folded his arms across his chest self-consciously.

"Exactly. That's the first thing everyone remembers. That's how you know you're dead, right? First you're going into the light, and then you're floating above your body looking down at yourself. Except not my client. Rufus doesn't remember dying, and he never saw a body. He just woke up in that dump all ghosty, with no idea what happened to him. As far as he knows, he never died."

Ryan silently admitted a possible connection. Being a ghost without dying was, after all, a situation he was intimately familiar with. But if Rufus had been extracted at the Clinic, he would have had days to prepare. He'd certainly remember it.

The rain slacked off as they sped into the city, and the hiss of the tires on the wet road turned into a dull, throbbing hum. As much of an infected scar as the Mass Pike continued to be, Ryan was grateful to be on it, and see the glow of Boston emerging out of the mists ahead. He recalled feeling in the landfill like he would never get back here. But here he was.

Lowell merged left to pull off the Turnpike into Cambridge and fished through his pockets for change without slowing down at all. Or, for those few seconds, steering. "We'll go to my office," he said.

"No," Ryan said, pointing ahead, "take me to the Clinic. I'll show you where it is. Head towards Davis Square."

Lowell slowed for the toll booth, veering into the cash-only lane. Ryan almost lost his connection to the car and sped through the EZPass lane on his own, but forced his particles back into the passenger seat with a hard molecular shove.

"Okay," Lowell said. "But on the way, you're gonna tell me everything."

"I already told you everything that matters."

"Then you're going to tell me everything that doesn't."

"Why? Are you going to solve my case too?" Ryan asked.

"You know, I was kind of hoping you'd solve mine."

They parked at a meter across from the Clinic. The rain had slunk away for the evening but the sky remained threateningly heavy, so the sidewalks were mostly deserted. Only a few brave pedestrians dodged puddles as they hurried home, while an assortment of ghosts who had no reason to care about puddles meandered right through them.

In ten minutes of stakeout, the Clinic entrance had not opened once. Yet Ryan ducked in his seat like he could be spotted at any moment.

"Is it closed?" Lowell asked.

The old wristwatch duct-taped to the dashboard suggested that it was about 7:30. And while the irregular movements of the second hand gave him plenty of reason for doubt, Ryan suspected it was roughly correct. "I don't know. Maybe they do night appointments. I'm going in." He pushed himself halfway through the car door.

"Whoa, and do what?" Lowell said. "Exactly what you did before? How'd that work out for you?"

"Then I'll do something different. But you have to come with me."

"Why?"

Ryan gestured towards the snow globe resting on top of the dash. Seeing it again made him love it more than ever, and then hate himself for how much he loved it.

"Even if it's open, which I don't think it is, they're not going to let me just walk around in there," Lowell said with a shrug. "Private property. I'm not going anywhere."

"Then we should go to the police."

"Have you been to a police station since the Blackout? 'Get in line' doesn't begin to describe it."

Ryan had already forgotten what the objection was to his original plan, so he returned to it. "I'm going in." He had both his legs through the door before Lowell's voice stopped him.

"Stop," Lowell said with a commanding edge. "That's stupid. You have to be smart about this."

Ryan hovered as Lowell studied the front of the Clinic and looked up and down the street, drumming his fingers on the steering wheel. Twice he rubbed his chin and at least once he let out a deep, thoughtful sigh. It went on for more than a minute at least.

"And?" Ryan demanded.

"And what?"

"You were going to suggest a plan!"

"No I wasn't. I said *you* have to be smart. I didn't say anything about *me*."

Exasperated, Ryan flopped back into the passenger seat. He felt a warm sense of relief being so near the snow globe again. He loved it unconditionally, and yet wanted it to know how much he hated it.

Ryan had a sudden thought. "There was a woman in there. A doctor, or whatever those people in there are. Margie."

"Dr. Margie?"

"She seemed like she would help me. She *tried* to help me. If we can find her…"

Lowell folded his arms. "You keep saying 'we' like this has anything to do with me. But it doesn't. This is all you. I'm not doing anything." He reclined his seat a few degrees, apparently to emphasize that his plan was to stay right where he was.

Five seconds later Lowell scrambled frantically to find the door handle, threw open the car door, fell out onto the road, picked himself up, stumbled against the hood of the car, and barrelled away down the street at a dead sprint, shouting

"Hey! Hey!"

This took Ryan very much by surprise.

He was so stunned that he neglected to do anything about it at all for several seconds.

Lowell was yelling something unintelligible and waving like he was hailing a taxi. Fifty yards away now.

Ryan got his wits together and forced himself through the passenger door, scrambling to catch up to Lowell even though he knew he couldn't. Ten yards down the road the yearning hit him and he stopped dead and spun around, straining to see through the windshield of Lowell's car. He desperately wanted a glimpse, anything to tell him the snow globe was okay and didn't need him. But he couldn't see it, not even the jagged top edge. So he had to run back and plunge his head in through the window. There it was, safe and sound on the dash and doing everything it could to make him happy. It infuriated him.

By the time Ryan was satisfied that the snow globe had no urgent need of his presence, Lowell was walking back up the street towards him, talking on a cellphone. He paused every few feet to double over and pant, gag, and hock something viscous from deep within himself onto the asphalt.

"What was that about?" Ryan called as Lowell drew closer.

Lowell dropped the phone into his pocket and barely managed to wheeze an answer. "I'm not... gonna... say."

Ryan had had enough. He threw himself back into the car. An insistent pessimism surged through his molecules, infecting them one by one. He didn't have the energy to fight it so he went with it. He wanted to be somewhere familiar, somewhere he could think. It occurred to him that he hadn't been home even once since leaving his body.

Lowell stumbled all the way to the car and leaned on his elbows on the hood, trying to force something out of his lungs.

"Do me one more favor," Ryan said. "Take me home. I'll show you where."

Lowell puffed. "What... are you going... to do?"

"I have absolutely no idea," Ryan said. Because he didn't.

TWENTY

Lowell scrambled frantically to find the door handle, threw open the car door, fell out onto the road, picked himself up, stumbled against the hood of the car, and barreled away down the street at a dead sprint, shouting "Hey! Hey!"

He wasn't at all sure how his passenger—was his name Ryan?—would feel about his sudden departure, but he didn't have time to consider it.

Because someone had just come out the door of the Post-Mortal Services Clinic. Someone who had no business being there. Hence his willingness to risk heart attacks and various other bodily breakdowns by sprinting up the street to catch up to him.

The figure was moving unhurriedly but with a kind of determination to his stride that suggested annoyance. The guy was moving like somebody had just wronged him and he was off to do something about it, dammit. But he was evidently unaware of Lowell pursuing him. He never glanced back, even when Lowell crashed into a Herald box and knocked it in front of a bus pulling over to stop.

Lowell picked himself up, but not the newspaper box, and resumed his pursuit as the figure ahead cut across the street into traffic. Lowell had closed enough distance between them that he tried calling out again. "Hey!" When that didn't get a response, he tried using the figure's name.

"Hey! Rufus!"

There was absolutely no way that Rufus Flowers hadn't heard him. Every single other person within earshot, both living and dead, turned towards him in response, some of them much further away from Lowell than Rufus was. But Rufus didn't so much as pause. He continued his stride across the street, ignoring even the car that had to screech to a sudden stop to avoid hitting him.

He's going to get himself killed, Lowell thought.

And the thought incensed him again. Because the last time he had seen Rufus, the "getting killed" had already been taken care of. And Lowell's paycheck from the case pretty much relied on that fact being true. Which it now seemed it wasn't.

Rufus being alive and walking angrily around in front of cars meant that he and his wife had lied to Lowell. There was no dead body for Lowell to find at all. He could spend weeks futilely looking for it, for no financial gain whatsoever. The couple were definitely liars, which made them that much more likely to stiff him on the check.

Lowell leapt off the sidewalk into traffic, waving at cars approaching from both sides to stop. They honked violently instead of slowing down. Lowell was forced to stop in the middle of the road and let them go past.

He craned his neck to keep track of Rufus. He caught sight of the man's enormous back as he stepped over a guardrail into a public parking lot.

As soon as the cars were clear, Lowell sprinted the rest of the way across the street and tripped on the curb, nearly diving headlong into a bus shelter. He went clear through a cluster of ghosts milling there and his wildly pinwheeling arms stirred them briefly up into a swirling mist.

He breathlessly mumbled an apology and cut left down the sidewalk towards the parking lot, weaving in and out of the various ghosts and occasional living people who got in his way.

By now he was already seriously out of breath and sweating, dismayed at how heavy and unwieldy he felt. He used to be able to run better than this, didn't he? He was being outrun by a three-hundred pound supposedly dead man.

Lowell grabbed a lamppost to stop himself. He clung to it, panting and clutching the stitch in his side.

Something wasn't right here. Something beyond all the other things that weren't right here. And he had just finally realized what it was.

He shifted sideways until he could see Rufus over the tops of the parked cars, moving across the parking lot.

Lowell remembered Rufus coming into his office. The man—or rather the ghost—was enormous. You could ski down this man. And yet he had glided with the grace of a speed skater on a smooth pond. Subliminally at the time, Lowell had attributed his movement to the fact that he was a ghost. But consciously, Lowell knew that ghosts always move exactly as they had done in life. Rufus must have been a smooth walker when he was alive.

Yet this figure that Lowell had been chasing moved nothing like that. He lumbered. He moved quickly for a big man, but his movements were massive, lurching. Encumbered, even.

For the first time, Lowell doubted himself. Was this Rufus at all? He had been so certain upon first seeing the giant figure emerge from the Clinic, but now he was losing his confidence.

Rufus—if indeed it was Rufus at all—stopped next to a silver Corvette, and fished through his pockets.

Lowell took a deep breath and forced himself to run again, despite the very convincing protests being mounted by every single part of his body.

He stumbled over the guardrail encircling the lot and squeezed between the parked cars, managing as he stumbled across the lot to set off no fewer than three car alarms.

By the time he reached Rufus, he could barely breathe and he thought he might be about to throw up and possibly to die, not necessarily in that order.

Rufus still had his back to him, and had only just found

his keys and was twisting sideways to force himself into a sports car clearly much too small for him.

Lowell clutched onto the SUV next to Rufus's car and tried to get a breath, to get a word out before the big man could get into his car and be gone.

Rufus seemed to sense his presence. There was a slight cocking of the head. But he continued to struggle into his car.

Finally Lowell managed a breathless, rasping word. The same word he had already tried.

"Rufus!"

The big man froze. He turned to Lowell.

It was definitely Rufus. There could be no doubt. The same jowls, the exact same spot of thinning hair just above his forehead, the tiny mole on his cheek that his ghost had decided to render as a brilliantly shimmering spot. It was all there, except opaque and in full color.

He stared at Lowell, and Lowell stared back between shallow, desperate, exhausted breaths.

Rufus said nothing. And there was nothing in his eyes. No recognition whatsoever. Just a baffled, vacant annoyance. Like Lowell had just stumbled up out of the gutter and asked for change.

Lowell had a million doubts at that moment but there was one thing he knew for certain.

This man, although he was definitely Rufus, had never met him before.

"Sorry," Lowell managed to choke out, "I thought... you were... somebody..."

Before he could say "else", Rufus had already forced himself into the car like cramming two buckets' worth of Play-doh into a single little Play-doh bucket. It seemed impossible for him to close the door but he did.

As the Corvette backed out, Lowell barely had the energy to get out of the way.

Halfway back to his own car, where the ghost Ryan waited inside for him with a dazed expression, Lowell thought how detective-like it would have been for him to have gotten the Corvette's license number before it pulled out. But he had not done that.

You, he reminded himself needlessly, *are not a detective.*

When he finally felt like he had his own voice back and wouldn't sound like walking tuberculosis, he pulled his cellphone from his pocket and touched a speed dial. Someone answered on the first ring.

"Mr. Mahaffey?" Lucinda Flowers sounded hopeful.

Lowell had been prepared to immediately launch into an accusation, but now that he was in the moment he decided on a different tack. Better to be sure when there's a pay check on the line. "Mrs. Flowers," he gasped, "is your husband there?"

"I'll put you on speaker," she said.

He's there? Lowell's breath caught in his chest, which was the last thing he needed when he had so little breath to go around.

Rufus's voice came on, close to the phone. "Mr. Mahaffey?" He had the same hopeful tone as his wife.

Lowell's mind raced, trying to piece together a scenario where any of this made sense. He couldn't come up with one. Not even one where these people were lying to him. He just couldn't buy that.

He got a bit of his breath back to speak. "Rufus, have you ever been to the Post-Mortal Services Clinic?"

"Never heard of it. Why? Did you find my body?"

"Yeah, I did," Lowell said. "But I think I'm going to have to find it again."

TWENTY-ONE

Lowell's car wobbled up to Ryan's house. The storm had cleared but the sun was long gone, and the nightly wandering spirits had taken to the gleaming streets. Ryan had always liked how the dense flow of ghosts looked on a rainy night, their shimmering forms suffusing the damp asphalt with an ethereal glow. There was a serenity about it despite the sheer number of ghosts it took to produce it.

A little cluster of ghosts that spanned at least three centuries conversed in front of the house, and had to scatter onto the sidewalk as Lowell pulled up. One of them waved his fist and hurled Dutch insults, but Lowell ignored him.

Ryan was just grateful to be home. Despite his hurry to find his body, and despite the fact that he could not get tired, and despite it being the least comfortable place he had ever lived, it was still home. And seeing it again was a relief.

But something wasn't right. He froze, staring.

Lowell got out the driver's door. He pulled the snow globe out and set it on the roof of the car. "Where do you want...?" he started to ask.

But Ryan cut him off. "Wait," he said urgently. He pointed up at the third floor windows. His apartment. "There's a light on."

There was a glow in the kitchen window, the one Sye used to sit in front of. The kitchen light made a dim orange circle on the water-stained ceiling. From their vantage point below, the ceiling was all they could see. But there was no doubt. The light was on.

"So you left the light on," Lowell said, shrugging.

"No, I specifically didn't." He had been very diligent about everything when he left the morning of the procedure.

He had shut off the lights, the heat, all the appliances that he counted on never needing again. The only thing he had left on was the fridge, because of the Algonquian ghost, who seemed to like the cold. He had definitely not left any lights on. And Benny the Poltergeist wouldn't have turned them on; he liked the lights off because it was scarier. And he hadn't ever managed to operate the switch anyway, though not for lack of trying.

There was somebody up there. Somebody living.

"So your landlord rented the place out again," Lowell tried.

Ryan shook his head. "I just renewed the lease."

He was sure he saw a shadow move, a slight darkening of a patch of the ceiling that slid away towards the living room. "Somebody's in there," he hissed. "What do we do?"

"Why are you asking me?"

"You're a detective! Don't you have a gun or something?"

Lowell snorted in reply.

Ryan glimpsed the shadow shift across the ceiling again, crossing the kitchen and then crossing back.

"Come on," he whispered. He started across the lawn to the front door. But Lowell stayed where he was. Ryan stopped halfway to the door and motioned for Lowell to come with him, but Lowell just leaned against the car.

"This has nothing to do with me," he called across the lawn.

Ryan made a cutting motion across his throat and ran back to Lowell. "Shhh! They'll hear you!"

"So? Isn't that good? Maybe they'll leave!"

"That's not a burglar up there! There's nothing in my place to steal. If there's somebody up there, it's because they're looking for me. And nobody ever, ever looks for me."

"Really? Ever?"

"Ever."

"That's sad, man."

"That is not the point! Whoever it is, they're looking for me for a reason. It could be whoever sent me to the dump. And that means they might know where my body is!"

"Or it might be you left a light on."

"I didn't leave any lights on! Please, just bring the snow globe and come upstairs. I might need help."

"I'm not getting into a fight for you! I don't even work for you!"

Ryan balled his fists and clenched his teeth. He didn't want to go upstairs unless the snow globe came with him. And he couldn't carry it himself. He had no choice.

"What's your rate?"

Ryan found it extraordinary how much Lowell's face lit up, and how quickly. "Four hundred a day. Plus expenses."

"You're hired. If you find my body, I'll throw in an extra thousand. But you have to start right now. And your first lead, clue, whatever you call it..." He pointed up at the window. "...is right in there."

Ryan crept up the stairs towards the third floor landing. He moved slowly, afraid of causing the stairs to creak. And he realized only after he had gone up halfway that with no mass, he couldn't make them creak if he tried. Any noises he made would be drowned out anyway by the squeak of the ventilation fan, and the irregular thumping from below that suggested a water heater approaching total implosion. So he hurried up the last flight as fast as he could float, unconcerned about creeping.

Lowell had placed the snow globe inside and then volunteered to stay at the front door watching the street, which he claimed was a good strategy. Ryan didn't know how to deal with a situation like this, and Lowell didn't seem to either. For a detective, he seemed unclear on exactly how to detect anything. Ryan felt the snow globe tugging backwards as he arrived at the door. He wished Lowell had come up with him. But the pull wasn't overpowering; he could resist it. A much bigger problem was that he was breathing fast, his fists balled, his mouth dry, and his teeth tightly clenched. Or at least, that's how his incorporeal form slavishly simulated an actual fear response.

He pressed both his hands against the surface of the door, letting the surface tension keep them from passing through. He was pleased that it worked; it made him feel almost material. He pressed his face into the door with increasing pressure until it broke through. He ignored the door's wooden despair and kept pushing, and then his face was inside the apartment.

Whoever had been casting shadows was not in sight. There was only Benny, trying to finger-write in the dust on a hanging mirror. He had finished a lowercase d and the bottom part of an i, but was struggling with the dot. It appeared he was trying to write "die", because Benny only ever wrote threatening messages even though he didn't mean them.

"Benny!" Ryan whispered.

Benny didn't hear him. He kept trying again and again to dot his i, without success.

Ryan whispered again, as loud as he dared. "Benny!"

Benny spun around, startled. He grinned as soon as he saw Ryan's face poking through the door. "Hey, you're dead!" he cheered. "That's great! Hey, man, Gabriel's really mad at you."

"SHHHHH!" Ryan expected somebody to come running, but there was no response. "Who's in here?" he whispered.

Benny looked puzzled. "You know."

"How would I know?"

"Um… duh. Did you forget?"

"No, I didn't forget! Who's in here?!"

"Your sister, idiot."

For a moment, Ryan wondered if the procedure had given him some kind of post-death amnesia where details of his life got scrambled in his memory. He imagined such a thing was possible. Things like that seemed likely to happen after thousands of volts of electricity was jolted through your brain. But he tested the theory by scanning his memory of every photo he used to have in his library. If he had a sister, it was probable she would be in at least one of those photos. But as far as he could recall, she wasn't.

"I don't have a sister!" he whispered. "I don't think," he added, just in case.

Benny looked perplexed. "Yes you do. She's..."

He motioned towards the bedroom. But he needn't have, because she had just emerged. She didn't notice them for a few steps, and even then she only saw Benny, and his finger painting on the mirror.

"You should write in uppercase," Margie said coolly. "Then you won't need to dot anything."

Margie.

Ryan was so astounded at seeing her that he involuntarily blurted "Hey!"

Margie spun and spotted him protruding from the front door. She stumbled backwards into a lamp and grabbed it to keep from knocking it over. "Mr. Matney?!" she gasped.

A memory rampaged through Ryan's mind, of a moment shortly before his ghost was extracted from his body. He remembered Margie flipping through his file. "Is this your current address?" she had said. "Nice place?" Up to that point she hadn't been prone to chit chat, so her idle curiosity had seemed odd. As though it wasn't idle curiosity at all.

Now she was in his home, comfortably dressed in sweatpants, a long T-shirt and fuzzy slippers like she was about to settle in and watch TV. Like she *lived* there.

Ryan had a surge of realization.

It wasn't Roger who had bound him to the snow globe. It

was Margie.

She had condemned him to eternity in a dump with a broken snow globe so she could steal his apartment.

Rage flooded through him. He could feel it tearing through his form like a hot wind, radiating through him in shock-wave ripples. He jabbed his finger at her and plunged through the door, preparing to unleash a barrage of accusations relentless enough to clear a beach of invading infantry.

He hadn't even yet pulled the trigger on his enraged volley when he noticed that she was fixated on his finger. The one he was pointing at her to focus his rage in her direction. The cannon that would launch all his indignation at her and, any second now, flatten her.

Before he could fire his first shot, she stepped forward. "What happened to you?" she asked. There was urgency in her voice.

For a moment he didn't know what she meant. She should know what had happened to him, shouldn't she? But she was staring at his finger, so he bent it towards his face and focused on it.

The tip of his finger wasn't there.

TWENTY-TWO

Ryan held his hand close to his face and forced his visual sense to zero in on his fingertip, ignoring everything else.

The last quarter inch of his finger was gone, and what remained was wafting away like sand coming off the crest of a dune. A thin, nearly imperceptible stream of particles cascaded up and away from the finger in defiance of gravity, carried on a spectral draft.

Ryan's breathing, or rather the simulation of it, accelerated. He felt his anxiety grapefruit expand into a watermelon. "Why is it doing that?" he managed to choke out.

"Come over here," Margie commanded. She pointed to the floor directly beneath the ceiling light.

Ryan shuffled under the light while she dragged a chair next to him and sat. He was still furious with her, but at least she was an expert. Apparently.

"Put your hand out like this, please," she said. He recognized the clinical tone he had heard from her during his extraction procedure. It commanded obedience, so he put his right hand out flat, palm down. His disintegrating finger released particles like the steaming spout of a kettle.

Somebody pounded on the door from outside. Lowell.

"I'll get it," Benny said, abandoning his calligraphy.

"You can't open doors, Benny," Ryan snapped.

"I can too!" He jogged to the door and swiped uselessly at the knob. "Whoever's there," he called through the door, "stay where you are! I'll have this open in half an hour at most!"

Ryan felt the emotional tug of the snow globe through the door. He liked it being closer. He wanted it next to him.

"That's a friend of mine," he explained to Margie. "He can help."

She strode past Benny and threw open the door. Lowell was on the landing, gearing up to kick the door down. He looked disappointed at having lost the opportunity.

"You," she said with no greeting, jabbing a finger at Lowell, "baking soda. Now."

Lowell must have had the same response to her tone that Ryan did, because without a word of protest he came inside and began opening cupboards.

Ryan waited, tense, as she pulled her chair in even closer to his side, peering at his outstretched hand with her eyes only inches from it. "What's going on?" he ventured.

"Shh," was all she said. She leaned far to one side, then the other, her eyes locked on his fingers. There was an urgency to her movements that concerned Ryan. Even Benny seemed to sense the gravity of the situation, because he hovered back and shut up.

Lowell stepped up with a box of baking soda and waited silently until she motioned to him.

"Take a handful," she said, "and drop it through him. Right here." She waved over Ryan's hand and pushed her chair back to give Lowell space.

"What's it for?" Ryan asked. His voice quavered, fear projecting ripples through it.

"Ions," she said, as if that explained everything. "Do it now please."

Lowell obeyed, pouring a little pile of the soda into his hand and holding it above Ryan's. Margie nodded, and Lowell tilted his hand and let the powder trickle off.

The baking soda plunged through Ryan's hand in thinning particulate tendrils. Margie leaned in close and squinted at Ryan's hand, watching the baking soda pass through it.

She leapt out of her chair. "There it is," she said, pointing at the end of his finger. "That's what I was afraid of. It starts in the extremities."

"What does?" Ryan studied his finger. To his surprise, where particles of baking soda brushed against the faded stump of his fingertip, a thunderstorm of electrical pops and flashes raged in miniature.

"Whoa," Lowell said. "That's cool."

"Hey," Benny said, pointing excitedly, "his other hand's doing it too!"

Ryan lifted his left hand to his face. The ring finger vanished into a vague fog at the tip. A steam of particles coiled off of it and dissolved into the air like smoke from a candle just blown out.

Margie pulled her glasses down her nose and studied both his hands over them. "It's important that you tell me where you've been since I last saw you."

Ryan's anger surged back, amplified by his fear. "Like you don't know!"

"How could I know?"

"You sent me there!"

"Sent you where?"

"You dumped me in a dump so you could steal my apartment!"

She blinked. Twice. "Those words made no sense to me. And two of them were the same word. A dump?"

"The snow globe!" he added.

"That's not helpful."

Ryan spun to Lowell. "Show her!"

Lowell fished in his raincoat pocket and produced the snow globe. The tiny plastic hotel shook loose and fell off, and he fumbled it from hand to hand before finally poking it back into place. He held the pathetic, cracked scene up towards her in his open palm.

A sense of security and well-being flowed through Ryan as the globe passed near him. He had to fight the urge not to try to snuggle it. He could tell that Margie recognized the trinket but he didn't get the guilty, cornered response he expected. Rather, she appeared perplexed.

"That's Roger's," she said, seeming to analyze its chemical composition with her eyes. "He has a timeshare in Myrtle Beach. Why do you have that?"

Ryan studied her face, hunting for any trace of deception. Finding none, he turned to Lowell instead. "She doesn't know."

Lowell nodded. "Also," he added, "just so we're on the same page, I don't know who she is. So I don't have a lot to contribute right now. But I'm still billing you."

Margie looked at Ryan sharply. "Wait... you said you were in a dump? With that?" She pointed at the snow globe.

"You used it to keep me there!" Ryan felt like pressing on with the accusation despite his newfound doubts, only because he had been so certain just moments ago.

"Why would I do that?"

"So you could steal my apartment!"

Margie blinked again. She flicked her eyes around the apartment. One of her eyebrows crept up to a skeptical angle. "You think I would do that. For this place. Have you *seen* this place?"

"She's got a point," Lowell put in. "I've only been here a few minutes and I already want to burn it."

Ryan spun on him. "Well then what is she doing here?"

"I don't even know who she is!"

Benny raised his hand like a kid in school with an answer. "She's his sister!"

Ryan's exasperation peaked. "No she's not!"

"She is! I vouched for her!"

"I don't think you know what 'vouch' means!"

"Shut up!" Margie commanded. "All of you!" They fell obediently silent. When she used that tone, it was impossible not to.

She picked up the snow globe. Ryan wanted to smack it jealously out of her hand. But he stopped himself, both because he couldn't smack anything, and because he wished he didn't so badly want to.

"You're telling me," she said, "that you're haunting this? Since when?"

"Since you… or somebody… attacked me at the Clinic last night."

"That's why you disappeared." It sounded genuinely like a revelation to her. "Let me see your hands again."

He held out his hands and she sat and studied the disappearing fingertips. Ryan averted his eyes, hoping that the act of not looking at them would somehow slow down their disintegration.

Margie sat back in her chair. "Well, that explains it," she said with a note of finality.

Ryan traded looks with Lowell, confirming that he, too, had missed the part where anything got explained. "What explains what?!"

"I knew it," Margie said. "I knew it, I knew it, I knew it, I knew it," she added angrily. She kicked her chair away and stormed into the kitchen and back, her eyes flailing around the room for something to glare at.

Ryan didn't know anything, and it seemed unfair that she apparently knew five things. "Knew what?" he demanded.

"I don't know! But, I mean, I knew it!"

"Start with the 'knowing it' part and work backwards!"

"There are two people who know how to use the Box. If it wasn't me who did this to you, it was Roger. He artificially induced a haunting, which bound you to this snow globe. Roger doesn't usually perform that procedure. He leaves it to me. There's a reason for that."

Ryan was in no mood for the dramatic pause she decided to insert. He filled it with a panicked cry of "Which is?!"

"Because it's difficult. Hauntings are created naturally by

emotional bonds established in life. They take time, and a complex interaction of the ghost with its host body and brain. Creating them artificially is like brain surgery on a ghost. Roger is terrible at it. And there are two possible results when an artificially induced haunting fails. One, is that the haunting just doesn't stick. It has no effect at all. But the other…" She pointed at Ryan's fingers. "The other is that."

Ryan had risked another look at his vanishing finger and as a result completely lost the train of her lecture at the end. "*What* is that…? What?"

She made a little explosion gesture with her hands. "Total axionic dispersal. Psssh!"

Ryan's watermelon squeezed tighter as he tried to process the word. "Dispersal?" He drew his hand even closer to his face. It was clear that the particles weren't just coming off the surface like a layer. It was the entire substance of his finger coming apart. When the particles departed, they left nothing behind.

She looked away. She didn't want to tell him. But she did anyway, softly. "It means the bonds that hold your axions together are breaking down. Within twenty-four hours you'll be unable to hold your shape. Within forty-eight all of your energy will have been distributed randomly."

"And what happens to me?"

"I just answered that, didn't I?"

"No, but, I mean, I go somewhere, don't I?"

"What do you mean by 'you'? If you mean the sub-atomic particles of which you are composed, then yes, you go somewhere. You go almost literally *everywhere.*"

Ryan couldn't even pretend to breathe anymore. He felt like he might pass out. He decided that his knees should give out, so they did. He collapsed into a quivering, crumpled squat. "Why?" he croaked. "Why would Roger do this to me?"

"I think, because he didn't want you to find out what happened to your body."

"What happened to my body?"

Margie shrugged, turning her hands to the ceiling. "I have no idea. Whatever it was, it had to be illegal. Or at least seriously unethical. He did this to you just so you couldn't figure it out and make trouble for him, so it has to be something bad. I knew it. That bastard." She swatted the snow globe, shoving it near the edge of the counter, and Ryan almost tore himself apart preparing to save it. "Right under my nose," Margie added, sneering.

Ryan couldn't move. He was locked into imagining what it might feel like not existing. Not good, he imagined. "What... what can I do?" he stammered. "There must be something I can do. To stop it. There's always something you can do. Tell me the thing I can do so I can do it!"

Margie pushed her glasses up her nose again. "The only thing that can stop it is getting back into your body. That would stabilize your form, undo the damage."

Lowell stepped forward. It startled Ryan; he had forgotten Lowell was there. "Can I ask a dumb question?"

"The only stupid question is the one you don't..." Margie started. She looked Lowell up and down and changed her mind. "Sorry, yes, go ahead."

"Why does it have to be *his* body?"

Ryan couldn't fathom even halfway what Lowell meant. And neither, apparently, could Margie because she said: "Meaning what?"

"There's lots of empty bodies lying around at your Clinic, right? So you put him into somebody else's. Temporarily, until we find his. Buy some time."

Ryan perked up, sensing hope. He looked up at Margie, hoping to see her nodding or excited, anything that might mean he wasn't going to disperse into the ether.

But she had her eyes closed, and was shaking her head. "That can't be done. It's been tried. It doesn't work."

Lowell looked disappointed. "Really? I thought I was onto something there."

Margie shook her head again. "It doesn't work. The body will reject the invader ghost. Never mind that it's an enormous breach of ethics."

Lowell shrugged. "It was just a thought."

"It was a bad one," she said frostily.

Lowell narrowed his eyes, evidently annoyed. He turned back to Ryan. "Why is she here again?"

"I vouched for her!" Benny called from the mirror.

Ryan had completely forgotten the issue of why Margie was in his apartment at all. And he decided to continue forgetting about it for now, given more pressing matters. "So we have to find my body."

"It's not at the Clinic," Margie said. "I checked every storage unit after you left. I even checked the dumpsters."

"I'm gonna go check out the Clinic myself, first thing in the morning," Lowell said. "Maybe have a talk with this Roger guy."

"And ask him what?" Margie asked, folding her arms skeptically.

"Questions," Lowell said, nodding and narrowing his eyes. Ryan doubted there was any kind of brilliant plan behind the look, but Lowell seemed to want them to think there was. He slid towards the door. "Meet me at my office at 10. I may just have some answers."

"Where's your office?" Margie asked.

"I can't remember the address. Harvard Square, I think. I always go in the side door. Just Google it or whatever. 10 AM!" He gave them a confident nod that inspired Ryan with no confidence whatsoever, and then slipped out the door.

Ryan waved his disappearing hand in the air, creating a smoke ring of particles. "Look at this!"

Margie straightened her back and stared at the ceiling. "I might be able give you more time. Without the original body, I can't stop your dispersal. But I might be able to slow it down."

"That sounds good. How?"

She pointed at the snow globe. "Unhaunt you from that. The permanent damage has been done, but the dispersal will slow down if we remove the artificially induced haunting. It's like removing the bullet from a gunshot wound."

Ryan sprang up, nodding. He liked this plan. It seemed manageable, and familiar, and it meant not sitting here doing nothing. "So we go to the Clinic! Do the whole thing with the Box! Unhaunt me!"

"It's a little more complicated than that."

"Why?"

She pushed her glasses up her nose. "Because I don't work there anymore."

Ryan seized up again. His anxiety watermelon had to be bigger than his torso now. "You... don't..."

"Roger fired me. Right after I searched for your body. All my keys, alarm codes, everything, is all gone. I can't get you to the Box."

The revelation hung expectantly in the air among them.

Lowell was the one who finally wafted it away. He opened the door a crack and stuck his head back in.

"I don't wanna sound, like, insensitive," he said, "but given the whole 'dispersal' thing, do you think you could pay me in advance?"

TWENTY-THREE

Ryan crouched behind a monolithic dumpster at the back of the Clinic parking lot and reflected that, though he didn't remember it, he had probably been inside this dumpster just the night before, thrown out with the snow globe. Being out with the Clinic trash seemed to be his thing.

The parking lot behind the Post-Mortal Services Clinic was much larger than it needed to be. Ryan found it hard to imagine that, even when the place was a funeral home, it could ever have hosted a ceremony large enough to warrant so many parking spaces. The rows were divided by dull concrete planters containing shrubs and perennials so neglected that they deserved funeral services of their own. This late at night the lot was vacant and unlit. It was a dark, Gothic forest of skeletal shrubs, drifting litter, and vaguely wandering spirits who seemed to be trying to remember where they parked.

"Do you think he'll do it?" Margie whispered. She peered around the corner of the dumpster at the back of the Clinic.

Benny the Poltergeist had been inside for ten minutes and there had been no sign of him. Ryan was unsurprised.

The plan was to get the door open. Ryan could easily get inside by passing through a wall, but if they wanted to make use of the Box, Margie had to get in too. Thanks to her insider knowledge, they knew that the alarm would be shut off because Ethan and Ewan the orderlies always cleaned at this hour. That part of the plan was good. They knew that the service door could be opened easily from the inside with the gentlest of pushes. That part of the plan was also rock solid. And they knew from the absence of cars in the lot that the place was empty except for the twin orderlies. If there was ever a time and opportunity to sneak in and use the Box to unhaunt Ryan from the snow globe, it was now. So the plan was for Benny to go in through the wall and push the door open from inside.

The flaw in that plan, of course, was Benny.

"I've seen Benny write on things, and sometimes break things," Ryan said. "But not once has he been able to open a door. I don't know why he'd start now."

"He said he could do it!" Margie said, sounding a lot more positive than Ryan felt.

"He says that every single time. Never true."

Margie bubbled with nervous energy and enthusiasm that Ryan didn't share. He was distracted by the fact that most of his fingers were down the middle knuckle already, and both thumbs were completely gone. His ability to point at things was seriously impaired, and hitchhiking was right out of the question. His only comfort at this moment was the snow globe. Margie had it nestled in a hip satchel, and he could almost make out the shape of it. He felt a steady ache of jealousy that she got to hold it and he didn't, but at least it was here where he could be close to its snowy globeness.

At the same time he hated himself for feeling that way, and couldn't wait to be rid of the thing.

"Look at me," Margie said, holding her trembling hand out for him to see. "It's the elevated adrenaline. I've never broken into anywhere before. I can actually *feel* my hypothalamus sending signals to my adrenal gland. It's extraordinary." She leaned back against the dumpster with her eyes closed.

"What are you doing?"

"Shh. Enjoying it."

Ryan decided to hold onto his impression, bolstered by mounting evidence, that Margie was a little odd. Not necessarily in a bad way. Just odd. And there wasn't any way he could tell if his own hypothalamus was sending signals to any other part of him, because he didn't have a hypothalamus or any other parts. Or rather, he didn't know where they were.

He returned his attention to the Clinic's service door, which Benny continued to not open. Ryan imagined Benny inside sweeping his hand again and again through the door handle, probably muttering something about terror from beyond the grave. Ryan wished they had a plan B, but they barely had a plan A.

"This is taking too long," he said. "I'm going to be part of the universe before he gets that door open."

"You're already part of the universe," Margie said.

"I mean a different part. You know what I mean."

"It hasn't happened yet. Don't think about it."

He needed to keep himself distracted, so he kept talking. "Hey, speaking of the universe, what were you doing in my apartment? You never said."

She looked at her feet. "I'll move out tomorrow."

"Wait... move out? Does that mean you moved in?"

She fell silent, staring across the dark lot.

Ryan took that as confirmation. "You *did* try to steal my apartment!"

"I didn't think you'd come back! They almost never do!"

Ryan's jaw dropped. "You've done this before?" His impression of her being a little odd disassembled itself and coalesced into an entirely new impression. "Oh my God, you work at the Clinic so you can steal apartments from dead people!"

She spun on him, trying to sound indignant but quickly looking at her shoes again. "No! That's a side benefit. And they're not dead."

Ryan's astonishment was interrupted by a faint sound from across the lot.

A cough.

They both pressed themselves against the back of the

dumpster. Margie risked a peek around the edge.

"It's Ethan," she whispered.

Ryan stole a look past Margie, hoping that his glow wouldn't give him away. The immense bull-like silhouette of Ethan the orderly was a featureless, hulking shadow looming outside the service door. As Ryan watched, the glowing orange circle of the end of a cigarette faded up and then sank back into darkness.

"Can you see Benny?" Ryan whispered. He couldn't see anything past Ethan at all. The giant man's enormous form was completely obscuring the light spilling out the open door.

Margie's fingers were tense against the corner of the dumpster. "Now that it's open maybe Benny can hold it open?"

Ryan doubted it, but the odds of that were marginally better than the odds of Benny getting the door open himself.

They watched together, staying silent, as the cigarette went orange, black. Orange, black. Orange, black.

Ethan's silhouette shifted. The cigarette sparked on the asphalt and went dark for the last time beneath his foot. His silhouette shifted again and heaved back towards the door. He had to squeeze through it, only slivers of light escaping around him. And then he was through and disappeared into the building.

Margie looked at Ryan sharply, stunned.

Ethan had left the door open.

It was propped open with half of a broken patio brick. The light from a naked bulb inside cut a bright trapezoid on the still-wet surface of the parking lot.

"Do we go?" Ryan asked, breathless.

"Of course we go!" Margie was already dashing across the parking lot, half bent-over so she could dive behind a planter if the need arose.

Ryan sprinted after her. "What about Benny? Where's

Benny?"

"Who cares? Just go!"

As they neared the building she ducked even lower, and Ryan with her. They both expected Ethan to reappear at any moment and kick the brick out of the door. But Ethan did not appear.

Instead, Benny did. He drifted into the doorway and looked with annoyance at the brick propping the door open. And then he started kicking at it. His foot passed through it again and again, but he kept trying.

He was trying to close the door.

TWENTY-FOUR

"What is he doing?!" Margie hissed.

"Benny, no!" Ryan didn't dare shout, but whispered as loud as he could, waving his arms.

Benny didn't look up. He crouched and cupped his hands near the brick, and started trying to push it out of the way so the door would be free to swing closed.

The brick shifted. Not quite far enough to let the door close. But it shifted. The most Benny had ever been able to move anything, and it had to be now.

"Benny, stop!" Ryan shout-whispered. Benny ignored him, or didn't hear.

Margie and Ryan crossed the last twenty feet to the door at a dead sprint.

Benny gave one last shove and caught the corner of the brick. It shifted just a millimeter. But it was enough for the pressure from the hinge to take over. The door started to swing closed, toppling the brick as it traveled.

Margie sprang ahead. She jammed her foot in the door and caught it an inch away from thudding closed. She wrenched her leg backwards and hauled the door fully open again.

Benny looked out at them like they'd just spat in his beer. "What'd you do that for?" he demanded.

"We need this door open!" Ryan snarled through angrily gritted teeth. "That was the whole plan!"

"Yeah, but some huge guy opened it! That's not scary! Close it again and let me open it right. I think I can even get it to squeak!"

Ryan expected that they would slink down the stairs the

way he had always gone, but Margie insisted that they use the casket lift. This was a small, cramped elevator expressly installed for the purpose of moving caskets, either occupied or not, from the basement up to the viewing areas on the main level. She reasoned that it would keep them further from where Ethan and Ewan were cleaning. But the lift descended haltingly, producing a cacophonous blend of squeaking and grinding that Ryan thought had to carry through the whole building. How this could be more discreet than the stairs, he couldn't understand.

While they rode the lift down he kept his arms folded so he couldn't see his hands dissolving. "Benny, what were you thinking?" he asked irritably.

Benny threw indignation back at him. "What?"

"If you had closed the door—"

"I'm telling you, I could have opened it a lot scarier."

"We're not here to scare people."

"Maybe *you're* not!"

"So you're not here to help me?"

Benny snickered in response. It annoyed Ryan more than any actual answer could have.

"Ryan, stop," Margie said. She had taken on that cool, clinical tone that Ryan had gotten to know from her.

"I've let him live in my place for three years!"

"It doesn't matter."

"I thought we were friends... sort of! I looked up scary Latin words for him to write in the steam on the bathroom mirror!"

Benny chuckled. "*Gladium mortis*! That was my favorite and I don't even know what it means."

Ryan held up his steaming, stumpy hand. "You don't care about this at all?"

Benny gasped at the flow coming off Ryan's knuckles. "Look at that! It looks like a finger tornado!"

Ryan was about to grab Benny's neck and squeeze, even

knowing that it wouldn't have any effect at all. He just wanted to do the action. But Benny denied him the chance.

"Look, I'm gonna go," Benny said. "This is taking way longer than I thought."

"You're leaving? You're just...?"

Margie cut in. "Let him go, Ryan."

Benny had already forced himself through the wall of the elevator and disappeared. Ryan couldn't help being offended. *All the times I've stuck up for that ghost...*

The elevator thudded into the bottom of its descent and the door screeched open onto the dim basement tunnel. Margie led the way along the length of the tunnel at a brisk pace, her footfalls echoing back at them off the pipes and ductwork. She walked with a kind of premeditated precision, like she was measuring the trajectory of her feet in three dimensional vectors before she moved them. But it didn't slow her down. If anything, it sped her up because she was placing her feet in precisely calculated spots. Ryan wished he could walk so efficiently.

He was still annoyed at Benny's betrayal, and Margie seemed to sense it. "Did you know Benny before he died?" she asked in a low voice.

"Of course not. He died in the 80's, before I was born."

"Then he doesn't care about you."

"So three years of living in my house—"

"Means nothing at all to him. He might as well have just met you today," she explained in a scolding tone, like he was a classroom full of disobedient toddlers. "You know this. It was all in the pamphlet. It's the same reason haunting this snow globe is tearing you apart. Ghosts are snapshots of their living selves at the moment of death. They can't form new emotional attachments, or break the ones they had when they were alive. Those things are handled by the body: brain chemistry, hormones, electrical impulses."

"Chemicals?"

"Correct."

"So emotional attachments are not real? They're just chemicals and electricity?"

She cocked an eyebrow disapprovingly. "So to you, if they're produced by chemicals and electricity, they're not real. But if they come from this—" She waved one hand through his torso. He felt it pass through him with no resistance. "—they're real? That makes sense to you?"

It had made perfect sense a moment ago. But now he found himself without a response.

They passed quickly through the morgue-like storage facility. Margie repeated that she had checked the whole thing and his body wasn't anywhere in it. But there was always a chance it had been moved back in since she looked. So Ryan poked his head through the wall of drawers a few times as he passed, just to look. He saw nothing that reminded him of himself.

She led him out of the storage facility and along the tunnel of pipes and ducts. As they neared the door to Margie's exam room, she slowed. Overhead they could hear the whine of a vacuum cleaner. Dulled through the ceiling and channeled through the ducts, it sounded to Ryan in his nervous state like an alarm. "Ethan and Ewan don't come down here, even to clean," Margie said. "Roger tells them not to. We should be fine." She seemed to be trying to convince herself. As she crept forward she kept glancing upwards, listening for the vacuum.

"Will they hear when we use the Box?" Ryan asked.

"Yes," she replied matter-of-factly. "And it makes the lights flicker in the whole building. Sometimes it throws the breakers."

"So how are we going to do this?"

She didn't reply. Her silence put Ryan's nerves on high alert. *Does she even know?*

"Margie? How are we going to do this?"

She dipped through the door and into her dark exam room.

He knew the room didn't look different than it had any of the other times he had been in it, but somehow being there secretly in the middle of the night made it feel even more oppressive. The light seemed harsher, the shadows deeper. Every sound seemed thunderous. Ryan wanted out of there quickly.

Margie was already pulling the Box out of the corner on its cart. The wheels screeched like attacking birds. Ryan winced, but Margie seemed unconcerned. She moved quickly, but not frantically.

Ryan headed for the exam table, remembering how the procedure had gone when they detached Sye from his chair. "Do I have to lie down?"

"No," she replied, checking that all of the Box's attachments were securely attached to the cart.

"So how do we do this?"

"Like this," she said. And unplugged the Box from the wall. She coiled the long cord around her shoulder.

Ryan would have scratched his head in puzzlement if he had a head and anything to scratch it with. "It works when it's unplugged?" he asked, knowing immediately that it was a stupid question.

Margie wheeled the cart towards the door. Its wheels shrieked in a chorus as though screaming for help. "Check the hall," she said.

Ryan was stunned. "We're taking it?"

"Yes, we're taking it!"

"That's why you made us take the casket lift! You were planning this all along!"

"Check the hall!"

Ryan's mind raced. If they took it, Roger would certainly know it was them. He would come after it. He could call the police and have them arrested. He could send his giant monster twins to hurt them and take it back. This was an action that could lead to any number of bad things. But all he could think to say in protest was: "But…"

"Ryan, check the hall!"

Ryan stuck his head out into the hall and looked both ways. It was as empty and subterranean as always. He could still hear the muffled drone of the vacuum overhead. "There's nobody," he whispered. "But…"

Margie charged into the hall, pushing the cart ahead of her. She turned hard left to head away from the stairs and towards the casket lift. The screech of the cart's wheels became even louder as they turned, and the noise echoed up and down the tunnel like the cries of panicked bats. Ryan froze, expecting to hear the vacuum noise stop. But it didn't falter.

Margie jogged down the tunnel. The squeaking wheels fell into a steady rhythm. Ryan winced on every screech.

"Why don't we just do it here?" he demanded.

"I told you," she said, "they'll hear it. And it makes the lights flicker. They'll know."

"They'll know we took it!"

"Do you want to get off this snow globe or don't you?"

"Yes! But…"

The cart stopped dead. One of its front wheels had caught the corner of a dent in the floor. The full force of Margie's momentum slammed into the back of the cart. It rocked forward, and the Box slid to the edge.

Ryan leapt, trying to stop it. But of course he couldn't. And Margie tried to yank the cart back upright. But it was too late.

The Box flipped over the edge of the cart and fell.

Wires whipped out behind it in a tangle, briefly dangling the Box above the floor before unwinding themselves and pulling free. The Box plummeted the last foot.

It hit the floor with a sound like a train broadsiding a truck. The echo washed over them several times and seemed to take minutes to fade completely.

They both stood frozen, waiting. The Box lay on its side on the floor.

The vacuum noise kept on, undisturbed.

And then it stopped.

The dull thump of heavy, fast footfalls pounded across the ceiling.

"They're coming!" Ryan knew it was obvious but said it anyway.

Margie yanked the cart out of the pothole that had stopped it, and swept past it to the Box. Even now she moved with a cool deliberation that Ryan had to admire. She crouched and lifted the Box, shaking it gently.

It rattled like a box full of old credit cards.

"That's unfortunate," was all Margie said.

"Hey!" a voice thundered at them from down the tunnel.

Ryan spun around to see the ghost brother—Ewan, was it? It was his head and shoulders only, upside down and poking through the ceiling halfway back to the exam room.

Margie ignored him and heaved the Box back onto the cart. She pushed the cart ahead of her as she broke into a run. "Come on! Come on come on!"

Ryan caught a glimpse of Ewan flipping himself upright and dropping to the floor of the tunnel. He was an immense, glowing form in the darkness. He came hurtling at them like a meteor on fire.

Ryan raced after Margie. She struggled to keep control of the cart, zig zagging through the storage facility. The cart's wheels protested with screams as though terrified of speed.

Ewan caught up to them just as they reached the other end of the morgue. Ryan glanced back and the huge man's form filled his vision. Ryan screamed involuntarily.

Ewan surged right through them and for a moment Ryan

felt like he was lost in a storm cloud. And then Ewan was blocking their path, a wall as wide as the exit. He folded his arms across his immense chest, a feat that served to emphasize both how enormous the chest was, and how gigantic the arms were to be able to fold across it. Margie pulled the cart to a stop, careful not to let the Box spill off of it again.

"Don't make me hurt you," Ewan growled.

"Just give it to him!" Ryan shouted. He tried uselessly to pull Margie back the other way. He just wanted out of here, away from this monster.

Margie glanced at Ryan. There was no fear in her face at all. "Why?" she said.

She shoved the cart ahead, straight through Ewan. Like he wasn't even there. Which, in the physical sense, of course he wasn't.

Ryan berated himself for being so stupid. What could Ewan possibly do to stop them?

"Sorry," Ryan said, and dove through the storm cloud that was Ewan to stay on Margie's heels.

But they had to stop again immediately, just outside the door to the casket lift.

Because the other twin, Ethan, was there, blocking the door. His arms were folded just like his brothers. And Ethan could most definitely do things to stop them. Bad things.

Margie stared at the big man, breathing fast but still showing no fear or panic. Ryan hovered behind her, not at all sure what to do.

"Ethan…" Margie said, as though scolding a child.

Ethan squinted at Margie, recognizing her for the first time. He unfolded his arms. "Dr. Sandlin?" He sounded surprised.

"Yes, Ethan, it's me."

"Ewan, it's Dr. Sandlin," Ethan said. And to Ryan's considerable surprise, he actually seemed to be smiling.

"What are you doing here? We didn't see you come in."

Margie glanced at Ryan with a look that said "don't blow this". And Ryan understood. *They don't know she was fired.*

Margie softened her face, took on a friendly tone. "Could you help me get this upstairs?"

Ryan tensed. She was pushing her luck. *That's not going to work. They're not that stupid.*

Ethan shrugged and stepped forward. He picked up the whole cart, Box and all, and hugged it to himself like a toy. He motioned back down the hall with his head.

"Come on," he said. "The lift sucks. Take the stairs."

He carried the cart and the Box up the stairs, chatting jovially with Margie the whole time, and all the way out the front door onto the sidewalk. It took all of Margie's persuasive powers to convince him to leave it there, and not carry it home for them.

TWENTY-FIVE

Myrtle Beach was on fire. The hotel, already half melted into the sand, spewed acrid smoke in a twisting black coil.

Margie blew on it to put it out. Ryan was relieved that she got to it before the smoke detector went off again. The landlord, Gabriel, had looked galled enough on his last time up the stairs that he might evict Ryan if it happened just one more time.

"Let's try again," she said. She balanced the still-sizzling snow globe on one of the paddles and held the other paddle out towards Ryan.

Ryan sighed. He was already resigned to the fact, which Margie refused to acknowledge, that the Box was broken. Nevertheless, he stepped forward and let her position the paddle in front of his chest.

She started the Box charging again. Rather than the steadily climbing drone he had heard it make before, it made an unsteady, warbling chord like a punctured accordion. Most of the readouts on it stayed dark, but the one that managed to light up said only "8888.86". He wondered about the 6.

Margie waited while the sick tone rose to a crescendo. There was no notification to let her know the Box had reached its peak, so she seemed to be guessing. "Ready? 3… 2… 1…" She squeezed the pedal, and the Box shuddered and let out a searing hiss. Both paddles blasted blue sparks and she yelped and threw them down, nursing her hands.

Myrtle Beach caught fire again. Any survivors still in the hotel would now certainly be dead. Margie blew it out and looked at Ryan questioningly.

Ryan walked across the room, putting as much distance

between himself and the snow globe as possible. It was only three or four steps before he started to feel the gentle tug, and by the time he reached the far end of the living room he desperately wanted to turn around.

He hurried back, shaking his head. "It's worse than before," he said. "It didn't pull nearly that hard back in the dump."

Margie made an exasperated noise and kicked the Box.

"It's broken," Ryan said.

"It's not broken. It's damaged."

The distinction was not clear to Ryan. "Can we get another one from somewhere?" he suggested.

She snorted in reply and twisted at the back of the Box with a screwdriver.

"Are you sure that's safe?" Ryan asked.

She smoothly lifted the top off the Box and set it aside. He watched as she deftly sorted through the components inside, tapping each one with the screwdriver as though taking inventory. She popped open a snap hinge, pulled a blackened circuit board out, studied it, and slotted it back in.

"Wow," Ryan said, impressed. "You've done this before."

"I should hope so. I built it."

Ryan blinked in surprise. And then he was surprised at how surprised he was. He had always assumed that she was some kind of junior medical assistant with a weekend's cursory training in how to remove ghosts from people with dangerous high voltage equipment. It didn't seem like something people got a university education in, or made a career out of. Not once had he considered asking her "so, how'd you get into ghosts?" And the Box, he had thought, was probably slapped together by Roger in his basement while listening to evil pipe organ music.

She glanced up at him and must have read the surprise on his face. "I didn't build all of it. It's about fifty percent defibrillator. The paddles are from a barbecue set. The case was two different toaster ovens." She yanked on the wires that attached the paddles to the main Box until they snapped free. It made Ryan wince. He couldn't help feeling like she was breaking it more when she should be fixing it.

"So, removing people's ghosts... that was your idea?"

"You're assuming that's what it was made for."

"It wasn't?"

She sighed and pressed her hand against the side of the Box as though petting a horse. "This was my PhD." She lowered her voice, and her eyes. "Supposed to be."

"PhD in what?"

"Neurophysics."

"Brains?"

"It's a branch of neuroscience incorporating the methods of experimental physics."

Ryan blinked. "So... brains?"

"Yes, brains."

"What do brains have to do with ghosts?"

She looked at him in a way that made him think he had asked a stupid question. "That's a stupid question," she said. He was quietly pleased that he had learned to accurately read her expressions. "The brain and nervous system control your body. It's your body's central processing unit. So when your ghost is in your body, giving it instructions, what must it communicate with?"

"The brain?"

"Correct. And when your ghost is out of your body, as it is now, it actually takes over some of the functions typically associated with the physical brain. Memories, for example. The ghost and the brain are intertwined in ways we haven't even begun to untangle." She hammered hard at something inside the Box with a rubber mallet. The sides of the Box rattled and shifted like the whole thing was going to fly apart.

Ryan raised his voice to be heard above the pounding. "So

you did your PhD in ghosts and brains?"

"Do you seriously think I could get any reputable institution before the Blackout to back a study like that? That would be parapsychology, where crackpots lived." She tossed the mallet aside and, to Ryan's astonishment, started wrenching at the Box with a crowbar instead. She seemed to think she was repairing an M-1 battle tank rather than a sensitive piece of medical equipment. "My study had to do with epilepsy and the angular gyrus. The Box was designed for probing unexplored parts of the brain with electrical stimuli in ways never thought of before."

"I bet it makes great tuna melts too." She didn't smile, so he explained feebly. "Toaster oven. Never mind."

There was the smile. She hid it by looking deep into the Box again, aiming her cellphone light around its corners. "But while I was tweaking the box, experimenting with different charges and targets, one of my test subjects reported an experience of having left their body. That wasn't totally unexpected."

"Roger told me about this. Out-of-body experience."

"Correct. It happens when you stimulate the brain in certain ways. We always assumed it was a malfunction in sensory processing caused by the electrical stimulation. But the thing is, at the moment she said she felt like she was out of her body... she *was*."

"How do you know?"

"I could see her."

"Before the Blackout?"

"Yes. There must have been some localized charge in the air, I don't know. But she was there. She looked at me." She threw the crowbar away and it clanged loudly and shook the walls. Ryan expected to hear Gabriel coming up the stairs again any moment. "Obviously I couldn't report that I had observed a ghost. Again, I had no desire to cross into the land of the crackpots. But I definitely saw it. This Box had done something I never intended it to do. I wanted to test it further. But nobody could know." Margie slammed the case back onto the Box and slammed it home with the heel of her hand. And then with the heel of her foot, which seemed to work better.

"I guess you figured it out."

"Not exactly. For three weeks, a month maybe, I was obsessed. I tried everything. Different voltages, different transmission methods, different subjects. When I didn't have test subjects I could fool into thinking I was trying to help them, I spent hours just firing electrical pulses into the air, hoping ghosts would just be there. Nothing worked. And then..."

"And then?"

She sat down and set her tools aside. The Box didn't look fixed, but she seemed to be done with it. She looked at her hands. "The Blackout happened."

Ryan couldn't figure out why that was bad. But the shift in her voice made it seem like it was. "And... that was good, right? It proved you right."

She ignored the question. From the way she kept her eyes down, he could tell he was way off somehow. And it was the first time he had seen her slouch even a little. "I found out there were eleven ghosts haunting the lab. Pretty typical. It was a big, old building. I was thrilled at first. I talked to them. They told me..." She closed her eyes. "They told me, all that time I had been doing tests, blindly throwing pulses into the air from this..." She jabbed the Box with her elbow. "I had been... hurting them."

Ryan sat down. *Oh. That's why it was bad.* "Hurting...?"

"I didn't know they were there, but they were. And my tests were tearing them apart, attaching them to objects in the lab, or to each other. Totally against their will. And I think..." She took off her glasses and rubbed her eyes. "They told me before I started there were twelve, not eleven. One of

my experiments... one of the ghosts was just gone. I think...
I think I..."

She still wasn't looking at him. He didn't know what to
say. So he tried: "You didn't know."

"No. I didn't know." She sniffed once and got her clinical
face back. She grabbed a screwdriver and tightened the bolts
on the back edges of the Box. She was stunningly fast at it.
"Anyway, I shut down the study. I was too scared what it
might do to the ghosts. And of course they made me pay
back all the financial aid I'd received up to that point. I'm still
paying it back."

"Which is why you live in apartments you steal from dead
people."

She lowered her eyes. "You're not dead. And I didn't steal
it." She shoved the Box into the middle of the table. "Let's
try this again."

Another question nagged at Ryan. "So when does Roger
come in?"

She plugged the paddles into the Box and the Box into
the wall. "A couple of years after my project folded. He had
heard about my study from some of my former backers, and
offered to buy everything. He was converting his funeral
business into some kind of 'post-mortal services' thing, all
built around helping ghosts. He thought the Box could be
adapted to give ghosts what they needed. And he would hire
me to operate it." She flipped the master power switch on the
Box. The warbling tone as it charged sounded even worse
than before, thanks to the addition of a high-pitched buzz.
"He made the idea sound good. Roger has a way of doing
that. And I was broke, and still had a lot of equipment I
hadn't taken a sledgehammer to. So I said yes, as long as he
agreed to my ethical standards. We would be messing with
people's lives, and people's afterlives. That's a whole lot of
ethics to violate. But as long as everything was on the up and
up, I was on board."

"And now what do you think?"

"I've had inklings for a while. I know he's done some involuntary un-hauntings. Detaching ghosts from their haunts without their consent, just to make living homeowners happy. They probably paid him a mint for it. He denies it, of course. And I can't prove it. So I've stayed on, waiting for the proof. But now... now your body is missing. I don't know what he's doing with it, but he's doing something. This is a whole different level. This is not what I signed up for."

"So what are you going to do?"

She tapped the paddles together and they angrily spat sparks. "What I'd most like to do is burn the place down, which is impractical because of the fire retardant materials used in the last renovation—I checked. So instead, I'm going to figure out what unethical, illegal, immoral, unimaginable B.S. that man is up to, and make sure he hangs for it. Ooh," she said, closing her eyes. "It felt good imagining that. Adrenaline surge. I can feel my ventral pallidum activating. Subliminal reward system."

Ryan didn't know what that was, but he worried that it might be personal so he didn't ask.

She shook it off and turned her attention back to the Box. "Come close again," she said, positioning one of the paddles once again next to the snow globe and the other in front of Ryan.

She lowered her foot gently onto the pedal, clamping her eyes shut. Ryan assumed she must know something he didn't, so he shut his eyes as well.

The pedal clicked.

There was a soft *pop*.

Ryan didn't feel anything at all. He opened one eye.

Dense white clouds billowed out of a seam on the back of the Box.

Margie dropped the paddles. "It's broken," she said.

Ryan's heart dropped. "So... this piece of crap is still tearing me apart? That's it? There's nothing we can do?"

The smoke detector went off, a shrill wail.

TWENTY-SIX

Margie was into her second episode of a house-hunting reality show. It seemed to have been made before the Blackout because none of the houses were noticeably haunted. Behind her, Ryan paced. The pacing turned eventually into circling. And the circling turned for some reason into hopping. The hopping didn't help as much, but he didn't want to go back to pacing. At least he could time the hopping to synchronize with the dull rhythmic thumps from the water heater downstairs. It gave him something to concentrate on.

For a few minutes he tried to imagine not existing. It wasn't something people had had to worry about for some time, since the Blackout pretty much confirmed that it didn't happen. Death had all but dropped off the list of the "great unknowns". And uninterrupted existence, even after death, became more or less a guarantee. It was reassuring. Now Ryan was staring into the face of not existing anymore. And the thought that there might not be a day after this one made him feel helpless. And made him wonder why all he was doing with his last night was pacing and circling and hopping.

But he paced. And he circled. And, to mix it up, he hopped.

"Your anxiety is understandable," Margie said from the couch. "But there's nothing we can do right now. We'll go back to the Clinic first thing in the morning and beat an answer out of Roger. But if you're going to stay here tonight, you can't keep moving around like that. It's distracting." She was eating something from a bowl in front of the TV. Even while watching TV and eating, she sat like a librarian waiting for a bus. Straight-backed, no hint of a slouch, legs directly out in front of her and folded in a perfect ninety-degree angle over the edge of the couch.

"This is my apartment!" Ryan retorted.

"Still." She took another spoonful and chewed distractedly.

Ryan could not shake the feeling that he should be doing something. He had mere hours of existence left. The Box didn't work. They had no idea where his body was. The detective he had hired seemed not to understand anything of what was happening. And why was the yuppie couple even considering that bungalow when it was out of their price range and clearly they would have to put on an addition? "They won't take number two," he said, stepping closer to the couch.

"Yes they will," Margie said, chewing.

"They can't. It's too small."

"They'll take it."

Several minutes later, to Ryan's great surprise, they did. He looked at Margie with newfound respect, but she just went on chewing. A dribble of milk escaped the corner of her bowl and she pushed it back in with one finger before it could fall onto the couch.

"They're fools," she said through a mouthful. "They're going to have to add on an entire half a house or the space will be well short of their minimum. But I've watched twenty-six episodes and house number two was chosen in twenty-two of them. So they're victims of the producers."

Ryan sat on the end of the couch farthest from her. "There's probably fifteen ghosts in that house and they have no idea."

"Won't they be surprised in a couple of years when the Blackout happens?"

Ryan glanced at her bowl, the contents of which were more colorful than he had expected. "What's that?"

"Cereal."

Ryan leaned in closer, almost involuntarily. He had to know. "What kind?"

She pulled the bowl away from him. "Just cereal."

"What kind?"

She sighed. "Sugar Frootz. Don't laugh."

Sugar Frootz, Ryan knew very well, was a cereal that emerged in the mid 80's, attached to a short-lived Saturday morning cartoon called "Breakfast Team 9". The cartoon had died, but the cereal lived on. Perhaps because of its name, which cagily combined what kids want in a cereal with what their parents could be conned into believing it contained. But for Ryan, it was that rarest of beasts: a sugar-coated cereal that he didn't like.

He couldn't contain his disappointment. "Oh."

"So?"

"Nothing."

"You think it's weird for a grown woman to eat Sugar Frootz?"

"No. It's just... nothing."

"Then you think it's weird to eat Sugar Frootz at night?"

"No. I could just never get into Sugar Frootz, that's all."

"Well when did you have it last?"

"I don't know. Maybe when I was nine."

She looked as if he had just said that he'd always wanted to visit Earth but didn't know where to find it. Her voice accelerated to the point where he could barely distinguish one word from the next. She reached out to grab his arm urgently, forgetting that she couldn't. "Are you kidding? Were they puffs?"

He kind of wished his arm was there for her to grab. "Yeah, little fruit-shaped—"

"You haven't had Sugar Frootz at all. In 2007 they went back to their original shape, which was little solid diamonds. They were modified to fruit puffs in 1991 and then in 2007 they changed back. What you had was not Sugar Frootz. *These* are Sugar Frootz. And even now you're missing out because they don't have blue or green anymore because of the manufacturer's inability to find a suitable natural alternative to the artificial coloring used in the blue and green variations. The artificial color had a unique flavor that is sorely lacking from the current blend, but still compared to 1997 Sugar Frootz it's absolutely night and day. Try them." She held out the bowl towards him.

Ryan stared at her, stupefied. It took his mind a few seconds to navigate its way carefully through her maze of words. "I would," he finally said. "I just..." He waved at his transparent form, just in case she had forgotten.

Apparently she had. Again. "Oh right. Sorry." She gave him a little accusing look and sat back.

What was that look about? "What?" he asked.

She scooped another spoonful. He got the feeling every spoonful she made had exactly the same number of cereal nuggets in it.

"I know what you're thinking," Ryan said.

"No you don't."

"You're thinking I brought this on myself."

"No I'm not. But you did."

"Come on, can you honestly tell me that, working there, you never once thought about having the procedure done yourself?"

"Never once."

Ryan didn't actually doubt her, but he pressed on anyway. He felt like he wanted to show her that he had faith in his own decision-making. Even though he didn't. "Why wouldn't you?"

"Because I like being material."

"You could like being immaterial more."

"Which one of us is eating Sugar Frootz?" She scooped the last spoonful and crunched it without looking at him, though he knew she could feel him looking at her.

The show was drawing to a close, with the yuppie couple freshly bungalowed and evidently pleased with their choice, though they were indeed already planning to put on an addition. Margie threw back the rest of the milk from her bowl. "Well," she said, "I'm off."

"There's two more," Ryan said quickly, before she could stand up all the way.

"Two more what?"

"They show four episodes in a row." He knew this from commercials but had never considered sitting and watching even one episode, much less four. But tonight, real estate held new appeal. It kept him from thinking what might happen tomorrow. And he was surprised to find how much more interesting it was with Margie there.

She hovered, not quite standing. Considering. "Would you laugh at me if I ate another bowl?"

"I would laugh at you if you ate less than two more."

"No promises."

She ate two more bowls and they watched two more episodes, and in both the couples chose house number two. And then they watched the first episode of the show about decorating that came on after.

During the course of the evening they agreed that Mr. T cereal had been just Cap'n Crunch in a T shape, but fundamentally disagreed on the merits of the various marshmallow-centric breakfast alternatives. Lucky Charms was the key point of contention.

When she finally went off to the bedroom to sleep, he realized that he had completely forgotten that he might not exist anymore in a day or two. And that he wished she wouldn't leave, but he didn't know why.

He also kind of wanted to try Sugar Frootz now. Kind of *really* wanted.

TWENTY-SEVEN

They were supposed to meet Lowell at 10:00, but reached Lowell's office on Mt. Auburn St. more than an hour early. Ryan woke Margie up with shouts shortly after 7 and finally persuaded her to move at nearly 8. By the time the taxi dropped them outside the office it was just before 9, and Ryan already felt like they were late.

Both of them were a little stunned at the building Lowell had somehow managed to get an office in. Based on what he knew of Lowell, Ryan had expected the place to be a water-stained rodent motel above a laundromat or palm reader. Instead, the address was just off Harvard Square, a modern seven-story brick-and-glass affair so squared-off and shiny it might have been made of Lego. The kind of place you'd expect to find a successful lawyer, not a detective—or whatever Lowell was—who seemed to own only one shirt and probably even fewer pairs of underwear.

But there his name was on the directory in the building's emphatically waxed marble lobby. "Mahaffey, Lowell". And beneath it, "I find ghosts!" Some of the other residents of the building seemed to have taken the cue from him and added enthusiastic descriptions of their own, like "Web design professionals!" and "We can help!" The accountants who had written "We do accounting" were the least imaginative, and the only ones who didn't seem to think their service was worthy of an exclamation point.

A couple of dozen badly wounded 17th-century spirits milled in the lobby, perhaps an entire settlement that had died somehow together in some colonial mishap. But when Ryan and Margie found their way off the elevator and into the richly appointed sixth floor corridor where Lowell's office was, there were only a couple of stray ghosts in the hall. Almost all of them hurried away when they saw living people approaching. Only one stayed put, and he happened to be standing right next to Lowell's door. But he stood with his face pressed so close to the wall, the tip of his nose might have been embedded in it.

Ryan felt a little awkward not saying anything to the ghost, but thought he'd feel even more awkward talking to his back. So he said nothing and just waved for Margie to knock.

She didn't have the same reservations Ryan did. "Sir, are you okay?" she asked the ghost's back.

"Fine, thanks!" the ghost said cheerily. He didn't turn around to look at them, and his face didn't pull away from the wall at all.

Ryan motioned to the door again. Margie finally relented and knocked twice, softly. After a silent pause she knocked again, louder. She tried the handle, but it was staunchly locked.

"He's not back," Ryan said. His voice was pinched with anxiety and he knew it.

"The Clinic just opened. He's probably just meeting with Roger now, so of course he's not back. So we wait," Margie said. She turned to the ghost next to the door again. "Are you sure you're okay?"

"Good, thanks! How are you?"

"You do know you're looking at the wall, right?"

"Sure do!"

Margie shrugged and looked for somewhere to sit, eventually deciding to just sit on the floor with her back against the wall and her legs straight out in front of her.

Ryan paced, and Margie watched him.

"That's interesting," she said.

"What?! What's interesting?!"

"I can't make out individual hairs on your head anymore,

and yet the logo on your T- shirt is still sharp and legible, and the grease stain under that rip is still the exact same shape it's always been."

"It's not grease," he mumbled. It was butter. He wasn't sure if that counted as grease.

The shirt, he now decided, was the exact center of a universe designed specifically to make him unhappy. Everything else in existence could boil away to nothingness and the shirt would still be there, floating in a butter-stained firmament.

"Not that one. That one," she said, pointing.

"Oh. Yeah. That one's grease." He folded his arms self-consciously over it.

"Turn around," she said. "I want to see if I can still read where it says 'Do whatever floats your boat'."

He refused to turn around, and stopped pacing so his back would never be to her. If his shirt still had a slogan on the back, he had no desire to show it off. Plus he was pretty sure there was more butter back there. She didn't push the issue, but she kept looking over at him sideways.

After a lot of pacing, 10:00 came and went with no sign of Lowell. Time was gnawing at Ryan and by now his hands had steamed away down to the wrists and his feet were little more than heels. "I can't take this," he said.

"You're surprised?" Margie asked. "Do I need to remind you, you found this guy in a dump."

"Technically, he found *me* in a dump." Ryan couldn't stand still. He approached the ghost standing with his face against the wall. "Excuse me?"

"Hey," the ghost said into the wall. He didn't move or even try to turn his head. "Nice day. I'm just guessing about that. I haven't looked."

"Do you know Lowell Mahaffey, the guy in this office?"

"Yeah I know him. He goes by me every day. Nice guy. Always says hi."

"Have you seen him today?"

"I never see him. I'm looking at the wall."

"I mean, has he gone past you today?"

"Not today. He went in last night pretty late."

"And when did he leave this morning?"

"He didn't. Far as I know."

Ryan thanked the ghost and called back to Margie. "Wait here. I've got a detective to fire." Then he pushed himself through the door, which he sensed was fairly indifferent about the whole "being a door" thing.

Beyond was an impressive space with a reception area, a small kitchen, and a spacious office. It had all the most expensive warm wood finishes that the highest-end offices install to approximate classic luxury. And the floor-to-ceiling windows provided an expansive view over building tops south to the Charles and Harvard Stadium beyond.

It was also, for the most part, empty. There was a leather office chair, and a plastic folding chair facing it across a modern black desk. Ryan thought he could see scuffed outlines and variations in the color of the hardwood floor where other pieces of furniture had once been, but they were not there now. Indeed there was no other furniture at all except in one corner, where sat what appeared disconcertingly to be an exam chair from a dentist's office.

Lowell was sleeping in it, snoring loudly.

Rage surged through Ryan, so intense that he thought he could see a reddish glow coming off him reflected in the floor wax. He badly wanted to stomp across and shove Lowell violently off the chair. But his stomping attempt produced nothing but silence and the shove just wasn't going to happen at all. So he yelled, which wasn't nearly as satisfying. "Lowell!" Though probably the loudest a ghost could possibly manage, the yell produced no response at all from Lowell.

Lowell was lying on his back at roughly a 45-degree angle, his head back on the headrest and his mouth lolling wide open, permitting some truly astonishing snores to thunder out. Ryan wondered if perhaps it was impossible to lie on such a chair with your mouth closed. Were they designed that way? Of course they would be.

Ryan yelled louder. "Lowell!" If he were haunting a place before the Blackout, a yell that loud would have curdled the blood of the living. Yet still, Lowell didn't move at all.

Ryan stepped up close to the chair and put his mouth right next to Lowell's ear. "Lowell! You're fired!"

"Hey, that's not fair," Lowell replied indignantly.

But the voice didn't come from the sleeping body in the chair. It came from behind Ryan, from the office door. Ryan jumped back from the chair and whirled around, stunned.

Lowell stood just inside the still-closed door.

Lowell also lay in the dentist chair, emitting snores that flirted with the Richter scale.

Door-Lowell was translucent, glowing, immaterial. Unquestionably Lowell, and definitely a ghost. While chair-Lowell was solid and very evidently alive.

Ryan's mind struggled to come up with an explanation that made any sense at all.

Lowell—ghost Lowell—grinned. "You can't fire me," he said. "I just found out what happened to your body."

TWENTY-EIGHT

Four years before the Blackout, Lowell Mahaffey wasn't a detective. He was a cab driver.

And he died because he didn't floss.

He brushed only irregularly, but it was the not-flossing that killed him.

It was the buildup of plaque and bacteria between his left mandibular second and third molars over a dozen years that caused a deep cavity and infection below the gumline. It was the infection that hurt. It was the pain that prompted him to make his first dental appointment in more than a decade. It was the dentist who insisted that he undergo routine surgery to clear the infection. And it was during the surgery that, due to an unpredictable interaction between a particular brand of local anesthetic and another particular brand of laxative, Lowell Mahaffey suddenly suffered cardiac arrest and unspectacularly died with a long tendril of stringy drool dangling from the corner of his mouth.

The drool stuck. The death didn't.

Because his dentist was a quick thinker. He had taken courses to learn the good way of hitting people in the chest. And he was able to drag Lowell back to life after 45 seconds of full-on, actual death.

But during those 45 seconds, Lowell rose out of his body and passed through the wall and saw the world teeming with the spirits of the dead. And it was incredible and terrifying to be one of them, and to realize with stark clarity that the mortal life is a blink, a grain of sand on a beach that never ends, a split second in an eternity.

Then the dentist hit his chest and he was yanked back into his body by some supernatural rubber band, and when he opened his eyes and breathed again all the ghosts were gone.

This, of course, was exactly the kind of shattering, revelatory experience that changes a person utterly and forever and makes them re-evaluate all their life's priorities.

It didn't, though.

Six weeks later he was back at the dentist having the exact same surgery on the right maxillary first molar. He flossed there somehow even less than anywhere else, even though he didn't floss anywhere else at all.

Most people who are nearly killed by their dentist tend afterwards to either avoid dentists altogether, or else look for a different dentist who doesn't almost kill people. Lowell did neither of those things. He positively scrambled back, hopeful that a bit of death might be involved. He even took the same laxative despite not needing it anymore, which had some predictable side effects well into the next day.

His dentist, though, was intensely focused on *not* killing him this time. For safety, he elected to use a different anesthetic. Lowell spent the entire surgery eagerly awaiting a death that never came. After a while he got bored and, lulled by the numbness in the side of his face and the white noise of the dentist's drill grinding into his tooth, nodded off.

It was just as good.

Once again he rose out of his body, and once again countless other ghosts were visible to him, milling in the streets. This time he started up a conversation with one, an 18th century gentleman who disapproved strongly of very nearly everything that had ever happened. Alive, Lowell would have walked away in seconds, annoyed. But talking to a ghost was so novel, he was enraptured.

For about 90 seconds.

Then the dentist, not taking any chances, pounded Lowell's chest again just in case he was dead. He wasn't, but it revived him anyway. He hurtled back into his body before he had finished opening his eyes.

He was disappointed to have been pulled back. But also thrilled with what he had learned.

Something, he decided, had changed when he died in that dentist chair. He had become untethered from the mortal world and could now, he assumed, cross back and forth at will.

"At will" turned out to be an overstatement. Because no matter how many times he tried at home, he couldn't make it happen again.

He tried everything. He tried it drunk and sober, asleep and awake, on his side and on his stomach and on his other side. Laxative-full and laxative-free. He tried it in daylight and midnight, hungry and full, hatless and wearing every hat he owned in a big pile so tight that it suffocated his scalp. He tried every single variation he could imagine, pouring every scant ounce of will he possessed into forcing his spirit to break free of his body. Nothing worked.

He finally came to an inescapable conclusion.

It was the chair. Had to be.

So he went back to the dentist.

The dentist was surprisingly unwilling to give him unnecessary surgery. Something about ethics. And he refused almost as strongly to let Lowell sleep there unsupervised.

Lowell could see two possible courses of action. Either he could stop brushing his teeth and continue not flossing while consuming unholy amounts of sugar until he needed surgery again, or he could steal the chair.

So he bought a hacksaw and rented a truck, and almost got caught but didn't. Afterward, he knew he would have to either find a new dentist, or stop going.

He stopped going. Easier.

He was completely correct about the chair being the key.

He had no explanation for it, nor did he ever seek one. The chair was comfortable to sleep in, but unsteady when propped against the wall. Twice it fell over in the middle of the night with him on it. But he kept at it, convinced that it was somehow the key to unlocking the secrets of the afterlife.

And then one night after consuming an entire bottle of red wine—partly out of desperation and partly out of just really liking red wine—he found himself once again drifting out of his body.

He was ready for it. He took his time and explored.

He was surprised, first, to find that his apartment had six ghosts residing permanently in it. He had never noticed signs of haunting, but there they were. And they seemed generally okay with him. They took his being a ghost in stride and struck up some light small talk.

Then he walked outside and spent a full hour wandering the streets among the drifting spirits. He was fascinated, and no longer drunk on the wine but rather on the untethered freedom of immateriality. He tried chatting with a few spirits, pretending to be just another ghost like them. Which he was, except that he could stop being one and they couldn't. He worried that this might make them envious or bitter, so he told none of them.

His newfound supernatural ability was a novelty for several weeks. He would leave his body and wander among the ghosts a few times a week.

After a while, though, it began to lose its appeal. Conversations with ghosts weren't really any more interesting than conversations with the living, of which he had more than enough with people in his cab. Even when they're transparent, boring people are still boring. And all ghosts ever talked about was how they had died.

He considered that it might be entertaining to tell some living people about his extra-corporeal excursions, but he worried that he'd be seen as a wacko. Before he learned to leave his body, that's certainly how he would have seen anybody claiming to have left their body.

He amused himself briefly by searching for his ancestors, seeing how far back in his family tree he could go. He hit a dead end only three generations back, and even those ones didn't seem impressed that he had descended from them. Some even seemed genuinely disappointed that their efforts at continuing their family line had led only to him. He had hoped to find his way back to ancestors from interesting times like the middle ages, but it didn't happen.

On top of all that, he felt like it was getting increasingly difficult to get back into his body. Like his ghost was getting used to the freedom of drifting around and didn't want to be caged up in a body anymore. Or perhaps like his body was getting annoyed with him: "In or out! Make up your mind!" Somewhere around two months after stealing the dentist chair, he entirely lost interest in leaving his body. For a while it only happened by accident.

And then he got lucky. When somebody got murdered.

He wasn't the murderer. Nor was he the victim. He wasn't even a witness. He had nothing whatsoever to do with the murder, apart from the fact that it happened in his building, three floors down from him. He woke up one evening to police lights flashing in his window, and went down to see what was going on. He got the story from a gathering of his neighbors already in the street, who had gotten it from one of the cops.

A man had been murdered on the second floor. Killed, they were told, by a meat thermometer jammed into his eye.

Every tenant in the building was interviewed by a detective. His name was Detective Blair, and he had a determined, hard-boiled air about him that positively insisted that he would be the one to solve this case. Lowell had no information to offer. He did inquire, though—out of pure curiosity—whether the police had used the reading on the meat thermometer to confirm that the guy was dead. He got only an annoyed grunt in reply. Detective Blair moved on, unburdened with evidence.

Lowell assumed that would be the end of it. Until two weeks later when he was interviewed again. Once again, Detective Blair came knocking, asking exactly the same questions he had asked before. All the gung-ho was gone. The case had lost its glamor and was dragging. Lowell had seen TV reports about it. The murderer was now called the "Turkey's Done Killer". Blair looked for all the world like he'd rather be off somewhere drinking than asking these questions again when he already knew the answers.

Blair showed up again two weeks later and brought the same desperate questions. "Is there anything, anything at all, no matter how small it seems?"

Lowell was annoyed at being interrupted a third time. And it was annoyance, more than altruism or interest, that led to his finally getting involved.

After Blair had moved on down the hall, Lowell dragged his dentist chair out of the closet and leaned it against the wall. He stabilized it with some milk crates, then popped a decongestant capsule and lay down. It had been weeks since he had made any out-of-body excursions, but he slipped easily back into it. Twenty minutes after lying down, he was drifting above his body and hoping the chair didn't dump him on the floor before he found what he was after.

He drifted into the hall and down three flights of stairs to the second floor. It was easy to spot which apartment the murder had taken place in because it still had police tape across the door. Apparently they intended to leave the place undisturbed until the case was solved.

He pushed through the tape and the door without any trouble, and drifted into an apartment nearly identical to his, except decorated. He marveled at what somebody who cared about their apartment could do with it, and vowed to spruce up his own place as soon as he had time. He was disappointed, though, that there was no chalk outline of a body on the floor. He wondered if the police actually did that.

He counted seven ghosts haunting the place, none of whom seemed perturbed in the slightest by his intrusion. Four of them were seniors from various decades, lounging and staring at each other. Two were in full football uniforms, which he was mildly curious about.

The other was clearly the victim. Clearly, because he had a meat thermometer protruding rather noticeably from his left eye. Really only the very end of it was actually protruding. The rest was decidedly not. He sat on the end of the couch looking sour, as probably anyone would be about having a meat thermometer in their eye.

Lowell drifted over to him and nodded a greeting, making no attempt to not stare. How could you not?

The murder victim, whom Lowell knew from news reports to be named Herbert Wendt, glanced up at Lowell with his right eye. The meat thermometer swiveled in his left eye socket as he shifted his gaze, like a giant cartoon eye on a stick. Lowell had to fight to keep from laughing. And to keep from checking what the temperature reading said.

Wendt didn't appear to want to talk, so Lowell kept it brief. "Who did it?" he asked, lifting his chin to gesture at the thermometer.

Ten minutes later, back in his body, Lowell pushed a piece of paper with a name and address on it through the window of Detective Blair's car. And the next day the Turkey's Done Killer was arrested, and Detective Blair received a citation and promotion. The public was disappointed to hear that the arrested man did not possess a psychopathic obsession with meat thermometers. The thermometer had just been convenient at the time he wanted to kill Mr. Wendt because of a wildly overheated argument concerning the Red Sox.

Buoyed by his success at solving that mystery, Lowell kicked himself for not realizing sooner what a unique business opportunity his special new talent offered. Surely if he played his cards right, got a private investigator's license, made some friends in the police department, and properly exploited his ability, he would be set for life. He could solve every cold case by simply asking the victim who did it, find serial killers by interviewing the people they had killed, assist the cops with every investigation either behind the scenes or in front of them. And he would make sure he was paid handsomely for it. His poor dental hygiene had granted him a gift, with which he could both change his own life, and help others in their time of need.

And then the Blackout came along, and suddenly everybody on Earth had that gift too.

Things went steadily downhill for Lowell after that.

TWENTY-NINE

"Please, come in," Roger Foster said, holding the door open and stepping aside to usher him in.

"Why thank you," Lowell said. "And thank you for seeing me at such short notice."

Try to look rich, he kept telling himself. *Look rich, sound rich. This is only going to work if he thinks you're rich.*

As he slid past, he made sure not to let Roger come into contact with his ghostly substance. If Roger even brushed through him he might pick up Lowell's emotions and sense the deception.

Roger closed the door and circled around the desk to face Lowell. "What can I do for you, Mr. Hammond?"

Hammond was the richest-sounding fake name Lowell could think of when he had arrived. He stole it from the rich guy who made dinosaurs out of mosquitoes in *Jurassic Park.*

In the hours leading up to the appointment, Lowell had gone over in his mind exactly how to have this conversation. He had rehearsed maybe ten different approaches. All of them felt fake. But rather than continuing to practice until he came up with one that he felt comfortable with, he did what he almost always did, which was to decide that he would wing it.

Now that he was here, the winging wasn't happening. Everything felt perfectly wrong. He wanted nothing more than to flee straight through the office wall.

"Yeah, yes," he started, "I needed to talk to you about a bit of a sensitive matter."

"I can assure you of complete confidentiality," Roger replied with a sympathetic smile.

This guy, Lowell thought, *is kind of awesome. I would buy a diamond-encrusted casket from this man.*

"I have heard," Lowell went on, "that your facility offers certain... services."

"We offer a number of services, yes. They are outlined in our pamphlet. Would you like me to read them to you?" Roger reached for a stack of pamphlets propped upright on the corner of his desk.

"That won't be necessary," Lowell said. He leaned forward conspiratorially. "I kind of think the service I'm talking about isn't in your pamphlet."

Roger's eyebrows descended so far they seemed about to absorb his eyes like bushy sponges. "All of our services are listed in the pamphlet."

"Yeah, no, I'm sure they are. Except for the ones that aren't. Am I right?"

"You are not," Roger said curtly. "In fact, it is specifically the function of the pamphlet to list all of our services. Were there any services not listed on it, the pamphlet would not be serving its purpose."

"Can I speak bluntly, Mr. Roger?"

"Foster. And yes, of course." Roger sat back in his chair, crossed his spindly legs and folded his hands in his lap. Lowell took note of the pose to use in his own office, because the casual I'm-approachable-but-don't-mess-with-me attitude it conveyed was astonishingly cool. He wished Roger taught a course in how to sit.

Lowell searched for a place to begin, and a way to begin there. "You've probably noticed by now that I'm a ghost."

"Mr. Hammond, I spend all day talking to people both living and not-quite-so-living. I scarcely notice the difference anymore."

Lowell was slightly annoyed that his point wasn't getting through. "Yeah. But I'm dead, is what I'm saying."

Roger smiled faintly. "But you appear none the worse for

wear."

"Still, dead. I'm dead. Are we clear on that part?"

Roger finally nodded. "I understand."

"Good. But the thing is, I find myself..." This was the part that Lowell had so completely failed to work out in advance. "...needing to *not* be that anymore."

Roger frowned. "To not be what anymore?"

"Dead."

Roger took in a long, slow breath that seemed to take a very long time to come out again. Lowell kept waiting for the exhale, but it stayed in for longer than he could stand. He found himself fearing a little for Roger's health. He was relieved when Roger finally let it out.

"I'm not sure I understand you," Roger finally said. But Lowell caught a hint of something in his tone, in the way he leaned forward across the desk. *He does understand. But he's testing to make sure we're talking about the same thing. He wants to be sure.*

Lowell leaned forward as well, so that their faces were barely a foot apart. They could whisper to each other. *This is how illicit deals are made,* Lowell thought. *I'm into it now.* "My body is gone, Mr. Foster. I died of disease. Heart, lungs, liver. It was a whole big disease thing, just awful. I won't go into the details, but there was a lot of pain. Sweating. Vomiting just absolutely everywhere. You don't need the gory details. Loss of bowel control. I'll spare you. Also pustules. Lots and lots of pustules. I won't even mention those."

"How awful for you," Roger said with silken sympathy. Lowell marveled at it.

"But I've heard that there might be a way to, shall we say, re-enter the land of the living, shall we say. In, shall we say, a different form. And that you're the man to, shall we say, 'talk to' about that."

Roger's face didn't change at all. He gazed at Lowell with

the kind of cool impassivity that Lowell had never been able to master. It took a long time for him to reply. "I'm sure I don't know what you mean, Mr. Hammond."

Lowell threw caution and subtlety to the wind. "I want a new body. Put me in a new body. That's what I want." There it was, all there for Roger to see. *If it works, it works.*

Lowell had come up with the idea in what he thought was a miraculous burst of deduction the night before. The seed was planted by his encounter with Rufus in the street. Rufus's body, anyway. But not Rufus. Somebody else in Rufus's body. It made sense. It answered a lot of questions.

Knowing full well that most of his theories eventually turned out to be wrong, he had tried subtly floating it to Margie, hoping for a hint that he might be onto something. And she had shot it down.

But he couldn't shake it. He had spent the night turning it over and over in his head, trying to convince himself that he was wrong. He was used to being wrong. Wrongness was a frustratingly comfortable state for him. And yet he strongly felt there was something to this idea.

Even if it was, according to Margie, totally impossible, he was going to run with it anyway. He had decided to trust his instincts, despite their consistent record of stabbing him in the back. If he was even close to right, he would be solving two cases at once. Which was two more than he was used to.

Roger's face remained inscrutable. He sat back in his desk chair. His eyes stayed locked on Lowell's, the slightest hint of a upturn at the corners of his mouth. "Mr. Hammond," he said finally. "I think you have been misinformed. Such a procedure is impossible."

Lowell had no idea if Roger was lying or not. None. He had never wished for intuition more than he wished for it now. He pressed on. "Yeah, but will you do it?"

"I sympathize with your predicament. I'm sure it's a difficult time for you. But ask literally any expert in this field and they will tell you. Ghost transplants, forced possessions, whatever term you wish to apply... they cannot be done. Full stop."

Lowell studied the tall man's face. *Is he onto me?* He couldn't get any kind of read on Roger at all.

"I do apologize," Roger said. "Is there anything else I can do to aid you through what must be a very trying period in your post-life?"

Lowell tried to look steely. "Money is no object, Mr. Foster."

He thought he saw a slight flutter in Roger's face. The corners of his mouth shifted downward ever so slightly.

"I own several genetics companies," Lowell pressed on. He hadn't planned on appropriating the character's job as well as the name, but there it was. "We work with mosquitoes."

Roger forced the corners of his mouth up again. Lowell could see him fighting it. "No amount of money can make the impossible possible," he said. His eyes unlocked from Lowell's and he fidgeted with a googly-eyed pet rock on the corner of his desk.

Lowell let the moment hang, hoping that Roger would crack further. But instead, after a silent pause, the Clinic Director lifted his eyes back to Lowell's again and returned his hands to their folded position in his lap.

"I'm sorry to hear that," Lowell said. *Is that it? Did I fail?* he wondered. He didn't want to just leave but he couldn't think of another approach to take.

He sat awkwardly, uncertain what to do. Roger didn't help him at all. He tilted his head in a way that somehow communicated how sorry he was to have caused Lowell so much inconvenience, and would Lowell like a complimentary mint?

Bail, Lowell thought. *Get out.* "Thank you for seeing me, Mr. Foster. I guess I should get back to my many businesses and theme parks." He stood and floated towards the door, struggling to find the right balance between looking casual and fleeing.

"Do we have you on file?" Roger said to his back.

Lowell paused and turned around. Roger hadn't stood. He remained folded behind his desk. "On file?" Lowell asked.

"Your information. So that we can inform you of changes to our services, specials, things of that nature."

Changes to our services? "I don't think so. Your receptionist didn't ask for any information. You know she doesn't have a head?"

Roger stood and clasped his hands neatly in front of him as though standing in a royal receiving line. "Well perhaps you could provide your information at your earliest convenience. You never know what might come up."

Lowell had to restrain himself from winking to let Roger know he was getting it. "Of course."

"Be sure to include your daytime business number, mailing address. Oh, and perhaps your Energy Signature. Your SES."

"Perhaps?"

"Perhaps definitely that, yes." Roger allowed his smile to broaden slightly. "For our records."

Lowell didn't know what Roger asking for his Energy Signature meant, but he knew it meant something. And he was almost certain Roger had just confirmed—without admitting it—that he was putting ghosts in new bodies. *I was right. This never happens! I was right!* Lowell couldn't wait to tell his client, Ryan, about it, probably in the form of a sizable bill. "I'll send it over right away," he managed to choke out past his own excitement.

"Excellent," Roger said. "Do have a nice day. I hope your pustules and bowel issues are not too troublesome."

Lowell drifted out of Roger's office. Then sprinted

through the corridor wall and finally out into morning traffic where he ran towards his office faster than he ever could have in his body.

THIRTY

"Did you guys bring any coffee?" Lowell asked blearily. "My ghost has been up for hours but my body's not what you call a morning person." He struggled clumsily to get his blinds closed and block the morning sun from streaming in.

Ryan was still stunned at how Lowell could get into and out of his body almost at will like that. Stunned, and jealous. He wished that all it took to get back to his own body was somebody slapping it in the face and waking it up, as Lowell had just asked Margie to do. It had taken three slaps, but his ghost had cannonballed back into his body like a circus acrobat into a net.

Lowell finally gave up on the blinds and flopped into his desk chair, sprawled. "Could you go get some coffee? I can expense it to my client."

"*I'm* your client," Ryan said.

"Oh right. That makes it easier. Just pay for the coffee."

Ryan sat in the folding chair across from Lowell and pulled his right foot up onto his left knee to keep an eye on it. He was worried about his feet, strongly suspecting that his toes had started to disappear the same as his hands. "What did you say about your Energy Signature?"

"Oh yeah. Roger—super cool guy, by the way. Have you met him? Evil, obviously, but so slick—anyway, get this, because this is the big deal. Roger said..." Lowell grinned wickedly, relishing the big reveal he was about to make. "... for me to send him my SES so they could keep it on file."

Ryan planted that in his mind and waited for it to bloom into something relevant to his body's disappearance. It didn't. Not a bud. "So what?"

"Don't you see what that means?"

"It doesn't mean anything."

Lowell looked crushed. "Really? I was hoping it did. Like a clue. Also, where are we on the coffee thing?"

Ryan leapt up, fiercely annoyed. "That's it? That's all you got?" He had waited all night for Lowell to produce results. Now he felt his one last faint hope leaving his grip. It made him dizzy with dread, and he had to sit down again.

Margie stepped around the dentist chair, which she had been examining with scientific interest. She looked intrigued. "That might actually mean something."

Lowell brightened and pointed at her enthusiastically. "See? She knows things! Ask her!"

Margie leaned against the dentist chair, then quickly gave up on that when it threatened to tip under her weight. "He didn't actually say he could put you in a different body?"

"Not out loud. But when he asked for my SES, it was like he was saying it without saying it, you know? I had like an intuition. I'm a detective."

Margie frowned. "Why would he need your SES? What's it going to tell him?" She pulled out her phone, turned her back to them and started swiping through something they couldn't see.

Lowell mouthed "coffee" to Ryan and mimed pouring with his hands. But Ryan was focused on Margie's back. She swiped over and over on her phone. It made a little musical chirp with every swipe.

A faint memory of the previous night crept into his mind, when he had sat and watched terrible TV with her. Hours of it. Stuff he would never have watched on his own. Why did he do that? It had seemed to make perfect sense in the moment but now that he looked back on it, he couldn't recall why he didn't find something better to do with his time, especially when there was so much at stake. He even had a vague recollection of not wanting her to leave, of wanting to watch even more terrible TV with her. It seemed plainly absurd in retrospect. He tried to recreate how he'd felt about her presence the previous night, but it wouldn't form up properly in his mind. It was full of interference and static, like an AM radio station he couldn't quite tune.

And then it was gone. Vanished. All that remained was him wishing that whatever Margie was going to think of, she'd hurry up and think of it.

"Okay," she said, still swiping through her phone. It was a tortuously long time before she said anything else. By the time she did, Ryan was sure the tips of both of his shoes had vanished. And then all she said in follow-up was: "Okay."

Finally she hurried over to them with her phone and held it up for them to see. "Look at this."

On the display was a complex grid of black and gray squares, like several highly detailed QR codes piled on top of each other in layers, forming a three-dimensional cube. "This is Ryan's SES. We scanned it when he came in for his procedure."

"Looks like a pirate," Lowell said.

Margie blinked at him. "It's a machine-readable matrix of binary modules representing unique patterns in an individual's spiritual energy."

"I know. With an eye patch and a beard." Lowell pointed at various spots on the image. "There's even a parrot on his shoulder."

Ryan had been thinking that it looked like a half-eaten chocolate chip muffin, but he decided against getting into a Rorschach debate.

Margie rolled her eyes. "Fine. The point is, everybody's is unique, right?" She flipped through a few more SES images, each completely different. One Ryan thought looked like a bird, one like a car, and one Abraham Lincoln in a baseball cap. "If you've been to the bank you know this."

"Of course. I go to the bank all the time," Lowell said, in a way that strongly suggested he didn't.

"The point is," Margie went on, "it's unique to you. I read about some studies done that suggest the pattern in your SES is tied to your DNA in some way. Which would make sense. Your ghost and your body are linked. It's why you can't put your ghost in somebody else's body. They don't match."

Ryan stared at his SES pattern on her phone. He found it amazing that this was everything that constituted *him*, codified and represented graphically on a screen that probably also played "Angry Birds".

"Except," Lowell said, "Roger *is* putting ghosts in other people's bodies."

"We don't know that," Margie said. "But what if he's *trying*? Roger is a funeral director, not a scientist. Maybe he thinks a ghost transplant is possible if he just has the right ghost and the right body. Maybe he thinks if they're close enough to a match, the body won't reject the ghost. So… say a client comes in looking for a new body. Roger doesn't just choose a body at random. He chooses one that's a close match for the client. Better chance of success, correct? So I searched the Clinic client database for an SES similar to Ryan's. That will be who Roger gave Ryan's body to!"

Ryan leaned forward, seeing where her wildly circuitous train of thought was going. "And?"

"No matches. Nothing closer than 20%."

Ryan sat back again. "So we're back to square one. I'm dead."

"Dead*er*," Lowell said. "You were already kind of dead."

"Not quite," Margie said. She swiped to a new SES on her phone and held it out towards them.

Lowell squinted at it. "Pirate again. It's Ryan."

"Wrong," Margie said. "It's somebody else's. By my analysis, it's a 97% match for Ryan's."

Ryan was puzzled. "You said there were no clients that matched."

"That's right. This is not a client." She pointed at the text under the SES image. "It's an investor. Specifically, the Clinic's biggest investor, Clifton Caldwell. The Clinic wouldn't exist without him. Well, without his money."

"Clifton Caldwell." Ryan stood up. He wasn't yet sure if he could be excited about this, but he wanted to be. "So, this is the guy who has my body?"

Margie shrugged. "If my guess is right... no, wait, technically, I just made about five or six guesses. If they're *all* right, it could be that Roger put this man's ghost in your body. Caldwell is wealthy. And Roger has never been above pushing the ethical envelope when there's a payout in it."

Lowell leaned forward across his desk. "You said ghost transplants don't work. If Roger gave this guy the body, how long before it'd go belly-up?"

"I don't know that. If the body didn't reject the ghost immediately, it could be days or weeks. I just don't know. There hasn't been extensive experimentation in this kind of thing."

Ryan leapt out of his chair. "So there's a chance it's still alive?"

"There's a chance."

"So I can be excited about this now?"

"I think so. But Ryan... think about it. If Caldwell has your body, he paid Roger a fortune for it. He's not going to give it up without a fight."

THIRTY-ONE

Clifton Caldwell's house was a big Colonial in Chestnut Hill with an expansive front lawn dotted with sprinkler heads. The property was surrounded by a waist-high stone wall that was an implied barrier rather than an actual one, although there was a cast-iron arch at the foot of the long driveway with a closed gate. From what they had read in an online article, Caldwell's money had come chiefly from his national chain of hardware stores. None of the three of them could say they had ever heard of these stores, much less visited one. But then, none of them were big on home maintenance. Apparently Caldwell had enough stores, selling enough hammers and caulking, to finance seven thousand square feet and a balcony where one could sit and think about teeing off at the very exclusive golf course across the street. They had also found the report of Caldwell's death a little over a year ago after a long and unspecified illness. Though by most accounts his death hadn't interfered with his success and he had continued to run his hardware business just as before.

"What do you think?" Lowell asked from the driver seat. They were parked some distance down the street where only the front of the house was visible through the old trees pressing in close over the road. A few ghosts meandered in the space between them and the house, but none showed any interest in them.

Margie had stayed behind to try again fixing the Box. Her reasoning being, even if Caldwell had the body, and even if he gave it up, they still needed to get Ryan back into it. And they couldn't do that without the Box. She had insisted that she could still fix it, although the tone of her voice suggested too much uncertainty for Ryan's liking.

"Hey," Lowell said with a hint of genuine concern, "you're not looking so good, man. Like, blurry."

Ryan's sense of disconnection was getting stronger by the hour. It had become all-consuming, like a fevered state that made him feel walled off from the world, in a bubble. He had to constantly fight it to concentrate on anything at all. So he didn't need Lowell telling him he looked blurry. He *felt* blurry. He *thought* blurry. His entire *existence* was blur.

He forced his awareness to center and watched the front of the house, wishing that by some coincidence Caldwell would happen to come out at that moment. Perhaps to walk his dog. Or, much better, to die and let Ryan take his body back. But if he came strolling casually out in Ryan's body, what could they do? Ryan weighed his various good options for a few minutes before deciding that he didn't have any.

"I'm going in," he said. "Follow me with the snow globe." He let himself gaze at it longingly for a moment. He dearly loved how chintzy and broken it was.

"What are you going to do?"

Ryan didn't answer. He forced himself through the car door and started down the street to the house. Parking so far down the road had seemed like a good idea at the time. Lowell's car stood out in this neighborhood and made them look like burglars scoping out target houses. The best they could hope for was that if Caldwell spotted them, he would assume they were there to rob some house other than his.

Every once in a while as they crept forward Ryan could catch a glimpse of the golf course through the trees on the other side of the street. There were a surprising number of ghosts on it. A few living golfers were gamely trying to carry on without letting the dead ones get in the way, but Ryan suspected it was a serious distraction. Some of the ghosts were going through the motions of playing the holes, though they couldn't hope to actually move a ball. Some of them had even been fortunate enough to die with clubs in their hands, providing their ghosts with immaterial versions of putters and drivers. Those few could at least do proper swings, even if there was no actual prospect of hitting anything. Ryan wondered how many of them had died right there, suffering hypertensive heart attacks from rage at some missed putt, and found themselves bound forever to the course. Eternity on the back nine.

He didn't bother heading for the gate at the end of Caldwell's driveway, just hopped the little wall and started straight across the lawn. He again considered what he would do if he went in and found Caldwell at home, walking around in Ryan's body. Bribery wasn't an option with a rich guy like this. That left threatening, except that he had nothing to threaten with. Or, as a last resort, begging. He decided that was probably what he was going to be stuck with.

Halfway across the lawn he stumbled and stopped. He was sensing something. The sensation was familiar, but sensed in an entirely unfamiliar way.

He felt, for the first time since leaving his body, hot. Like he had just stepped into bubble of thick, humid air.

He shook off the feeling and took another few steps.

He felt like he had stepped into a furnace. He yelped in pain and looked down at his body, expecting to find himself on fire. Instead all he could see was his particles swirling in miniature hurricanes, bubbles of energy forcing their way to the surface and popping there, creating craters in his form that other particles immediately poured into to make new bubbles.

His substance was boiling, and he didn't know why.

He took a step back, and felt the sensation cool a little. He could see the roiling of his substance slow down and all the various particles fall back into place. But a single step forward and he felt the heat surge back.

He weighed his options. Go back and give up, or make a

beeline for the front of the house and hope to get there before he boiled away into steam.

He was just about to take his first steps when he heard a cry from Lowell behind him. "Ryan! Stop!"

Ryan caught himself and stepped back, relieved to feel the boiling sensation cool off.

Lowell waved him back to the road. "You can't do that! Sorry, man, I didn't notice!" He pointed at the nearest lawn sprinkler, just a few feet in from the wall.

Only now, Ryan could see that it wasn't a lawn sprinkler at all. It was a cluster of miniature parabolic dishes aimed in all directions. All the other objects protruding from the lawn that he had thought were sprinklers were little dish arrays as well.

"It's a Ghost Wall," Lowell said, doubled over and out of breath from running. "Like an electric fence for ghosts. This guy likes his privacy." He scanned the array. There were maybe twelve of the little units, arranged in a grid covering the entire lawn. "Man, he got the full package. That's probably worth more than the house. And that is one serious garden gnome too."

The heat was surging up and down Ryan's form and making it even harder for him to stay focused. He felt himself swaying on his feet. "What happens if I keep going?"

"You can't. Don't try."

Ryan stared at the house, frustrated, trying to spot anyone moving inside the windows. The sunlight was too bright. All he could see was reflection, and hints of curtain and blind.

"Then *you* need to go in," Ryan said, hopping back over the wall onto the sidewalk. A pleasant cool washed through him and he sighed with relief.

"I'm not breaking in there," Lowell said. "You don't think a house like this has an alarm?"

"Ring the doorbell."

"And say what?"

Ryan kicked at the ground in frustration, and the lack of impact just made him more frustrated.

Lowell beckoned him to follow back to the car. "Come on, good old fashioned stakeout. I might even have donuts. Not so much for you, I guess. But you're not missing anything. They're a week old if I'm lucky."

Ryan shook his head emphatically and scanned the house and the yard. But even a quick scan of the Ghost Wall units made it clear that they had full coverage of the yard, front and back. There was no way for him to approach the house.

Ryan stopped. There was something he wanted to try.

He hopped the little wall again and started across the lawn, headed straight for one of the little energy projectors.

"What are you doing?" Lowell called after him. He looked nervously up and down the street. "When you creep like that, it looks really suspicious."

Now that Ryan was aware of it he could hear a soft buzz emanating from the little unit. *It must consume a lot of power*, he thought. He paid close attention to exactly when he could start to feel the burn from it. He stepped slowly, pausing to check for any sensation before stepping again.

There. He was about five feet from it, and the burn came on fast and sudden. He stepped back quickly to escape it. The unit had a definite range, and it wasn't long. And the next unit, closer to the house, was ten feet beyond.

"Ryan!" Lowell hissed at him from the other side of the wall.

"Shut up," Ryan demanded. He had to concentrate.

He assumed the little device projected its field in a circle around itself, and the circles from all the devices overlapped slightly to completely fill the yard. So there weren't any gaps between them to squeeze through. And presumably they projected upwards as well, probably the same five feet. If he could only pass over them higher than that...

Ryan looked up at the house. There. French doors on the

second floor balcony right over the front entrance.

"Ryan!" Lowell whispered again. He looked up and down the street like he was expecting a SWAT team any second. A passing ghost in Victorian garb frowned at him, and at Ryan. "It's okay," Lowell said to it casually. "We're just breaking in."

Ryan ignored the ghost. "You have the snow globe?" he asked, staring at the balcony.

Lowell patted the pocket of his raincoat. "Yeah. So?"

"I need you to throw it." He pointed at the balcony. "Up there. When I say."

Ryan hopped back out of the yard and strode past Lowell and across the street. He remembered that bungee cord elastic snap back at the dump, when the distance between him and his haunting was too great. The more distance he could put between him and the balcony right now, the better chance he had of being slingshotted all the way up there. He didn't want to fall short and wind up right in the middle of the Ghost Wall.

Lowell followed. "I see what you're doing. And it's stupid."

"Don't follow me," Ryan demanded. "Get close to the house so you don't miss."

"Even if I get you in there, how are you going to get out?"

That gave Ryan pause.

Lowell seemed to sense that he had made a good point, because he pressed it. "Even if everything goes perfectly and you get in there and this Caldwell guy is walking around in your body, what do you do? And that's assuming he's even home."

"I don't know," Ryan said. Because he really, truly didn't.

But what was the alternative? Wait all day for Caldwell to come out? Ryan felt like he had hours at best before he'd waft away to nothingness. Of all the things he could not do right now, the thing he could most not do was nothing at all. He picked up his walking pace to get ahead of Lowell. "Just get ready to throw. When I say."

Lowell threw up his arms in exasperation. But he gave up protesting, and as Ryan continued walking away he could hear Lowell fishing around in his pocket for the snow globe.

Ryan kept walking until he was all the way across the street and into the trees. He went right through the golf course fence and onto a fairway for extra distance. Some of the golfer ghosts complained and gesticulated angrily at him, though it was as impossible for him to interfere as it was for them to play.

Lowell looked up and down the street, checking for witnesses. Even from a distance, Ryan could see him shaking his head.

Finally Lowell relented and hopped over the wall into Caldwell's front yard. As the snow globe in Lowell's hand moved away from him, Ryan could feel the pull of the haunting getting stronger. He badly wanted to run to it and throw his arms around it and declare it his most precious thing forever, but he resisted. He dug his feet in, such as it were, and stayed put.

Lowell seemed to lose his nerve halfway to the house and started looking for a good vantage point to throw from. Ryan found himself getting irrationally furious at Lowell for making off with his lovely, precious snow globe. *How dare he toss it so casually from hand to hand? Does he not understand the indescribable joy that is plastic Myrtle Beach in winter?*

He fought against the anger. *You told him to take it, you idiot.* What little concentration he could muster through the snow globe rage and the battle to keep himself cohesive, he had to commit entirely to resisting the overwhelming urge to leave this spot.

He saw Lowell look back at him and mouth "Ready?"

He braced himself, and nodded. The compulsion to lift

his feet off the ground and let himself be pulled was staggering. *Do it, Lowell. Do it now.*

There was a sudden blast of piercing sound, the warning bleat of a siren.

A police car hurtled towards Lowell and squealed to a stop in front of the house.

He hard Lowell shout "Oh no!"

Another police car came hurtling around the corner from the other direction. It ripped through the last stretch of road to the house in no time flat.

Ryan let go.

He released himself from the ground and felt the tension accelerating him forward.

He heard the shouts of the police as they leaped out of their vehicles and sprinted for Lowell. Ryan would be upon them in seconds.

Somehow in the blur as he hurtled through space he could make out the panicked look on Lowell's face as he raised his hands and backed away from the circle of cops closing in around him.

They were telling him to lie down on the ground. And from the looks of it, he was going to obey.

Yet in the last second, Lowell dared to spin around, swing his arm back, and lob the snow globe.

And then the officers tackled him, and he disappeared beneath them.

Ryan's course pitched upwards. He hurtled straight over the melee. He felt his feet heat up as they grazed the energy field like a space capsule hitting the atmosphere. He pulled his knees up to his chest, and he was rising over the lawn, arcing up towards the balcony.

He caught sight of the snow globe as it cleared the railing and bounced, threatening briefly to pass right through the balusters and tumble into the yard beyond. But it stopped just short and settled.

And then he was upon it, and felt the wash of relief at finally being with this, the one thing in all the world that he loved and wanted to be with forever. The most awful and nonsensical trinket ever made, but it was his and he was back to it and all was right with the world.

He was so consumed with relief that he stopped hearing the shouts of Lowell vehemently not resisting arrest on the ground below. And it was several seconds before Ryan remembered where he was and why.

He ducked straight through the closed and wildly indifferent French doors, and into the house to look for his body.

THIRTY-TWO

The inside of the house was cool. Or so Ryan imagined, because it was dim and he could hear the soft whirr of the air conditioning. It didn't make a warm impression, at any rate.

Caldwell wasn't home. He couldn't be home. If he was home, he'd be out looking at the commotion on his front lawn, or making calls, or at the very least, moving around. But the stillness in the house felt oppressively total. A neighbor must have seen Lowell and Ryan skulking around and called the police.

A flood of vagueness surged over Ryan and he struggled with his consciousness, pounding it mentally until it agreed to do what he wanted. *Get moving.*

He passed through an obscenely huge bedroom with the biggest TV he had ever seen, and onto a landing that overlooked a vast living room with an even bigger TV. It felt unfamiliar to see such a large, old house with no ghosts at all in it. The Ghost Wall certainly did its job.

There were four other doors along the landing and he gave a cursory glance into each room, sticking his head through, seeing nothing but shadows and shafts of sunlight from outside, and then moving on to the next. There was no sign that anybody at all was in the house.

Ryan finished with the upstairs rooms and drifted down the grand staircase into the living room. He could feel the tug from the snow globe out on the balcony as he moved further away from it, but it was not so strong yet that he couldn't press on.

The living room was brighter than upstairs because of the enormous picture windows looking out over the pool and the expansive back yard. Ryan had already mostly given up hope of actually finding Caldwell at home, in Ryan's body or otherwise. But he still hoped to find some kind of clue, something that would give him somewhere to go next. Besides which, now that he was in the house he had absolutely no way to get out past the ghost wall. So he kept searching.

In the kitchen he finally found signs of life. Or at least, signs that somebody had been there relatively recently. There were dishes in the sink, a couple of bowls encrusted with bits of dried cereal. Apple Jacks, Ryan noted. He had never cared for Apple Jacks. The fruit content threatened nutrition.

In the adjoining laundry room he found baskets of clothes, some clean and some dirty. Without being able to pick them up he couldn't discern any details of them other than that they appeared to be men's.

He finished searching the entire ground floor and still hadn't found anything useful at all.

And then the doorbell rang.

He rushed back to the front foyer. The wide double front door had frosted glass set into it, so he could make out the silhouettes of two people on the front step. And behind them, the hazy red flash of the police lights. No doubt it was the cops who had tackled Lowell outside. They were probably here to make sure Caldwell was okay, find out if he wanted to press charges, or whatever it is that police do in situations like this. Finding nobody home, they would probably just leave and not come inside. Or so he hoped.

From the foyer he could see another stairwell down into the basement, so he drifted down there, still faintly hoping to find some lead he could follow. The basement was much darker, lit only by slivers of light from behind blinds pulled down over ground-level windows. But it was an impressive basement indeed. It was furnished like a pub, complete with bar stools and pool table and two TV's mounted high in the corners. And there was a movie room attached, with theater seating and a giant screen and projector. Everything was powered off. The silence was complete, apart from the air conditioning being slightly louder down here.

The doorbell rang again, and one of the cops rapped hard on the door. They had to be making sure nobody was home. Ryan wondered what had become of Lowell. He was probably handcuffed in the back of one of those cruisers. But there was nothing Ryan could do about that now.

This was it. A dead end. He had searched the whole house and found nothing. Caldwell could be anywhere. He could be on vacation. He could have decided to take his brand new body out for a spin in Costa Rica or someplace. Which was more than Ryan had ever done with it. He had a strange thought that maybe his body was grateful to have somebody in it who would actually make good use of it for a change.

He sat on one of the bar stools to ponder. Without the need to focus on standing, dizziness closed in around his awareness and he had to shake his head and fight it off. He lifted his hand to his face again, struggling to focus on it.

But there wasn't anything to focus on. His hand was gone. His arm had vanished nearly to the elbow. He struggled to get the molecules back into place and was able to form a blob shaped somewhat like his arm, but completely without detail.

He didn't have long. And not only had he run into a dead end, but it was a dead end that he was trapped in. There was no way for him to leave this place.

The terror of that gave the dizziness a new opening to exploit, and Ryan teetered on the stool. Shadows made a dim frame around his vision that closed in on him from all sides.

And then he snapped into clarity. Because he saw something.

He saw feet.

Two of them, extending out from behind the bar.

Someone lying on the floor.

Ryan leapt off the stool and circled around the end of the bar. And he froze.

There was a dead man lying face-down behind the bar.

It wasn't Ryan's body. It was too large, startlingly so. This guy had to be at least six-six, and three hundred pounds. But he was lying on his stomach so Ryan couldn't see his face, just the bald patch on the peak of his scalp. And he appeared quite dead. What little skin Ryan could see—the hands and the back of the neck—was sallow gray.

Ryan had expected to find his own body with someone walking around in it. He had prepared for that, as much as one can prepare for such a thing. He had not prepared to find an extremely large dead man lying face-down in the basement. He didn't have a reaction pre-planned for it, which normally he liked to have. So he stood and stared while his mind careened acrobatically.

Finally he decided that he wanted to see who this was. He didn't expect to recognize him, but he wanted to see. So he put his natural revulsion aside and crept forward to lie down next to the body, trying to get close to its face. But the face was turned to the side and nearly pressed into the bottom of the counter. There was nowhere Ryan could position himself where he could make out details of the features.

The doorbell kept ringing insistently, and the pounding on the glass was getting more urgent. Ryan ignored it. Other things to worry about.

Like why was there a dead man in the house? It wasn't Ryan's body, and it certainly wasn't Caldwell's—Ryan had seen pictures of him online during Lowell's search. Caldwell was a fit man in his late 50's. This body was nowhere near that in fitness or age.

Ryan needed to know who he was, and what he was doing here. He tried again to see, hunting for a sweet spot where he could lie and get some sense of the face. If he could just get into that inch between the forehead and the bottom of the bar. He almost had it.

But the huge man's eyes sprang open, and he let out a dry, strangled gasp.

THIRTY-THREE

Ryan reeled backwards in a panic, clear through the bar and several stools. Had he been substantial, he would have knocked down every piece of furniture in the place as he stumbled, flailing, away from the huge man who wasn't dead, not completely.

The man fell silent again, but Ryan couldn't see anymore if his eyes were open. The man's feet went on twitching, like he was trying weakly to flee.

Ryan had no idea what to do. He spun around twice, looking for some action to take, as though there might be a sign on on a wall nearby with instructions on how to deal with an almost dead man in an empty house.

The police, he thought. *They're already here.* He would have to make some excuse for why he had broken in, but maybe they could help the man. And maybe the man would know something.

The doorbell had just stopped ringing, so Ryan dashed up the stairs two at a time, sprinted through the foyer and forced himself without hesitation straight through the front doors. The second he was out into the open he yelled "wait!" He instantly felt searing heat as he hit the Ghost Wall, and he backed up almost all the way to the door before it cooled. He fought to ignore the feeling that his entire form was being microwaved.

The officers were gone. The cruisers were gone. In their place, there was only Lowell standing on the front step and eating a glazed donut. It crunched.

Ryan blinked in surprise.

"Find anything?" Lowell asked around the donut.

Lowell broke a window with a flower pot from the back patio. It took him several minutes to clear off all the glass shards around the edge while Ryan paced frantically.

Lowell explained something about having a friend on the police force who had called off the arresting officers, and who would have to forgive him breaking the window as well. But Ryan couldn't focus on his words or what they meant. What portion of his mind wasn't spinning in circles trying to figure out the almost-dead man in the basement, was functioning only in brief, dim spurts. He felt like he was already intermittently popping in and out of existence.

Once Lowell got through the window he followed Ryan into the basement and up to the enormous gray man behind the bar, who had gone still again. Ryan silently cursed Lowell for taking so long.

As soon as Lowell saw the body, Ryan could tell that he recognized it.

"No... way," Lowell said. He sounded at once horrified and giddily excited, like he had just run over someone in the street only to discover that it was his favorite A-list celebrity.

"Who is it?!" Ryan demanded.

"I know this guy! This is messed up!"

"Who is it?!"

"This is Rufus Flowers!"

The name meant something to Ryan, but in his dazed, unfocused state he could no longer remember what names were.

"My other client!" Lowell explained. "The guy I was looking for in the dump! This is his body!"

He raced to the big man's side, and for a moment Ryan was surprised at Lowell's apparently legitimate concern for his client. But rather than any of the helpful medical things Lowell could have attempted, he instead grabbed the man's left arm and yanked it out from under his body, then peered closely at the hand. He cursed under his breath.

"What are you looking for?" Ryan asked.

Before Lowell could answer, the body's arms twitched violently, and another choked gasp escaped it.

"Hey! He's not dead!" Lowell said with only mild surprise. "What do we do?"

"I don't know!" Ryan said. "Get him out of there!"

There wasn't enough space behind the bar to turn the man over, so Lowell had to drag him by the ankles out into the open and then crouch to put all his weight into flipping the man over.

As the man's enormous girth rolled up, Ryan had a flash of recognition. "I've seen this guy before too."

"Where?" Lowell demanded urgently.

Ryan remembered cowering in the body storage units at the Clinic while Margie was being fired by Roger. The wheezing breath of the very large man in the cabinet had been too much for Ryan to take, so he had shifted to an empty one.

"At the Clinic," he finally said. "I think this body was in storage."

Lowell shook his head. "Rufus wasn't a client at the Clinic. He never heard of it."

"He was definitely in there."

The man's arms twitched like he was trying to reach out to them. His eyes opened briefly and then rolled back into his head as the lids drifted closed again. Ryan and Lowell stood and watched helplessly.

"Is this like a CPR situation?" Lowell said.

"Do you know CPR?"

"I always wanted to learn."

"Just call 911!"

Lowell fished through his raincoat pockets for his phone. Not finding it in the outside ones he tried the inside ones. On the fourth pocket he stopped. For a long moment he didn't do anything.

"Call 911!" Ryan said. His voice went high with panic.

Lowell was staring, dumbstruck. "I think it's too late," he said.

The man's body heaved as though trying to expel water from its lungs. Only it wasn't water that came out. It was light.

Energy coursed over and through the body, all surging towards a single point. As Ryan watched, the point gathered more and more energy, getting brighter. It reached a pinnacle of intensity and floated up away from the body. It flickered and sizzled like an ember, appearing somehow angrier than a single point of light should ever be able to look.

Ryan looked down at the body. It lay still and pale, lifeless.

When he looked up again he was surprised to see that the point of light had expanded to a nearly human shape already. As he watched he could see the fingers separate, the feet expand like inflating balloons, details of the face separate and gain definition

Margie and Lowell had apparently been at least partially right. The ghost looked nothing like the body. It was less than half the size of the big man on the floor. As the face came into focus, Ryan found that he could recognize it from the pictures he had seen online.

It was Clifton Caldwell, the hardware baron. Completely bald, with a hard, sullen, 50-year-old face that Ryan couldn't picture ever uttering words like "strawberry" or "dainty". He had a single cruel, thin eyebrow high at the ends and deep onto his nose in the middle.

"Mr. Caldwell?" Ryan tried tentatively.

Caldwell's head twisted to look at Ryan. His eyebrow went even deeper in the middle. His eyes scanned up and down Ryan like he was searching for where a wallpaper pattern repeated.

To Ryan's great surprise, Caldwell said: "You're that one!"

His voice echoed backwards on itself, like it emerged only partly into this dimension and retreated back to another.

Ryan stammered. "Th... that? One?" Caldwell recognized him. Why did Caldwell recognize him?

Caldwell's face changed. But in a way that made no sense. The left half of his face slid downward and the right half slid up, so that his nose and mouth stretched horribly between them. He seemed to sense it happening and buried his face in his hands.

His *three* hands.

He had an extra arm, splitting off from the left one somewhere near the elbow. The hand was over-sized, twice as big as the others.

"Okay. That's..." Lowell started, horrified. He seemed to realize he didn't know the rest of the sentence, and stopped it.

Caldwell stumbled backwards, changing shape constantly. He developed several new legs and lost others as he walked. And for a moment Ryan wasn't sure which of the three was Caldwell's original head.

Caldwell roared furiously as though expending great effort, and all his extra parts snapped back into him. When he turned to Ryan again he looked much more normal. And much more outraged.

"Where's Foster?" he snarled.

"I... I don't know. The Clinic?"

"I'm going to kill him," Caldwell said.

He lurched away from them and up the stairs.

Ryan and Lowell looked at each other. Lowell's face looked exactly like Ryan imagined his own did right now: wide-eyed and dumbfounded.

They chased after Caldwell. "Mr. Caldwell!" Ryan called after him. He was afraid to talk to this man who seemed constructed mostly out of rage. But he needed to know.

Caldwell was already at the front door when they caught

up to him. He spun on them, and for a moment seemed to be facing both forwards and backwards at once. He shook himself until he snapped back together. "Eight nine eight six," he said.

Ryan didn't know what he had expected Caldwell to say, but it wasn't that. "What?"

Caldwell developed a new hand with a finger far too long for it. The finger pointed at a keypad set into the wall next to the door. "Eight nine eight six," he growled again.

"The Ghost Wall," Lowell said, nodding. "That's the PIN to shut it off?"

Ryan dared a step forward. "Mr. Caldwell, you've seen me before! Why have you seen me before?"

Caldwell's eyes shifted back to Ryan. Two other eyes on a different head partially overlapping the first one stayed locked on Lowell. "Eight nine eight six," the voice said from another universe.

"Please," Ryan pleaded. "Did Roger Foster give you my body? Where is it?"

Caldwell made a guttural noise that seemed to come from his center of gravity. "He didn't have it," he spat.

Ryan couldn't make sense of it. *He didn't have it?* "What... what do you..."

In a blink, Caldwell expanded to twice his size. He spread five arms and loomed over them, leaning like a gigantic tree about to fall and crush them. "Eight! Nine! Eight! Six!" he bellowed.

Lowell, frantic, scrambled around him to the keypad. His elbow slipped through Caldwell partially as he passed, and a surge of something almost knocked Lowell flat. "This guy's *really* pissed off," he said. He flipped open the cover on the keypad.

"Lowell, don't!" Ryan shouted.

Lowell, finger poised over the number buttons, stopped and looked back at him.

"Mr. Caldwell," Ryan said, trying to sound calm and forceful like Margie always did. It was hard when his voice kept trembling like a nervous chihuahua. "We'll let you go. As soon as you tell me what I need to know."

"Punch in the code," Caldwell snapped at Lowell. One of his heads ignored Ryan while the other stared him down. The newer third head seemed unaware what was going on.

"You recognized me," Ryan said. "Did Roger Foster try to transplant you into my body?"

Caldwell's heads all turned to Ryan at once. They merged into one and Caldwell almost looked like a normal human ghost again. His eyebrow bent up at one end and down at the other. "He was supposed to. Never did."

"What happened? Tell me everything, and we're done."

Caldwell grunted. "He was supposed to find a body that would work," he growled. "Only reason I invested in that damn place. Put me in five different bodies. None of 'em worked. All died with me in 'em. And every time they died, I got a little more messed up. Look what he did to me." His head turned inside out so that for a moment they were looking at the back of his face through the back of his head. He forced it back to its usual shape. "Then he showed me you. Said yours was it. Some kind of perfect ghost match."

Ryan's heart, such as it were, skipped a beat. Margie had been right about everything. He was close.

"But when the time came," Caldwell went on, grimacing, "he didn't have the body anymore. So he gave me the next closest match he could find." He jabbed a finger towards the floor, beneath which Rufus's body lay somewhere, empty. "From my employee records. He worked in one of my stores I guess. I dunno."

Lowell gasped. "Toilet parts." When Ryan threw him a confused look, he elaborated. "Rufus told me he sold toilet parts. Didn't say where. But he didn't exactly volunteer to have his body taken."

Caldwell sneered. "Didn't ask him to. Foster took care of everything."

Ryan stepped forward and fought to keep his voice steady. "What happened to my body? Why didn't Roger have it anymore?" He clenched his fists. He was afraid of the answer, but desperately wanted to hear it.

Caldwell grunted again, a deep, hollow sound like a drain backing up.

"He told me."

Ryan wanted to grab him by the neck and shake him. "Told you what?"

"The day I was supposed to go into it, take it over for good. He didn't say why. But he told me. It died the day before. It was dead."

THIRTY-FOUR

Lowell was concerned about Ryan. The poor ghost had looked seriously bummed when he left Caldwell's house. The most likely reason was that he had just lost virtually all hope of survival and would be gone forever in a day or so. Or maybe he had other personal stuff going on. Whatever. Lowell didn't know him well enough to guess. Either way, Lowell decided that he'd better get his payment from Ryan tonight, or he might never get it.

More vexing to Lowell at the moment was how he was going to get Rufus's body into the car.

His first plan was to not move the body at all. His clients —his *other* clients—were less interested in the body than in the ring it was supposed to be wearing. Except it wasn't wearing the ring anymore. The deep indent was easy to see on Rufus's finger, but the ring itself was gone. If Lowell were to find it, he could deliver that and they would presumably be satisfied.

So he spent the better part of an hour tearing the house apart looking for it. And the better part of another hour tearing apart Caldwell's liquor cabinet.

The ring was nowhere to be found. There was a good chance it had been removed long before Caldwell was ever put into Rufus's body and was not in the house at all. So Lowell shifted plans. He would have to move the body. The clients had asked for a body, so he would deliver a body.

He brought his car around the house, grateful that Caldwell was rich enough to have an extra delivery entrance on the back. And he found a wheelbarrow parked next to a garden shed at the far side of the pool. The wheelbarrow, while being the spacious, wide-wheeled and smooth-rolling kind befitting a hardware baron, proved to be utterly useless on stairs.

Still, somehow Lowell managed to brute force his way through a *Weekend at Bernie's* nightmare. And an hour later he was sweating, exhausted, possibly herniated, and on the road with Rufus's body upright in the passenger seat next to him because it was too big to fit in the back with all the liquor and beer Lowell had stolen.

He crept through the Beacon St. rush-hour glut, trying to get around Boston College and hoping that none of the strolling students would notice how the gigantic body in the car was bent at an unnatural angle with its face pressed against the window, and was also dead.

As he drove, he thought about how best to play this.

Obviously he couldn't return the body to Rufus and Lucinda today. That would be madness. He had been working their case for barely a day. And while he was proud of having solved it, it was almost not worth even typing up a bill for that.

So that left the question: what would seem a realistic amount of time for him to have spent tracking it down? How long before he could expect a phone call from them requiring him to explain what he had been doing? And how long after that phone call could he call them back and say that he was working on a lead, thereby setting up his usual 48-hour delay before actually delivering the body and handing them a bill? These calculations were an inexact science at which he was well-practiced. But calculating how long it would be before a dead body started stinking was new to him. One of many reasons why he typically hunted only for ghosts.

He would need ice. Lots of ice.

As he turned a hard right onto Commonwealth Ave. and imposed himself into the line of impatient traffic, the G-force of the turn shifted the big body in the seat next to him. It leaned off the window and a little closer to Lowell than he liked, threatening to topple into his lap. He reflexively thrust out an arm and shoved it back into place.

To his great surprise, the body made a noise.

Not just an escape of trapped gas, or any of the other noises Lowell had heard bodies can make. It sounded like an actual, driven-by-the-nervous system vocalization.

A grunt.

Lowell slammed on the brake.

Rufus's body slumped forward, and its forehead thudded into the dash.

It grunted again, eliminating Lowell's doubts about whether it had actually grunted the first time.

Lowell stared at it, breathing fast and gripping the steering wheel. He ignored the honks of protest from behind him and studied the body. Its eyes were closed. Its mouth hung limply open. Its arms were pretzelled into the scant space between its torso and the dashboard. It looked, as he had assumed it was, dead.

Except that now, he saw it was breathing. Definitely breathing. A steady, shallow rhythm.

Lowell gingerly reached out and pressed his fingers to the body's wrist. He had never had reason to check anyone's pulse before, so it took him a few tries to find the spot. But there it was. A heartbeat.

So, not dead. Another deduction proved wrong. And one that seemed like it should really have been a gimme.

The honks from behind had reached an intensity that he couldn't ignore any longer, so he accelerated into the hole he had made in traffic ahead and as soon as he could, pulled into the parking lot of a college administrative building. There were no empty spots, but he stopped in the lane between rows of cars to catch his breath and think.

The body breathed softly in the seat next to him. Aside from how bent its limbs were to fit into the seat, and how its face was pressed hard into the dashboard so that one eye was pulled open, it looked almost serene.

If he understood Margie's science correctly—and that was far from a guarantee—the body had rejected Caldwell's ghost because of a mismatch of pirate DNA or whatever. It was now a shell, alive but lifeless. What did that mean he had to do with it? How did it change his plan?

If he brought the body back to Rufus and Lucinda alive, what then? They had already accepted its death and begun to deal with it. Forcing them to actually be present for that death would just be cruel, wouldn't it? At the very least, they'd have to keep the body somewhere, taking up space. That was likely a couch or a hammock that they wouldn't be able to use for god-knows-how-long. Who was he to subject them to that kind of inconvenience?

Some small part of his mind also acknowledged the possibility that Rufus could be put back into his body. Yes, there was that. But really, again, they had already moved on. Rufus seemed to be adjusting to his ghostly life quite well. The pain and re-adjustment of going back might be too much for the big man's heart to take. Maybe. Or something.

After a few moments' consideration, Lowell thought he knew exactly how much his "keep the body as long as possible" plan would need to change.

Which was hardly at all. Except that now, he wouldn't need to buy all that ice.

He was whistling as he pulled back out into traffic.

THIRTY-FIVE

"Why aren't there any blue ones?" Ryan asked. He leaned with his elbows on the table so that he could be at eye level with the cereal bowl. Or rather, he approximated such a lean because he didn't have any arms anymore. He could still pretend to have them, and found that his form behaved as if they were there, but they weren't. The top half of his form, too, was mostly disconnected now. It floated a few inches above his hips, sometimes not quite keeping up with his walking pace and then bobbing forward like a helium balloon on a string. His shirt, however, remained as intact as ever. He wondered if, when there was nothing else left of him, the shirt would somehow remain as an eternal butter-stained Float Beer blight upon the Earth.

"They don't make blue anymore," Margie said. She stirred up the bowl with her spoon, making little Sugar Frootz rock slides. A pinkish nugget tumbled out of the bowl and she flicked it back in. "They decided, for the sake of PR, to replace the original artificial dyes with all-natural food coloring, which is harder than you think. Artificial dyes have no flavor, and are loaded with preservatives. Natural dyes are made from things like vegetables, which add their own flavor and tend to spoil. They couldn't find a natural blue dye that worked so they stopped making blue."

Ryan was dimly conscious of hearing all of that, but retained virtually none of it. He did know, though, that he didn't like what it implied. Why would he want natural ingredients? Sugars manufactured in a lab for maximum flavor and minimal nutrition was the whole point. He didn't want cereal to contain anything that could also be found in spinach.

He struggled to focus on the nuggets of cereal. For the past hour he had been finding it difficult to focus on anything at all. Just remaining conscious required most of his energy. With increasing frequency he found himself missing entire minutes, slipping through them without noticing their passing. Sometimes he would snap back to awareness in an explosive surge of panic like a driver waking up to the oncoming headlights of a dump truck.

"Put the milk on," he said. His voice, like his vision and his thought, was losing coherence. He sounded like he was a mile away and inside a phone booth.

Margie gave him a concerned look. "Isn't there something you'd rather be doing? Don't you want to call your family? Your parents?"

He couldn't blame her for asking. Of course, he really *should* have something else he would rather be doing. He was, after all, about to die. He definitely had to use that word about this. Because although leaving his body did not fit the traditional definition of dying, what was happening now came a lot closer. And people who know they are about to die usually have people they want to see for the last time to make amends with, to say goodbye to, or even just for comfort.

He didn't. He just wanted to try Sugar Frootz.

All these years he could have been trying it, the new Sugar Frootz that he didn't even know was a thing, and now here he was with maybe only minutes left of existence, staring at a bowl of it that he couldn't touch, couldn't smell, couldn't taste. Maybe it was still terrible. Maybe it was worse than before. He would never know. Even the colors were becoming harder to make out as shadows intruded around the edges of his vision and a hazy filter went up between him and the world. He could tell there were no blue nuggets, but only because he thought they would be darker than all the others. They all looked gray.

He leaned forward to put his nose over the bowl and inhaled deeply, keenly aware that he wasn't actually inhaling. There was no sensation of his lungs filling up, no sense of warm or cool, and certainly no scent of Sugar Frootz, either natural or artificial. He was just miming the act of inhaling: expanding his chest, making a noise that resembled air moving into his nostrils, ballooning his lungs. He got nothing from it except a sharp stab of anger at how empty the experience was. Or was he just miming the anger too?

He noticed that Margie had her hand over her mouth and he thought he could see glistening in the corners of her eyes.

"What?" he asked, alarmed.

She kept her hand over her mouth and shook her head. "Nothing." This was not the blunt, analytical Margie he was used to. Right now he needed the Margie that would, with dry enthusiasm and at very little prompting, explain how photosynthesis works. This wasn't her.

"What is it?" he asked, more demanding.

She shook her head again. "You don't have a nose," she said. "You're trying to smell it, and your nose is gone. Your face is... it's..." She couldn't finish.

He had no interest in checking a mirror. He fully expected that by now his head was a roundish bubble of steaming soup. There was nothing he could do about that. All he wanted to know was exactly what he had been missing.

Sugar Frootz.

"I'm going to make sure he hangs, you know," she said. "Tomorrow. Lowell already said he has police friends and we're going to tear that place down. He won't get away with —"

"I know. Put the milk on."

She composed herself, and there was the Margie he needed again. He marveled at how quickly the clinical mask came back onto her face. She had amazing control over her emotions, more than anyone he had ever met.

She upended a milk carton over the cereal and he watched the little pebbles try to flee the dairy tsunami as the bowl filled. They bobbed and settled, reorganizing themselves. He recalled hazily how he had always thought cereal smelled best right after the milk went on. As though the milk released the scent like rain invisibly opening up little fructose-frosted flower buds.

"What does it smell like?" he asked. "Tell me."

She leaned over the bowl and inhaled. "Sweet."

"Duh. I know that. It's like ninety percent sugar. What does it smell *like*?"

She inhaled again, this time with her eyes closed. She seemed to be swishing the aroma around in her nostrils. "Corn meal. Fruit. Some kind of citrus. Orange. Lemon. That must be the natural fruit flavor."

Ryan concentrated hard, trying to remember what it felt like to smell these things. To smell at all. The memory, like everything he now consisted of, was indistinct.

She sniffed again. "And I think… calcium carbonate. Yes. I'm sorry, I have to…" She scooped up a heaping spoonful. He watched her chew it at a measured pace, again with her eyes closed. "It's loaded with sugar but it's the corn syrup that gives it the stickiness, that glaze on the outside before the corn meal crumbles and the tumeric extract mixes with the sugar. That's when you get that little burst. There it is."

"Just tell me what it tastes like."

"I *am* telling you what it tastes like." She took another spoonful. "The recipe is precisely calculated to activate all five elements of taste perception in a specific ratio. It's genius, really. Years of lab work went into this. But I do miss blue."

She opened her eyes and reached to scoop another spoonful. But her hand stopped halfway to the bowl. She was looking at him, and her professional cool fell away again. He saw something that looked like guilt flash across her face.

She put the spoon down. "I'm sorry. I shouldn't…"

"Why not?" He had been enjoying listening to her. The rustle of the spoon digging into the nuggets, the crunch as she chewed, the little dribble of milk snaking down the side of the bowl and mounting a failed escape attempt across the table—all of it was stirring up fragments of memories. Bits of sensations that he couldn't quite piece together into a whole experience. But he was still relishing the bits. All of them were mere instants, gone in a flicker, barely noticed at the time. And yet somehow now at the end, he wanted desperately to have them back. And to have more like them. New ones. He wanted to try the new Sugar Frootz, and he never would.

Margie pushed back from the table. "There must be something you want to do. Anything. It's not right that we're just sitting here."

"Why not?"

"Because there has to be something more important that you want to do before…" She stopped herself from finishing the sentence.

Ryan had a sudden idea, and he wasn't certain about it, but it came out even before he convinced himself it was good. "We could watch TV."

She blinked at him. "That's it?"

"What else do you suggest? Something bigger? Climb Mount Everest? I've done that. I want to watch TV." He paused, considering, and decided that he needed to add something. "With you."

He had a nebulous recollection of his feeling the previous night watching real estate shows. He knew that he had enjoyed it somehow, and not because of its surprising insights into the Boise real estate market. He had enjoyed it because she was there. He hated real estate shows, so what else could it be? But he couldn't recall what specifically it was that had made him enjoy it. He studied her face, trying to find his way back to what he had felt the night before. The feeling was flitting around the edges of his mind but refusing to land.

But he had enjoyed it. He knew that much. And he really wanted to enjoy something right now. Because he was about to stop existing, and he felt like that would be hard to enjoy.

"Okay," she said, utterly perplexed, as though he had just asked her to shave the word "bingo" into the back of her head.

They moved to the couch, and she propped herself in the corner, precisely perpendicular to the cushions as always, and folded her hands in her lap. He smiled, and then immediately wondered why he had done that.

It was too early for the real estate marathon, so they were stuck with decorating shows. He hated those even more than real estate shows. Margie wasn't saying anything, so he found his mind sometimes fading out completely, and other times wandering of its own accord. Trying to make sense of what tomorrow would be like.

There wasn't going to be a tomorrow. Or there was, but he probably wasn't going to be here for it. The party was going to keep going, but he was leaving it early. And for the first time in any party ever, he wanted to stay.

"Don't do that," Margie said, in response to nothing he was aware of.

"Don't do what?"

"I can tell what you're thinking about. Don't."

"What should I be thinking about?"

She motioned towards the TV, which he hadn't been paying attention to at all. "That guy thinks he can lay bathroom tile himself."

"So?"

"So, have you ever tried to lay bathroom tile?"

"People do that? I always assumed the tiles were already there in nature, and they built the house around them."

"In about ten minutes, you're going to see this guy have a meltdown because he has no idea how grout works. Watch."

The meltdown arrived in eight minutes after only four tiles. And in the next episode, the same thing happened because somebody else didn't understand the intricacies of toilet installation. And they were disappointed in the next episode because the couple was actually pretty good at putting up wallpaper and it didn't push them perilously close to divorce, as Margie had predicted. Although the wallpaper was ugly.

And in the fourth episode, as Margie was giggling with giddy delight at a man struggling to decode an arrangement of decorative pillows, Ryan realized in a blinding blast of clarity why he wanted so badly to watch TV with Margie again.

But before he could examine it, the feeling wafted away just as his arms had done. He couldn't even remember what the feeling was but he knew he badly wanted it back.

"Ghosts can't form new emotional attachments." That's what she had said. It hadn't occurred to him at the time, but *he* was a ghost. So her statement included him.

As he tried to make sense of it, his mind felt like it sank far back into mud behind him and he had to yank it back into place. The shadows around his vision crowded in, and he fought against them, shouldering them back, forcing his way back through them to the man on TV and his pillows, and to Margie. But the shadows fought back, and his mind sank again.

This is it, he thought. *I'm done. And it's my fault. I did this.* He wanted to stay with Margie just a little longer and see if he could trap the mysterious feeling even just for his last few seconds. But he was nearly certain he wouldn't be able to. It was too elusive, too hazy. And, if what she said was true, as long as he was a ghost it always would be.

He had made a terrible mistake.

Just as the shadows seemed about to wash over his vision and overtake the light completely, Lowell came in with a bill in his hand.

THIRTY-SIX

"This is absurd," Margie said. She had the full heat of her volcanic stare directed at Lowell. He had already asked her three times to stop looking at him that way.

Ryan tried the ATM again. "Ryan Matney," he attempted to say into the voice-activation microphone. But he couldn't move the air the way he used to. Fine detail in sound was impossible in his incoherent state, and he could hardly get any volume at all. So the sound he produced was like a swarm of mosquitoes that had figured out how to work as a team and move the pitch of their whine faintly up and down.

The ATM buzzed negatively, a sound much more cohesive than anything Ryan could manage. "Please try again," it said, as though he just needed a little encouragement and everything would be fine.

It was late, and there was very little traffic on the street. Living pedestrians had long since abandoned the night to the ghosts, who now seemed mildly annoyed at having someone here invading the time when they did some of their best glowing and flitting around. Some scowling 18th century farm hands leaned on their hoes and kept looking over Margie and Lowell's shoulders at what Ryan was doing. Lowell had to keep giving them "you want to make something out of it?" looks.

"Ryan Matney," Ryan said again, leaning in close to the microphone. He didn't like how his head disconnected from the rest of him when he leaned like that. For a moment he couldn't even find the rest of him, and his head was on its own. He located his torso a few feet to his left and had to float his head over to it and then drag the whole thing back.

"Please try again," the ATM replied with the exact same encouraging tone.

"Let me do it," Lowell said, stepping forward.

"You're an ass," Margie spat bitterly. "He may only have a few minutes left and you want to *bill* him?"

Ryan appreciated that she was outraged on his behalf, but he wasn't actually mad at Lowell. At this point, moments away from annihilation, it gave him some small sense of satisfaction to honor a commitment and do something nice for someone. "It's okay," he said to Margie gently, concentrating hard to make himself understood. "I hired him. He helped. He deserves to get paid."

"He deserves to get kicked in the teeth," she muttered.

"It's okay," Ryan said. He chose whatever part of himself was most well defined at the moment—somewhere around his hip, he suspected—and pushed it into the softly glowing SES scanner on the side of the ATM. It was designed for ghosts to put their fingers in, but it would have to take what he could manage. He nodded at Lowell.

"Ryan Matney," Lowell said.

The SES scanner brightened for a moment as it confirmed Ryan's identity. Then the ATM's display lit up with a menu of options.

"Transfer," Lowell said into the microphone.

Ryan fought to keep as much of himself as possible inside the scanner, but his particles kept spilling out. The ATM buzzed and the screen turned red. "Please keep your finger inside the SES scanner," it said pleasantly. Ryan twisted and contorted, searching for a part of himself that would work.

The only cohesive part of Ryan left was the shirt. Nearly as well defined now as in the moment he had unwillingly formed it. He pushed his stomach into the scanner so the bottom of the Float Beer logo was directly within the scanner's beam, and the main menu flashed back up. "Do it fast," he said to Lowell.

"Are you sure?" Lowell asked. Apparently Margie had convinced him to feel guilty. He avoided Ryan's gaze. Or perhaps he just couldn't tell anymore where Ryan's gaze was.

"You earned it," Ryan said. He wasn't sure it was clear enough to be understood, but Lowell apparently guessed from the tone. He fished around in his coat pocket and produced a slip on which he had written his account number.

"Transfer," Lowell said into the microphone.

More options popped up on the display. But Ryan was distracted by his shirt. Even the letters on the logo were coming apart now. And the little illustration of a floating scoop of ice cream was swirling out of focus as though being sucked down a drain. Ryan started to slip backwards, and the ATM lost connection again. "Please keep your finger inside the SES scanner."

"That's it," Margie said. She took two fast steps over and shoved Lowell backwards with both hands and all her weight. He stumbled, flailing his arms. "Get out of here!" Margie bellowed. "I'm taking him home."

Lowell looked stunned. "But... it'll just take..."

"Is this who you are?" Margie demanded, coming at him again. She was ready to knock him flat if she had to.

"Apparently!" Lowell said, annoyed. He held out the slip of paper with the account number on it.

Margie slapped it out of his hand. "Get out of here!"

Lowell snapped up the slip of paper and backed away. "I'll leave this on your..." he started to say. But Margie charging him again cut him off. He spun and dashed straight through the farm hands, and stormed angrily across the street, glancing back frequently.

Margie turned back to Ryan. He had sunk to the ground, and struggled to focus on her as she came back to him. "Ryan? Can you describe what's happening? Are you still..."

She froze, staring at the ATM.

After a moment of staring she swerved past Ryan and

pressed in close to the ATM display. Something on it had caught her attention. She jabbed at the screen with her finger. "Look! Look!"

In the corner of the display was Ryan's name next to a small thumbnail of his SES pattern. Ryan couldn't tell why she was pointing at it.

Margie waited for him to clue in. Finally she spat it out. "It's not a pirate!"

Ryan leaned in closer and struggled to focus on the SES thumbnail. She was right. The signature on the screen looked nothing like a pirate. He thought it more closely resembled some kind of crested lizard. He focused for a moment on remembering the name of the particular species, and completely forgot to figure out the significance of what Margie was saying.

Exasperated, she did it for him. She tapped on the lizard-shaped pattern. "*That* is you. The ATM just scanned you, so we *know* that's you. That means—" She poked at her phone until Ryan's Clinic file came up again. She held it up for him to see the SES record, and even pinched to zoom it in for him. It had the familiar pirate shape. "—this is *not* you! This scan was taken right before your ghost was extracted, but it's *not you!*"

"Please keep your finger inside the SES scanner," the ATM suggested unhelpfully.

"What does that mean?" Ryan's mind was trying to reach understanding, but kept bumping hard into an invisible wall like a fly trying to find its way through a window.

Margie turned her phone towards her and studied it. "I don't know," she admitted. Ryan was grateful to hear her say it. It wasn't just him. "We have two scans on file for you." She swiped back and forth a few times. "They're both the same. Pirate."

"When was the other one taken?"

She frowned, uncertain. "Just a few days earlier. Did you

have another procedure done? An unhaunting? That makes no sense."

Ryan's mind fly found an opening in the window and bolted through. "That wasn't me. I mean, I filled out the forms in my name. But it wasn't me. That was Sye."

Margie looked at him without seeing him. He could see a thousand mental calculations going on behind her eyes. Her jaw fell slowly open as the results of the calculations came in and added up to something. "So this... the SES in the Clinic file under your name is Sye's. Not yours. That means..." More calculations began processing. Ryan could almost hear her mind clicking.

"Please keep your finger inside the SES scanner," the ATM put in, for the first time with a hint of impatience.

Margie's mind stopped clicking. She looked down at her phone once again. "When I scanned you before your extraction, I scanned *you*, but Sye's SES came up."

"But you scanned *me*," Ryan said. "My ghost was still in my body."

She looked at Ryan again, searching for where his eyes were and finally deciding on a spot. "Yes, it was." Her face lit up with realization. "But Sye's ghost must have been in there too!"

"How...?"

"When I unhaunted Sye's chair, how close were you? Do you remember? Did you come in contact with Sye at all?"

Ryan scanned his memory of the procedure. It seemed so long ago, and even his recent memories had a haze around them now. One so distant felt like it might not have actually happened, like a far-fetched story he had been told. But there were pieces of it. Sye's expression. Margie holding the paddles. The Box charging. The back of the chair coming loose.

The back of the chair coming loose.

"I touched it," Ryan said. "I touched the chair. While you

were doing the thing, I touched it."

"That's it!" she said. She almost threw her phone in the air, but instead just punched at Ryan. Her fist went through his shoulder. "You must have come in contact with Sye when you did that. The procedure forced a possession. It detached him from the chair and attached him to you. He possessed you, and you didn't even know it!"

"But I walked home with Sye! I could still see him!"

"Yes, but his ghost was attached to your body! It's possible for a ghost to be attached to a body without being inside it. He'd be able to go into it at will. Do you remember having feelings you couldn't identify the day after the procedure? Thoughts that weren't yours? Confusion?"

"Now that you mention it, that was the day I decided to have myself extracted. I wasn't totally sure why I wanted that."

"Maybe you didn't. But Sye did! He was hiding in your body, encouraging you to get out so he could take over!"

Ryan sank further onto the ground. His form was coming completely apart. He felt like a cloud, a fog, an assortment of wisps. Yet still he tried to force the wisps to piece together the implications of what Margie was saying. Thoughts evaded him, but he chased them. When he tried to speak he could manage only the faintest whisper, grass in a breeze. "So Roger didn't give my body away."

Margie shook her head. "He doesn't know where it is either. Because right after your extraction, Sye just got up and walked away with it."

THIRTY-SEVEN

They raced back to the house the same way they had gone to the ATM: on foot, because Lowell had insisted that his car was too full of other things. What other things, he didn't specify.

Even with a renewed sense of purpose, Ryan could barely hold his form together. By now, he suspected that he was only a shirt ballooned up with vapor. Huge portions of his volume were leaking out through the holes in the fabric. He had to keep drawing them back to him like re-inhaling smoke rings. But with his senses fading fast, it was getting harder to pay attention to all of himself at once.

Margie kept saying that there was still a chance. If they could figure out where Sye went, they could find Ryan's body. And there was only one place they could think to look for any clues about where Sye might have gone.

The chair. The chair was all they had.

When they finally arrived at the house, Ryan drove the shadows back from his mind. He gathered up every part of himself and forced himself onward. It felt like rolling an enormous water balloon, but he kept moving. By the time he got upstairs, Margie was already turning the chair over, examining it from every angle.

It had no markings, no manufacturer labels, no hints at all as to where it came from.

"It was here when you moved in?" Margie demanded. She was moving fast, but not frantic. Spinning the chair in ninety-degree increments. Professional and analytical to the last.

Ryan nodded in reply. He could feel himself spreading like a cloud of gas. He was fairly certain he had no identifiable features anymore, not even the shirt.

Margie walked the perimeter of the apartment. She seemed to have divided it into sectors and was visually scanning each one. She stopped in front of each piece of furniture and each decoration to study it. "Was anything else here when you moved in? Any of this?"

Ryan didn't think so, and didn't know why it mattered.

While she was scanning, Margie walked right through him without seeing him. She didn't react at all. No shiver, no chill. No indication that she had absorbed his emotion at all. It was like Ryan wasn't even there. Which he was increasingly feeling that he wasn't.

"Think think think think think," Margie was saying as she circled the apartment.

Ryan let himself spill onto the couch, spreading over it like dry ice steam. He could see tendrils of himself going around and through it, but his consciousness seemed focused more or less on top. The shadows were pressing in around his vision again, and even sounds had become muted, senseless. He remembered sleep, and wanted it more than anything.

"There has to be something! Ryan! Ryan?" She couldn't find him. He was dimly aware of her searching the couch for him. Looking behind it, under the cushions, scanning the room.

I'm not here anymore, Ryan thought. *This is it.*

Margie sat on the couch next to him. Next to him, and also partially mixed with him. He could feel her there, a warm patch. He focused on it, and it anchored him slightly.

She was saying something. He wrestled with consciousness, drew himself in. He concentrated on his chosen field of vision, centred right on her face, and shut off every part of his mind except the part interpreting the sound waves from her voice. They seemed miles underwater but he drew them to the surface.

"There's still a chance," she said. "You have to try.

Remember anything."

Ryan couldn't remember why it was important. He wanted to try, but he didn't understand what he was supposed to try to do.

"Anything," she said. "Anything about Sye. Did he say where he was from? Did he ever say his last name?"

Ryan had nothing. He couldn't form his own last name. He spread out more over the couch like a pat of butter on a hot pan.

"Were there any other ghosts here who might..." Margie didn't finish her question. The look in her eyes said that she had already answered it for herself.

She sprang off the couch and to the fridge in a single step. "Was this fridge here when you moved in?"

It had been, but Ryan couldn't form words to say so.

Margie threw her arms around the fridge, leaned her weight back and shimmied it out of its alcove. It came unplugged as she pulled and the light inside the open freezer door went dark. When she swiveled the whole thing to face the dining area, Ryan could see the Algonquian tribesman's face glowing softly in the back of the freezer, casting a faint blue illumination over a frozen Salisbury steak dinner.

"That chair," Margie said. "Do you know it?"

The man in the fridge looked at the chair. Then turned to Margie silently, surprised, like someone who hadn't been meaningfully spoken to in three hundred years.

"Please," Margie implored. "Where did the chair come from?"

The man in the fridge looked at the chair again for a moment.

Then his eyes drifted around the room, searching for something. Something that he didn't find.

He looked at Margie again. He lifted one of his hands from the fridge below and held up two fingers next to his face.

"There were two chairs? Like that one?" Margie asked.

The man in the fridge nodded once.

"Where's the other one?" Margie asked.

The man in the fridge looked down. He let his hand extend out of the fridge and pointed straight down at the floor with his index finger. He nodded at Margie with wide eyes, insisting silently that she should understand exactly what he meant. He jabbed his finger downward.

Ryan was used to random noises in the apartment. So much so that he hardly heard them anymore. But now that he paid attention to it, he was surprised by how loud and insistent the banging of the water heater in the basement was. Louder than a water heater should be. Now that he focused on it, he couldn't imagine any water heater ever sounding like that.

Ryan didn't wait for Margie. He didn't bother with the door, or the stairs, or most of the laws of physics.

His form was so nebulous now that he could just let himself drool through the spaces between atoms in the floor. He poured into the second floor apartment and pooled on the floor there for a moment, spreading. And then, ignoring the firm tug of the snow globe from above, he dribbled through the second floor atoms and down to Gabriel's apartment on the first floor. This one had dense ceramic tiles, but he found the gaps and sifted through them. And then he was in the basement.

And there it was.

Seeing his own body in the third person had been seriously disconcerting the first time. But this time turned out to be significantly more so. Because his body was doing things without him, and every wisp of human instinct left in him told him that they're not supposed to do that. He felt slightly betrayed.

It was at the top of the short flight of wooden stairs,

beneath a dangling bare light bulb. It lay sprawled, like one who had just crawled out of the desert. Its face was haggard, unshaven for days at least. Its eyes were rimmed with red, the skin under them dark and sagging with exhaustion. And it was wearily pounding with a balled-up fist on the basement door against which its upper body was leaning. The basement door that had once trapped Ryan down here for a whole afternoon might have this time kept his body down here for days.

And it was still, he noted with dismay, wearing the shirt.

"Sye?" Ryan said. It emerged as a faint, dry whisper. But in the cool stillness of the basement, it carried. And Sye heard him.

The body—Ryan's body—stopped pounding and twisted its head unsteadily, blearily, to look at him. And Ryan recognized on his own face Sye's usual frown. The eyes fell on Ryan, searched for a focus point. Finally they locked. Sye could see him, and knew who he was. He didn't say anything, or betray any new expression, but there was definite recognition.

After silently acknowledging Ryan, Sye's eyes shifted to look past him. Ryan swung his own vision around to see what he was looking at.

Across the basement, half hidden in the shadows behind an ancient furnace, was another chair virtually identical to Sye's. It was the same wood, the same mismatched varnish, the same lashes of stripped bark and the same rusted bolts only barely holding it all together. The same blunt ugliness that dared you to point it out and make a big deal about it.

And in the other chair was the ghost of a woman.

She was likely within a decade of Sye's age, and wearing a plain, long dress that was, like Sye's outfit, probably from the 1940's or 50's. Her hair, though it was difficult to tell for sure given its translucency, seemed to have retained most of its dark color well into her senior years, and it was styled long with curls in a way that made her seem younger than she was. The years that weren't in her hair were all in her face. But in a graceful way, each one adding layers of perfectly balanced expression and character. She projected good nature just from her posture and the angle of her head and her faint, sweet smile.

Ryan fought to piece together a narrative that made sense of this. The woman was on a chair like Sye's. His wife? She had to be. Had Sye made the chairs for them? Maybe. It didn't matter. The chairs belonged to them. And then somehow, in years past, the chairs must have been separated. One of them put aside here in the basement. Perhaps before the Blackout, when nobody knew there was a ghost haunting it. No wonder Sye wanted out of his chair so badly. No wonder he had borrowed Ryan's body.

The shadows that had for so long ringed Ryan's vision tightened around him like pythons, and he felt himself crumble. The last bonds holding him together broke completely, and he couldn't pull them back together.

The last thing he heard was footsteps approaching outside, and someone trying to break down the basement door. Dust showered from all corners of the ceiling as somebody on the other side pounded again and again. "It's stuck!" he heard Margie yelling. "Gabriel, get your key! Hurry!"

He felt his mind separating, breaking, shutting down.

He drifted, not into dark, but into nothing.

THIRTY-EIGHT

Ryan slammed back into consciousness like a cop beating down a door: shoulder-first, bull force, and roaring. His eyes blasted open and the world surged through them and flooded his head.

He was so stunned by the shock wave of sensation that for a moment the reality of how he was sensing did not occur to him.

He had eyes.

He was in a body. And it felt familiar. It felt like *his* body. It had to be.

He could feel all eleven pounds of his head pressed down hard by gravity. He had forgotten what gravity felt like. In this case, it hurt because his head had a chunk of cold metal beneath it. He could feel the pressure of long metal legs, a claw gripping his skull from the back.

His whole body convulsed violently and he was certain his ghost was about to be wrenched back out. He braced himself for the disorientation and the dizziness.

But it didn't come.

Instead, his body relaxed. And he was somehow still in it.

He felt, briefly, fevered. Heat coursed through him. And then a gentle cool. And stillness. His arm hairs, standing on end, relaxed. They felt singed.

He breathed. He breathed again. Breathing was great. The air was damp and close, and smelled like disinfectant and sweat.

He blinked. Blinking was great too. He would enjoy every blink to the utmost from now on.

He could feel his heart beating. If he wanted to, he could measure his heartbeat in his eardrums. He had rarely paid attention to it before, but now he was intensely relieved to have it back.

He breathed one more time, just to be sure he was here for good.

Margie had done it. Somehow. He was back in his body, and apparently not vanishing into the ether anymore. Everything was going to be okay.

Now. What happened?

He tried to sit up, but found that though his muscles responded, he couldn't move. Had he forgotten how to make his body move? Shouldn't it be like riding a bicycle? It should just come back to you.

But that wasn't the problem. The problem was a vinyl strap cutting into his shoulders, another across his chest, and another over his knees.

He was on his back, staring straight up. His head was immobilized. He felt again a hard lump of cold metal behind his skull, the pinch of spindly arms digging into his cheeks and neck.

A silhouette cut across the light. The silhouette cocked its head, studying him. Its proportions were wrong. Too tall and thin to be human. For a moment, Ryan thought he had been abducted by aliens, and that his day was therefore looking up.

"You're conscious." Roger's voice oozed over him.

Why is Roger here? Did Roger save me?

Roger's soothing voice drenched him again. "I can only imagine what you have been going through. Oh dear oh dear. What a terrible thing to have happen. I feel for you."

Ryan tried to respond, but found that there was some kind of restraint holding his lower jaw shut. Part of the restraint was inside his mouth, pressing his tongue down. Likely to keep patients from biting their tongue while being electrocuted. Trying to open his mouth made it hurt more. He was past enjoying pain and back to generally not being a fan of it.

Roger's silhouette slid out of view and Ryan strained to follow it with his eyes. He lost sight of it completely.

A moment later it slid back into view from the other side and shone a medical penlight into each of his eyes in turn. "It has always been my vocation to help people through the most difficult times in their lives," Roger said. "In your case I happen to be the *cause* of that difficult time, and quite deliberately so. But I don't see how that changes things. So if there is anything I can do to make you more comfortable..." Roger jerked one of the straps tighter. It cut a deep gouge into Ryan's thigh and cut off the flow of blood down his leg. "...you have only to ask."

How did I get here? What happened to Margie? The questions went unasked. He could only make frantic mumbling noises.

But the answer came anyway.

"Don't torture him." This voice wasn't Roger's. It was someone else's, cool and clinical. Not a trace of sympathy. "Remember, if you damage any tissue, it's Caldwell who will have to deal with it. He won't like that"

Another silhouette slid into view next to Roger's. It took Ryan only an instant, even in the halo of the light, to recognize it.

Margie.

Ryan's mind, now bottled up within his physical brain and making use of its various receptors, was a battleground. Rage and fear and hurt all grappled each other. For now, rage was trouncing the others, but he sensed that the balance could shift.

How long had Margie been planning this? Perhaps she hadn't stolen his apartment for herself at all. Could it be she was only there to follow him until he found his body, so she could bring it back to Roger?

Ryan pressed against the straps, enraged. There were a

thousand names he would call Margie right now if he could, none of them flattering.

"Are we ready?" Roger asked her.

Margie shook her head irritably. "I told you, his biological systems need some time to stabilize. It was nearly dead when we located it. Executing the possession now, it would likely kill them both."

Roger pinched the bridge of his nose and shook his head, maybe trying to shake the impatience out. "Mr. Caldwell will be arriving shortly. He won't want to wait."

"He won't want to die either. He's done that enough times lately."

Roger circled halfway around the table with a fist pressed to his chin, never taking his eyes off Ryan. "This will all be over soon, Mr. Matney," he said. "Won't that be a relief? You've been through so, so much." Finally he spun around and strode out of sight. Ryan could hear his long footsteps receding down the hall and up the stairs.

Ryan stared hard at Margie's face. But she wasn't looking at him. She was staring at the door, listening to Roger moving away.

When the hall was silent, she leaned in close to Ryan's. "Ryan, listen to me."

Ryan didn't want to listen. And at the same time, desperately wanted to. He strained against the straps again and roared as much as he could with his jaw held shut. He knew none of it would do any good, but he wanted her to know how offended he was.

"Shhh!" She gently pressed down on his shoulder and jabbed a finger towards the door. "Ethan and Ewan," she whispered. "Right outside." She took a few steps out of sight, was gone for a second, and then reappeared on his other side. Maybe she had looked out in the hall? "Ryan, I'm sorry. After I extracted Sye, I tried to restore your ghost/body connection myself. But the Box was just too damaged. It wasn't going to work, and you were close to total dispersal. The Clinic's equipment was the only way to save you."

There was a cough from the corridor, and Margie looked sharply over her shoulder. She stared at the door, waiting for somebody to come in.

When nobody did, she leaned in to Ryan again. "I made him a deal," she said. "If I brought your body here, he would let me put you back in it temporarily. Your body is keeping your ghost stable for now. But the deal is, we're going to extract you again. And Clifton Caldwell will take over your body. Permanently."

Ryan struggled to understand. *What happens to me?* He tried to ask it with his eyes.

Margie glanced back at the door again. "We don't have much time, so listen. When I extract you, I can 'borrow' some of Caldwell's axions. He won't miss them. He's lost millions of them already. I think I can stabilize you for good, reverse the damage done by the snow globe. You'll be a stable energy field again. You'll have your post-mortal life back, exactly as you wanted. And with a new shirt. It's nice. I picked it myself."

Ryan sniffed deeply. He knew the shirt's usual baked-in grease-and-sweat aroma very well, and it was not here. In its place all he could smell was fresh cotton and heavily scented detergent.

A clean shirt. I'm sorry I doubted you, Margie.

"Caldwell's possession isn't going to work," she went on, shifting again to the other side of him so she could watch the door as she whispered fast. "Your body doesn't match Caldwell's ghost. It will die within days, and Caldwell will be out-of-body again. Roger doesn't know that, and he doesn't need to. We need him to let this procedure go ahead. Without this procedure, your ghost will never repair itself. Even if it stayed in your body for the rest of your mortal life, as soon as your body died, your ghost would disperse immediately. Do you understand?"

Ryan tried to nod, but could produce no head movement at all.

She must have noticed the flexing of his neck muscles, though, and interpreted it as a nod. "Good," she said. She put a hand on his shoulder. "You're going to have everything you wanted."

Ryan's heart pounded like a flurry of punches inside his rib cage. His mind flipped over and over. Everything he wanted. Everything he came into the Clinic for in the first place. An end to the nightmare. Right now. What did he care if the Hardware Baron of Boston got his body? Just minutes ago he had been facing total oblivion. And now? Now he could ensure that he never faced it again. Ever.

So why was he not sure?

Margie's eyes snapped back to the door. Feet were coming down the stairs. Roger's voice, shifted now from sympathetic to sycophantic. "How nice that you've managed almost the typical number of torsos today," he was saying to someone in the hall. "Well done!"

The exam room door *thumped* closed. The *clack* of a deadbolt invaded its echo.

Margie stepped back, and Caldwell's ghost thrust into view, peering down at Ryan skeptically. He seemed to have two constantly shifting torsos facing opposite directions and his head drifted fluidly between them like a blob of goo in a lava lamp. It was hard to imagine that he could focus on anything.

Caldwell frowned at Ryan. "This is the one that was at my house. He's the perfect match?"

"Better than ninety-five percent!" Roger replied.

Ryan checked Margie's face, but she was steadfastly refusing to show a reaction.

"Guaranteed to work this time!" Roger chirped. "A *lifetime* guarantee, in fact. But just one lifetime. After that, we'll have to discuss options."

"It's not as fat as the last one," Caldwell finally said. "Let's do this." He drifted out of sight.

"Very good," Roger said, rubbing his hands together as though anticipating a lovely dinner. "Let's begin."

THIRTY-NINE

Lowell reclined in his office chair, using the plastic folding chair as a footrest. He was slightly buzzed from Caldwell's mid-priced rye and wanted to sleep, but was afraid to lie down in the dentist chair because he might leave his body. He didn't want to. He had thought about putting Rufus's body into the dentist chair instead, but getting it out of the car and up to his office was an impossibility.

Is this who you are?

He drowned out Margie's voice in his head with another sip of the rye, and balanced the glass on his gut as he stretched out. A couple of his usual office ghosts watched him silently from across the room and whispered to each other, but he ignored them. He didn't need their judgment. Passing headlights from the street below threw shifting silhouettes of his window blinds across the ceiling. They made him dizzy. He wished he had a couch to sleep on. And a home to put it in. And maybe a bed in that home, so he could sleep in that instead and save the couch for other things.

He wasn't going to get anything from Ryan. Ryan was probably gone by now, along with all access to his finances. That was a loss. A pretty big loss for Ryan too, obviously, but still a significant loss for Lowell. He could perhaps have stood up to Margie. Ryan seemed more than happy to pay him. But something about what she had said made him back down.

Is this who you are?

He took in a deep breath, and his gut rising almost overturned the glass and spilled the whiskey across his pants.

Screw it.

He pushed himself off the desk chair, threw back what was left in the glass, and stumbled to the dentist chair. He lay back on it, adjusting his back and neck to its familiar curves. This was better. He would sleep. If he left his body, so be it. He'd find something to do while his body got some rest.

Except...

What if I can't get back in?

He reluctantly rolled off the dentist chair and made his way back to his desk chair/folding chair setup. They both made irritable grinding squeaks as he tried to get comfortable.

He didn't want to leave his body. If he couldn't get back into it, this was who he'd be forever. The answer to "Is this who you are?" would be "yes", and would always be "yes".

He couldn't get comfortable enough to sleep in the desk chair, even with the footrest. He briefly attempted curling up on the top of the desk, but that was worse. That left his car, down in the parking garage. But Rufus's body was in there.

That was his one hope. Keep Rufus's body in the car for a few days, and the payout from Rufus and Lucinda would cover him for another month. Maybe he could get some kind of traction, start to build up some savings and get a place, and a couch in it to not sleep on because he was sleeping in the bed. Turn things around. Like he had tried to do every month for five years.

He had to admit, Rufus's body's breathing had seemed to be getting faster and shallower when he left it down there, like it was in some kind of distress. But it didn't matter. If it died, he'd deal with it. Five days, maybe six. That seemed like the magic number. Then he'd call and start the ball rolling.

He made me coffee. He drove me to work every day.

That's what Lucinda had said, through tears. But so what? It was a play on his sympathies so he'd lower his rate. Wasn't it? And it hadn't worked.

Lowell gave up on sleeping and pulled the blinds open to

stare down into the street. There was little late-night traffic so the street was almost all ghosts, from this height faint white blobs drifting around each other. Lowell wondered if they were all fine with who they were going to be forever. Probably not. Probably hardly any of them were.

And there wasn't anything they could do about it. Their time to change was over.

His wasn't.

Dammit.

He drained the bottle and pulled his coat on, dialing Rufus and Lucinda's number as he staggered to his office door.

FORTY

Roger shoved Ryan's gurney. The wheels shrieked, and the ceiling spun around Ryan.

"I do apologize if you're claustrophobic," Roger said, "but this procedure requires somewhat more specialized equipment than you're used to."

The light overhead revolved and twisted out of sight, and then something else filled his entire field of view, just a foot or so above his face. He was inside a metal cylinder. All around him was smooth, shiny metal. His breathing, fast and shallow, echoed hollowly around him. He had never had an MRI but he imagined that they felt something like this.

Claustrophobia gripped him, and every muscle in his body jerked as he fought panic, squirming to get free.

As the gurney plunged into the metallic hollow and jolted to a stop, Ryan could dimly make out his own reflection in the surface of the tube above him. It was distorted by the curvature into a grotesquely wide version of himself that, he was not surprised to note, was also panicking.

"Are you warm enough?" Roger's voice reverberated down the tube at him. "Your comfort is... well, clearly not my *first* priority. But let's say my third. Fourth at worst."

Ryan focused all his strength on the shoulder straps, thinking maybe if he concentrated on just those he could summon enough force to break them. He strained every muscle in his back and stomach, but the straps seemed not to give at all. And then he thought, *why am I fighting? They're giving me what I wanted.*

"Mr. Caldwell," Roger said from outside the tube. "If you would be so kind as to enter the chamber as well."

Something moved at the foot of the tube, diffusing what

faint light made it as far as Ryan's eyes. In the distorted reflection above him Ryan could see a mist flowing into the tube with him, swirling around his feet and flooding up over him. Shapes of Caldwell's body parts—feet, hands, even his face—shifted in and out of existence throughout the cloud as it swirled around Ryan's legs, past his waist, all the way up his torso. He could feel Caldwell's ghost beginning to mingle with his, the sharp static tingle, the intrusion of emotions that weren't his. Mostly greed, impatience, and rage. Caldwell's ghost filled the chamber so completely that Ryan started to lose any sense of which emotions were his and which were Caldwell's.

In the distorted reflection above him Ryan watched through panicked eyes the mist flowing over his shoulders and neck, up to his face. He felt like he might drown. He seized control of his mind and threw every remaining ounce of his strength into flailing all his limbs. But none of them moved beyond a furious tensing of the muscles.

The mist rolled over his face and formed briefly into a grotesque distortion of Caldwell's head, giant eyes bulging and sinking back and bulging again, the mouth fully open on one side and fully closed on the other.

"Anything I should know?" Caldwell asked sourly. "This body allergic to anything? It doesn't have any, like, rashes or anything, does it? That last guy had this thing on his foot. Drove me freaking nuts."

From somewhere over his head there was a hard, sharp *thunk*. And then a sound that Ryan recognized immediately. An electric drone that started deep and rose slowly, steadily in both volume and pitch.

Just like the Box, the cylinder was charging up.

"Thirty seconds, Ryan," Margie called in from outside the cylinder.

Ryan felt the hairs on his arms stand up. Electricity hummed through the spider on his head and through every inch of the metal cylinder. The air was thick with static. This was it. It was happening.

And yet he still wasn't sure.

It had seemed so clear when he first came into the Clinic. Give up a few mortal years for a perfect eternity. What decision could be easier? It was trading a penny for a billion dollars, a matchbox for a castle, a thimble for an ocean. Going post-mortal was inevitable anyway, so why put it off? What could he possibly do in those few mortal years that would remotely compare to an eternity spent doing very nearly anything, without the limitations of a physical body. He had climbed Everest in his first week; he could climb a billion of them in an eternity. Even now, he felt the logic hard to contradict.

And yet he was not sure.

"Twenty seconds."

Sugar Frootz. He tried to imagine the taste of them. How he wanted them to taste, not how he remembered them. There would be that hint of some kind of fruit flavor, but it would be sealed in an impenetrable armor plating of processed sugar. And that was the beauty of it. That was all he wanted from them.

He would never taste them.

Ever.

Unless... what if he refused the procedure? Could he do that? Margie had said it would mean his ghost would never stabilize. But he'd still have those mortal years in his body, wouldn't he? He'd disperse at the end. But still, he'd have all those years.

Don't be an idiot. You'd really give up living forever just for some Sugar Frootz?

"Ten seconds," Margie said.

"Both of you relax, please," Roger said. "This will only take a moment."

But it wasn't just Sugar Frootz. It was also Froot Loops,

Honey Combs and Lucky Charms, Franken Berry and Frosted Flakes, Cocoa Puffs and those squares with cinnamon he couldn't remember the name of. He would never taste any of them again.

But it wasn't just those.

It was Everest. He wanted to maybe try Everest again, but he wanted it to be cold. He wanted it to hurt when he got to the top. He wanted his feet to ache and his lungs to scream at him because the air was too thin, and the bitter wind to tear the flesh off his face. Or, almost as good, he wanted to be able to say that he had never climbed Everest because it was way too hard for someone like him.

But it wasn't just that.

It was also Margie. It was that evening spent watching terrible, terrible TV with her. He had felt nothing that night but now that he looked back he felt… something. He wanted to watch trash TV with her again. As often as possible. And if she reached over to touch his arm again he wanted his arm to be there. And when she wasn't there he wanted to miss her and if it turned out that he was misreading her and her interest in him was entirely professional, he wanted it to hurt a little. Even that would be good in its way.

Even if it was only fifty or sixty years of those things, he wanted them anyway. Even if it took just five minutes to eat a bowl of Sugar Frootz, and even if it took few years to figure out he would never climb Everest because it really was far too hard, and even if the marathon of *House Shopping* episodes ended at eleven, and Margie brushing his arm only lasted a fleeting second or two, he still wanted those things. He couldn't imagine anything his ghost could do for eternity that he might want more.

But it wasn't even just all of that.

It was definitely the Sugar Frootz too. He wanted to try those Sugar Frootz.

And for that he needed a body for them to be deliciously

unhealthy in.

"Three, two, one…"

Ryan braced.

Fight this.

FORTY-ONE

Ryan clung onto his body, braced himself in it as though clutching the inside of a lifeboat about to smash into rocks.

There was a deafening electric *crack.*

The spider on his head superheated, and the cylinder filled with searing plasma. Hot bursts of white light surged down Ryan's entire nervous system, concentrating into knife-points of pain at his fingertips and toes as it crackled out of him. His nose hairs burned down like fuses. He tried to cough but couldn't open his mouth, so he snorted smoke and ozone.

The all-too-familiar sensation of the world plunging out from under him took over, and he was in the emptiness again, lost and formless and careening.

The pain was gone as his body fell away, and the escape from it was profound relief.

He was fine with his situation. This felt better. Everything was going to be okay. Why had he even considered resisting?

His body's face dipped into view below him, and he didn't recognize it. It was a stranger. It didn't matter.

No.

He locked onto the face. Forced his attention to stay on it, to focus on nothing else. *That's me. Right there.*

He demanded that the world stop spiraling, locked his rotation to match that of his body so he was hovering in place above it. He gathered everything that he consisted of into a pressurized bubble of force.

And he propelled himself straight down, body-slamming his own body.

As soon as he sensed the hard *pop* of passing through his

skin and ribs, he forced his molecules outward and expanded as far as he could, as fast as he could.

He flowed himself down his spine, along all his nerve pathways to every extremity, up his neck into his brain.

Caldwell was in there with him, already working himself into the nervous system. Ryan wrestled half control of one eyelid and managed to flutter it before Caldwell resisted.

What are you doing? Caldwell's voice roared in his head.

Ryan didn't know how to think back a response, so he focused on getting control of something, anything. Some part of his brain. There! The smell center! He conquered it with overwhelming force. The hot stink of burnt hair flooded into his mind and he gripped onto it.

"He's still here!" Caldwell screamed out loud. The echoes of his voice thundered through the cylinder, deafening. Ryan heard them through the left ear, but Caldwell was putting up a ferocious battle for use of the right one.

Ryan surrendered it, but retaliated by invading the left pinky toe. He twitched it triumphantly, and that seemed to enrage Caldwell further.

Roger's shadow darkened the bottom of the cylinder. "Mr. Matney, don't be a fool!"

Ryan suspected that Roger was right. He *was* being a fool. But he did it anyway. He crammed himself down the length of his left leg and made a concentrated effort to kick Roger ferociously in the face. He was still far too restrained to manage it, but Roger saw the twitch and got the point. He reflexively ducked back.

The temperature in the cylinder plummeted. The crackle of electricity went out of it, and darkness drove the searing plasma away. *It's shut off! Why?*

"Margie!" It was Roger's voice, enraged, outside the cylinder. And Ryan realized what had happened.

Margie had shut off the cylinder. She had figured out what he was doing, and was trying to give him a chance.

"Back away, Roger!" he heard Margie say. Not raising her voice. Clinical, and commanding as always.

There were thumps and scuffling sounds from outside. Something thudded into the outside of the cylinder. Ryan worried for Margie's safety. He wished he could see something, anything.

He felt the first rush of real fear from Caldwell. It buoyed Ryan. He could win this.

"What's happening, Foster?" Caldwell shouted. Both of his voices merged into one enraged, frightened one. The echoes inside the cylinder magnified the fear in his cry.

But his fear made him fight.

He mounted an assault on Ryan's spinal column, coiling himself around it and squeezing into the spaces between vertebrae. Ryan pushed back, but Caldwell's fury was too much and Ryan had to retreat head-ward. He got the use of both eyes and could feel his scalp hot with lingering electricity. He gasped for air, but couldn't feel anything below the neck. That was all Caldwell's territory now.

From outside, the hum of a fresh charge began to rise. Roger must have seized control from Margie. Ryan hoped she wasn't hurt.

"Sorry for the interruption!" Roger's voice echoed. He sounded uncharacteristically flustered. "We should have this done in thirty seconds!"

Caldwell surged up Ryan's neck and Ryan could feel him coming like a dragon roused from its cave. The sheer force of him shoved Ryan completely out the top of his head, and his body dipped away from under him. He heard a shout of triumph from Caldwell.

Sugar Crisp, Ryan thought. He had forgotten about that one. Light and airy. The choice of cloudy summer Tuesdays.

Emboldened by that, he dove back in, straight down through his skull cap, compressing himself into a dense spectral battering ram and hammering Caldwell downward, not stopping until he had the furious ghost all the way down to his feet.

Sensation flooded over Ryan again. He was sweating. His skin felt singed. His hair was standing on end. His eyes were watering and something was dribbling out of both ears. But he was in and loving every miserable discomfort.

Caldwell was losing his grip on Ryan's feet. His ghost was flowing out of Ryan's ankles, the churning steam once again spreading through the cylinder. His scowling faces went past Ryan's vision in several pieces, the space between them widening as he lost cohesion.

He's out, Ryan thought. He tensed all his muscles, testing them, trying to form a physical barrier to keep Caldwell from making another attempt.

He could feel a chilled static charge and flashes of anger as Caldwell churned around him.

"Foster, I swear to God if you don't get me in there right now—" Caldwell's voice was feeble, choked, echoing like it was miles away.

Ryan judged from the sound thrumming in the cylinder that it wasn't fully charged yet. Surely Caldwell couldn't hold himself together much longer. The mist was losing density, particles streaming apart in rivulets, pouring like fluid out the end of the cylinder between Ryan's heels and wisping away on the air conditioning.

Roger's shadow again blocked the light at Ryan's feet. "Clifton, change of plan! Come out of there please!" he said. He was wrestling to get his cool back.

"Why?"

"Because I'm going to overload the cylinder. It should obliterate him. For good."

"And then I can get in?"

"And then you can get in! I apologize that this has been so difficult. I do try to make things easy."

Caldwell surged around Ryan's head for a moment. Ryan

could see two halves of a face floating near each other, and both of them were smirking.

And then all the mist cleared out of the cylinder, and Ryan was alone in his body. Breathing hard, and clutching the fabric on the gurney.

Whatever device powered the cylinder rose to a pitch so high, it left the audible range. A dread silence descended, though Ryan could still feel intensifying vibrations in the cylinder all around him.

Roger's voice was icy. "Ten... nine..."

Ryan closed his eyes.

Obliteration. There would be no fighting this one.

He concentrated instead on taking in every sensation, enjoying every last aspect of his final moment. He took note of where on his body every feeling was coming from. He studied how his mind was processing them and he savored every one. None of the sensations were good—heat and pain and burning—and yet he savored them because in a moment there wouldn't be any of them anymore. He marveled at the cool of the fabric under his arms, the bite of the spider's arms into the sides of his head. He loved the scald on his tongue like he had just swallowed boiling water, the pulsating pressure of electricity building all around him. He listened hard to the buzz of the fluorescent lights outside the tube, the hollow dripping behind the walls, the *click* of the deadbolt on the exam room door snapping open.

Ryan's eyes snapped wide.

Did the door just open?

The sound was followed by the ancient crypt squeak of the hinges as the door swung inward a few inches. And that was followed by a voice, just inside the room.

Benny's voice. Pleased with himself. Thrilled, even.

"Hey!" he cheered. "I did it!"

Someone kicked the door open the rest of the way and barreled into the room.

The inside of the cylinder ignited searing white again, and Ryan's ghost was on fire.

Ryan knew very little of what was happening outside the cylinder. His senses were coming apart along with the rest of him, blasted by a howling, hot wind. He thought he heard voices shouting. He thought he saw shadows passing by the end of the cylinder one way, then the other. He felt the whole cylinder shift sideways, kicked by some external force, and he thought he might pitch over.

But he was losing all sense of anything. He could feel his ghost being ripped from him, his body's connection to it snapping like seams being ripped. *Hold on,* he kept telling himself. *Just hold on.* But his will was breaking down. His mind was being sand-blasted apart. He could no longer feel terror because he didn't know what it was.

Through the maelstrom ripping at him, he dimly sensed something surging around his feet. A mist filled the cylinder. Multiple faces of Caldwell, climbing up him. A last-ditch effort to seize control of Ryan's body. Ryan had nothing to resist with, no resources left to fight him.

And then the gurney moved.

The cylinder was sliding past. He was moving out from under the mist that was Caldwell. Leaving the white fire inside the cylinder behind.

Someone was pulling the gurney out. Ryan could already feel his feet cooling, his legs, his torso.

Caldwell's howls of rage echoed from within the cylinder. Becoming less like a voice and more a primal noise.

Ryan was out under the lights in the open air, and his mind spun and rearranged itself into something he could think with.

I'm still here. I'm out.

Arms of mist, vestiges of Caldwell, flailed like tentacles around Ryan's face and dissipated. Caldwell's shouts went silent.

The cylinder darkened. The mist inside it cleared. Ryan could no longer feel the electric charge from it tugging at his hairs.

It was shut off, and Caldwell was gone.

Ryan breathed. He thought he would never do that again. But here he was, doing it.

For a few moments, it was all he did. There was nothing to look at and nothing to hear. So he breathed, and savored the stillness.

A ghost drifted into his view and regarded him silently.

Its outline and its features were faint, unformed. He thought it must be freshly out, a new ghost that hadn't found its form yet. He watched it, uncertain, as dark areas in it shifted, joined together, formed into features. A face emerged.

It scowled at him.

Roger.

It looked like it wanted to strangle him. It hovered above him, dripping resentment, while Ryan wondered what he should do.

He didn't have to do anything. Roger's ghost composed itself, trying to look dignified. And then it silently strode away and was gone.

Moments later, a human form cut into the square of the light, also looking down at Ryan. Ryan blinked, trying to force his eyes to adjust.

The silhouette blurred gradually into Lowell, just as another shape entered across from him. Ryan could see its shoulders rising and falling, breathing fast. It became Margie, holding paddles from the Box, one in each hand. They steamed.

She threw them down and started pulling at Ryan's restraints. "Ryan? How do you feel?" she asked. "Be specific."

Before Ryan could answer, Lowell interjected. "Charge

up this thing again," he said to Margie. Then to Ryan: "And you, get up. I need you to help me bring something in from the car."

FORTY-TWO

Three months later.

The dry, long grass scratched against Ryan's legs as he pushed through onto the beach. He had his sunglasses perched in his hair even though the persistent bank of clouds didn't so much block the sun as spread the brightness across a wider area. He carried his sandals so he could feel the sand cold between his toes.

"They didn't have any either," he said. He sat next to Margie, who was sitting in an Adirondack chair on the sand and gazing out over the steel grey ocean.

She hung up her phone as Ryan sat down. "Lowell again. He brought in the desk from his old office but he says it won't fit."

"So he wants Roger's office."

"I strongly suspect he already *took* Roger's office. I'm fairly certain my stuff will be piled in the basement when we get back."

"He'll come in handy. I have a feeling."

"I have the opposite feeling. If he screws up, I'm firing you both." She closed her eyes and turned her face towards where the sun seemed to be.

Ryan inhaled ocean air that smelled equally of sea salt and hot dogs. One from the ocean, the other hopefully from the stand about a quarter mile down the beach. Both compelling. He kind of wanted fish, and a hot dog.

They were the only living people on the beach. But the chill of November had no effect on the hundreds of ghosts who lay sunbathing on the sand despite the lack of either skin to tan or sun to tan it with. And there were hundreds more meandering in and out of the surf, trying unsuccessfully to feel the cold waves on their feet. It was hard to make out any details of individual ghosts in the daylight, but Ryan thought he could see some fully armored Spanish Conquistadors debating whether to mount an attack on the hot dog stand.

"Maybe they'll have some in the summer," Margie said without opening her eyes. She pulled her knit sweater closer around her as a shield against the wind coming off the ocean. Even in a chair like hers, which reclined naturally at a steep backwards angle, she managed to sit like she was on a church pew. He admired her consistency.

"No," Ryan said, "they said they don't have snow globes, they've never had them, and if somebody offered them a box of them, they'd ask that person to leave. They seemed to feel pretty strongly about it."

"Where next?" Margie asked.

Ryan looked down the beach the way they had come. The SkyWheel, so towering when they had stood in front of it that morning, was barely the size of a nickel now. And it still hadn't turned at all. He turned to look up the beach the other direction. The wall of absurdly hued condo hotels seemed endless, and impenetrable enough to block a naval bombardment.

"There's a Hilton right there," he said, pointing.

Margie stood off the chair. Getting off an Adirondack chair is clumsy at the best of times, but the way she did it was a marvel of precision movement. "Let's go." Before she started walking, she dug her toes deep into the sand and squirmed them into it, as she had done at every stop they'd made.

They started walking, away from the hot dog stand and the SkyWheel, weaving a serpentine path around whatever ghosts drifted near. They fell into a leisurely pace. Ryan kept his face mostly pointed into the wind so he could feel the salt against his cheeks. Margie's hand was cool in his, and she squeezed.

"You know," Margie said, "even if we find one, it won't be the same one."

"I know."

"And even if it's the same one, it won't be the *same* one. Completely different molecules. You'll have no axionic attachment to it whatsoever."

"I know."

"Strange. Do you feel some kind of irresistible draw? Is it physical, mental, subliminal? There shouldn't be any residual attachment whatsoever."

"I don't know. I just want one."

They turned off the beach and into the long grass again, headed for the nearest resort. The tips of the grass brushed against the hairs on Ryan's legs. He was glad he had decided on shorts despite the November temperatures.

"What day is the flight back?" Margie asked.

"I didn't book one," Ryan said.

Margie nodded, untroubled. "What do you want for dinner?"

"I think you know the answer to that."

"I don't think any of these places will serve that stuff after noon."

"I'll bring some in. It comes in a convenient box."

There were rocks buried in the grass, hurting the soles of Ryan's feet. But he didn't want to put his sandals back on. He wanted to feel the rocks.

"Hey," he said, "if we stay long enough, do you think it will snow?"

Did you enjoy this book, but wish it had slightly more words?

Visit the author's page to get the free companion short story
"Ghosts Don't Believe in Marshall Lloyd".

dmsinclair.com

ABOUT THE AUTHOR

If you've ever turned on a television, and are not picky about what you watch, you've probably seen something written by DM Sinclair. He's done more than hundred hours of that stuff, and will happily take the blame even for the shows he didn't write.

Later he switched to writing books because he thought it might be nice. It isn't, though.

Nevertheless, he plans to keep writing as long as he is alive. After that, he intends to visit Australia.

Like many Canadians, he currently lives in Canada.

For more information, you could try going here:

http://dmsinclair.com

Made in the USA
Coppell, TX
30 November 2019

12179944R00185